The Tattooed Detective

THE TATTOOED DETECTIVE

David Craig

Constable · London

First published in Great Britain 1998 by Constable & Company Ltd
3 The Lanchesters, 162 Fulham Palace Road, London W6 9ER
Copyright © 1998 by David Craig
The right of David Craig to be identified as the author of this work
has been asserted by him in accordance with the Copyright,
Designs and Patents Act 1988
ISBN 0 09 478000 5
Set in Palatino 10pt by SetSystems Ltd, Saffron Walden
Printed and bound in Great Britain by
MPG Books Ltd, Bodmin, Cornwall

A CIP catalogue record for this book
is available from the British Library

Author's note

The geography of Cardiff and its dockland in this book is correct in outline. Much of the detail is also right: there is a Cardiff Bay project, though further ahead than is described here. The former Bute Dock East is an ornamental lake and Victorian warehouses have been flatted. There is marina-type development. Rat Island and Mount Stuart Square exist. So does the theatre which was formerly a church: I was christened in the church. The zeppelin-shaped piece of architecture still looks out towards the Bay.

Some locations and all incidents are fictional. There is no Toledo club. Bethel Baptist Chapel, which, in a switch of denomination, I attended as a child, used to be in Mount Stuart Square, but has long gone, though the building remains. There is no police station in Bute Street. Likewise, the geography of New Cross, London, has been slightly changed. This is a story.

Part 1

1

If you planned a job and needed tasty recruits you dropped a word or two in the public bar of the Starboard Light. Obviously, you talked vague, oblique, non-committal – at the start, anyway. Things could leak, even from the Starboard Light. There were a couple of dockland police, Brade and Glyndwr Jenkins, who heard a lot, and guessed a lot, often spot-on. So, keep it murky. But the message would reach the right people: *Paul Yeo's got a project, needs staff.* All right, some would go back to sleep: *Yeo? Leadership? You must be fucking joking.* Others might perk up, especially others who had heard a murmur, or half a murmur, about Yeo's four hundred or so grand, earned in less than two years, still deposit-banked and growing, all collected without wounds or worse, and without law comeback, even from bright know-alls like Dave Brade and Glyndwr Jenkins.

'Business still bright, Paul?' Julian Corbett said in the bar one lunch hour.

'Great, but I want other openings. I'm thinking bigger. Opportunities, Jule.' He saw Corbett turn meditative.

Yeo's own thinking was, get yourself the funds and you could buy a sweet and hefty and permanent slice of this city. The place dreamed non-stop these days of its own rebirth, and there would be pickings. He reckoned it might be worth the money, as long as you went strong and big enough. The scramble had started. He would be part of it. He did not much care where the money came from. It had to be plentiful, so how *could* you care? He needed investment that would wipe out a long past, win a long future, give a true stake, establish solidity. But especially wipe out a long past. He thought of himself so far as a Nowhere Man – to pinch that old Beatles title. And he thought of turn-of-the-millennium Cardiff, that one-time brilliant and rich Coalopolis to all the world, as a Nowhere Place. One way and the other, and especially the other, he had already piled up loot and, for a while, had nearly convinced himself it would do – that £400,000, in cash, naturally. Also naturally, he realised all along that 400K, or even the full half-million, left him far from the 'seriously rich', such as – talking of Beatles – McCartney. But there had been a spell when he thought he needed no more. The effort and peril could not be worth it. Didn't he know of enough bodies early in the ground or locked away to prove that? The sort of gains he had in mind were not handed over nicely, like the Nobel Peace Prize, but ripped from their owners or keepers in rough and chancy expeditions. Although he stayed clean, occasionally the police had come close. Carol would have worried and grown angry, if she had known. He must not lose Carol. Settle for home contentment?

Yes, he had asked himself this a while ago, and asked himself again, and could find no reason against. Not then. But there were twenty reasons. They came down to a conviction . . . Jesus, that black word . . . They came down to a feeling he was still nobody, nowhere. Big money would see you right, conferred lasting identity – made sure you were not like all the other nobodies, about to be squashed to even less by the runaway renaissance of the city.

Take his name. He went as Paul Yeo – legally and properly went as Yeo, a fully documented job, far back in the family. But his great-great-grandfather's and great-grandfather's, and even grandfather's name for part of his life, was Köller. The family were destitute German immigrants who settled in the English West Country then moved here, across the Bristol Channel, to Cardiff, when the city hummed with all that sweet wealth and work late last century.

'You're someone who sees horizons, Paul,' Corbett said.

Yeo bought him a burgundy topped with soda, Corbett's tipple. 'Well, I'm looking around, Jule.'

Corbett was right for this kind of cue, with tabs on all sorts of special, hard, recruitable skills. About thirty, educated – some said even college – he looked like milk and water: tall, pale, a little-boy face, with trusting eyes and a neat mouth made for singing canticles. Yet he had all sorts of friends, or not friends, contacts. In fact, Jule Corbett was a quiet credit to villainy, the type Yeo would ditch first if he ever did make it straight. They were the worst, the ones who looked mild: a special, dirtier deception. Corbett listened now with everything he had, while acting polished, relaxed. Jule would get the project under way.

10

Yeo felt he was at last starting to put things right, starting to bury history.

His great-grandfather changed the name in the First War because Germans were hated. He had married a West Country girl called Mary Yeo. Her brother ran successful tug-boats in boom-time South Wales, so Paul Yeo's great-grandfather took her surname – to lose the German connection, and to lift his fortunes by going into tugs himself, trading on brother-in-law's reputation. There were still old docks folk around who knew this tale, and even some who would make a slip, or no slip, and call him Köller. That could rock Yeo. Who the hell was he?

As he had been told it, his great-great-grandfather Köller made a flimsy living winding and repairing clocks in mansions around Axbridge, Somerset. *Got this little German fellow who comes in and does the lot for threepence and a cup of broth. Can't understand a word the grubby bugger says, of course, but he knows his stuff.* Not many mansions survived over there now or Yeo might have crossed the Severn Bridge with a friend one of these nights and done a couple of burglaries and exhaustive vandalisings. Fuck up a few clocks, especially. Yes, clocks – for old times' sake.

'I wouldn't mind if you put out an inquiry, Jule. One or two really decent boys. Standard aptitudes. But not from this area. I don't work with locals. As you know. This would be a prime kind of operation, worth their travel, from any distance.'

'What I love to hear.'

'Jule, you're a grand judge of talent. Management Selection could have a career for you.'

'I can mention your name?' Corbett asked.

'Not straight out at the start.'

'Would I, Paul?'

'When people seem ready to bite.'

'Exactly. Your name would clinch it, then. They'd know it's a fine project.'

But to Yeo his name had always been fragile, a nothing name from nowhere, and he was in search now not just of gain but of that basic item – solidity. You bought it or won it, then held it. Lately, an obsession had taken a grip on him: to show he could organise and lead, instead of just tagging along as before. He looked for dimensions, grandeur.

Of course, Dave Brade would regard all this as high-class,

high-flown shit – a big-talking attempt to justify big crime. It was definitely best not to upset Brade, and Brade was easily upset. He had a fierce belief in the glorious prospects for dockland, and could grow venomous with anyone he thought might foul it. Well, Yeo had the same fierce belief, wanted a hefty piece of the new scene. However, Brade would not see their aims as similar. Although he would be busy with all the routine docklands gang stuff and pimp stuff and drugs stuff – which were all pretty much the same stuff – Dave's big, brainy ears never stopped flapping.

Corbett said: 'And I might like to go along myself on anything worthwhile. You could make an exception for one local?'

'Well, of course.' Would Jule hold together under heat? You could not tell that about anyone, until it happened.

Yeo was unsure what sort of project he wanted, except he thought it must be something head-on and physical, something calibre, with plump gains, or it would fail to establish him in the style he wanted, needed. He would buy what lineage had failed to deliver. Paul Yeo yearned to be jumped-up, *nouveau riche*, Johnny-come-lately, as long as he could stay where he jumped to. Burglary, even from the biggest houses, did not fit. Burglary was furtive, plus it was getting fleeced by fences. No, it had to be juicy cash, some figure to thicken his savings noticeably. This meant a bank again, or possibly cash in transit. Something that took logistics, not a ladder.

Yeo and Corbett drank quietly for a while. The talk moved back to day-to-day stuff. That had its importance, too. Corbett said: 'So, they keep you at it?'

'Non-stop.' On the legitimate side, Yeo ran a small dredger out of Cardiff, sucking sand from the bottom of the Bristol Channel near Flat Holm Island, a unique, miniature, single-ship operation, but in profit. He had followed the family's sea tradition, with the dredger, though, not tugs. From the windows of the Starboard Light you could look out over mud flats or the dark, covering tide to the dredging grounds. Suddenly, there was a fat market for sand. Civic re-creation ate cement. And it was not just roads and buildings. If these beautiful plans ever worked, around the docks entrance there would one day be a broad lagoon behind a barrage, not, as now, the filthy, lapping tide, or long, ugly, bird-rich mud flats at low water. That barrage

12

was already nice business for Yeo. One of his grandfather's yarns had been how, as a kid living in Magenta Street, he and his gang would cook crabs in tin cans on the mud. The whole area – houses, roads and the flats – was called Rat Island, not a name to woo investment with, and they left it out of brochures. Perhaps Cardiff Bay really could bring revival. The city would still be a nowhere place without any clear way of earning its keep, but a handsome nowhere place, a lovely thing to look at and possess a chunk of.

'Running a neat little vessel like the *Splott* is fine, Jule, but a slow way to build real money. Plus, the big buggers undercutting and bringing in three times as much in the tank. And then tax. I need genuine infusions of funds now and then. I mean genuine.'

Yeo watched Corbett interpret this. 'Genuine' would say to him big, unaccounted for, and, of course, untaxed. 'I may be able to help, Paul.'

'I knew it.'

Even if the Bay dream turned out to be nearly all dream, a public relations, beautifying job only, there might still be fortunes to be made. Yeo had his one small ship and wanted more, to fight the big lads. But when it came to buying dredgers, four hundred grand was chickenfeed. This degraded him, marked him a nobody.

'Well, I'll leave that with you, Jule.'

Another plus about Corbett was he apparently had a link to fine, anonymous gunnery. Some of the usual suppliers had disappeared lately, what with age or reciprocal violence or Dave Brade, so Corbett was emerging. The suit he wore this afternoon did not say wealth, more Next, but his shirt might be handmade and the shoes non-plastic.

At 4 p.m. Yeo met an estate agent to look over a country house in the Vale of Glamorgan belonging to the estate of the late Martin Clode, or Magnificent Martin, as he had been known to colleagues and the law. The Vale was highest quality rural, near Cardiff, sprinkled with fine properties, genuine old money and spruce village churches. The Clode place proclaimed excellence, proclaimed durability. Martin had been quite a figure: young but very loaded, and a top-class leader. In fact, leader of the project that killed him – a bank in Manchester where it seemed there had been advance word to local police, and a fire-power ambush like the valley of death. That, for instance, might have been one of those Starboard Light leaks. Perhaps Magnificent had not been such a golden leader, after all, then – poor on security.

As a matter of fact, Yeo might have gone on that outing but drew back early. It had looked wrong, somehow. Occasionally, you smelt nothing but haste and information gaps and error, and you opted out. Yeo still could not tell how he had sensed catastrophe. Some had wondered about the tip and about him, he knew that. But it had been brilliant instinct, that's all: one reason he felt ready to do leadership himself.

The house, called Highcross Farm, was empty since shortly after Magnificent's end. For a while, Clode's woman, Enid, had stayed there, but then moved on with their baby. Buying this place would be symbolic. It would tell of changes – what were known as *vis à vis* changes: that is, *vis à vis* him and Magnificent. Martin had abruptly stopped being Magnificent, and Yeo might be moving up. He no longer felt satisfied living with Carol in their big, modern, detached place at Cyncoed, a prime suburb, but so utterly and dismally a suburb. He deserved more space and a quality view. And Carol deserved more, too. Highcross Farm would help bind her to him. It supplied a man with roots, a place on the map. Good God, 'The green, green grass of home' star, Tom Jones, had a spread not far away.

2

Brade said: 'Oh, yes, new life everywhere. We're so lucky to be part of the resurrection.' Standing alongside the girl's tattered corpse, he very gently pushed her hair back off her face with the toe of his fashion boot. 'Poor Olive. A lovely kid. This really tears at me, Glyndwr.'

'Well, it would,' Jenkins said.

Brade moved away a little from the body, glancing about what had once been some firm's forward-looking offices, now empty, except for soiled spears of broken glass, a couple of wrecked concertina files, ancient papers and brick fragments.

'She was run by Maximilian,' Jenkins said.

'Prince of pimps.'

A set of emergency lights had been set up near the girl and Brade's shadow jumped and swayed on the walls, ceiling and boarded windows as he did his little tour. The Scene of Crime people had been here hours ago, and there would be nothing for him to discover. He wanted to get the feel of the place, though. It was one of those things detectives did, part of the job myth, and myths mattered: helped you work long hours.

Brade said: 'Yes, Maximilian has a gorgeous pedigree, but he'll disappear soon, with the rest of them. That's what I mean, new life. Give it ten years and this will be a transformed area, right through – no whores, no punters' knives, no pushers' wars, no pimps. And no protection battles. It's happening already. Brilliant.'

'Well, I hope so, Dave,' Jenkins said.

'Captain Scott's *Terra Nova* sailed from here to the South Pole.'

'Yes, I'd heard.'

'There's a model of her in Roath Park, and a pub full of pictures.'

'Yes, I'd heard.'

Brade said: 'I like that – *Terra Nova*. New land. Definitely what we'll get here.'

'Yes?' Jenkins bent down and touched the girl's cheek for a second. 'She could still be at school, for Christ's sake. Not the sexiest of them, Olive, but really buoyant.'

'A treasure. The childlikeness would get through to many. Did.'

'Not marked, even now. If the floor dirt was scrubbed off.'

'*Hardly* marked. Above the left eye? It was a tonic to watch young Olive flash her vim in West Bute Street.'

'Dave, I was hoping you'd break it to the parents,' Jenkins said quietly. Brade had noticed before how his voice went right down when he asked a favour. Glyndwr was still a bit tender for this job, but a great talent. 'We think not quite eighteen. That your impression?'

'Clothes?' Brade replied.

'Scattered. A skirt in another old office suite two storeys up here – where that bolshy law firm, Peters, Johnson and Johnson used to plot.'

'Those sods. You saw them off, Glyn. I still don't want to know how, and nor do the brass.'

'Olive's leather jacket in the doorway of the NatWest, cut about, bloody. Erica's going to confirm. You know her fine colleagues, Erica and Louise?'

Brade did another stroll, shorter this time, and again saw nothing of use. 'This building will come down in the next stage, yes? We'll get a sea-view hotel instead – pool, gym, helicopter pad, external glass-walled lift like a Michael Douglas movie, unrivalled conference facilities.'

'Along those lines.'

'Oh, take my word. I've seen drawings. Lovely wide area in front, with a big, ample fountain. When you set yourself up somewhere, don't skimp on the fountains, Glyn, it looks mean.'

'Erica and Louise say Olive would never bring *clients* – their word – wouldn't bring a tom to any derelict office block, though there are plenty of ways in through smashed window boards. Not even for the shortest of short-times. She worked in cars or took all-nighters back to the flat. Olive's nice temperament jibbed at indoor rubble and wino shit.'

'Dumped here dead? All her teeth OK? Yes, Maximilian can pull a punch, and in his modest way wears no blockbuster rings. Handbag?'

'Not yet.'

'So, some business tiff? Max himself did her? Gone rogue? But, no, he couldn't, could he, he's – ?'

'Yes, still in hospital. Out of Intensive, but one leg in a sling still.'

'Damn disgusting street battles,' Brade snarled. 'So primitive.'

'Staff say he didn't leave his bed – couldn't conceivably. And definitely not climb through a window with a body, alive or dead.'

Brade prepared to go. 'So, who ran Olive on her beat this week? Was she free-agenting? Or Maximilian's got a locum?'

'We're looking at that, Dave. Plus there's some rumour about a special client. Possible Londoner. Jule Corbett brings very ripe folk into the area lately, looking for business opportunities in the New Bay – metropolitan developers, builders and so on. All big-time. Most big-time and straight. Some not. There are grant pickings to be had.'

'Ah, yes, Jule. Mr Middleman,' Brade said. He brushed his clothes with one hand. Brade believed entirely in the Bay regeneration, but Jenkins might have it right: the scale of opportunity could bring in large-scale London interests, not all of them pure. These deaths might be the edge of something. 'Do we tie Olive's death to the street fracas?' And the street fracas to God knew what.

'Possibly,' Jenkins replied. He brought four index cards from his inside pocket and held them spread like a fan. Glyndwr believed in stationery. Under the glare of the emergency lights, Brade could see a main name in capitals at the head of each card, with more in smaller lettering below. 'This was a very fluid and hearty rout starting in the Toledo club but spilling out on to Martha and James Streets et cetera, involving ultimately forty heavy people at least, all colours, naturally. Some women, naturally. Varying sites. What looks like all four of our principal trafficking and/or protection outfits.'

He separated one card at a time and held it up, like an ice skating judge. 'Simeon's lot. Maximilian's. Sweet Bachelor Percy's. And Les Sendanta's International Corporate Enterprises. The old brigades. They were chopping and slashing at one another for more than an hour back as far as the bridge, around the Exchange Building, and over towards the Big Windsor. This went on until 4 a.m., by when we had enough people to cope. Charting every combat incident is tricky, Dave. Maximilian's the only one hospitalised but there must be others in need of wide bandages, so we're asking around.'

Brade lingered. He took the four cards and examined each slowly. Then he bellowed despairingly: 'Jesus, only hours after that butchery talented people would start arriving on the same site for a day's gifted work in their Mount Stuart Square studios, making current affairs films and whimsical cartoon shorts, and hatching happy Welsh language telly ads for S4C. Inventive and decorous medialand by day, fucking Passchendaele at night. I won't have it. Glyn, we're going to make life here twenty-four-hour peaceful soon – no more savage night blood underfoot fouling the creative director's slip-ons.' He walked to one of the windows where boarding had been pulled loose and stared out. 'Already, just around the corner, bijou marina housing, for God's sake. Old warehouses gloriously refurbished into smart flats.

17

Such a thorough killing on their doorstep – it's indelicate. These are properties advertised as "Live now in a waterfront future", silk tie people.'

Jenkins took his cards back and then bent over Olive again. 'Oh, yes, the girl's death is almost certainly connected to the Toledo thing. She might have helped Maximilian with the pushing and crossed one of the other teams. It easily happens. Or maybe collected protection for him on someone else's ground. They're all so nervy now, with these new barons trying to move in. She's just a kid. Eight wounds, six front, two back. Oh, eight at least.'

Once more Brade prepared to leave. Jenkins remained bent over the girl again, his face a rich mixture of gleams and shadows under the lights. Probably, he was the only bilingual Welsh-English black detective in South Wales, which would mean the cosmos. His parents, themselves Cardiff dockland West Indian, had wanted him to integrate, and so the Welsh language education and his first name borrowed from that famous, ancient prince, Owain Glyndwr. Brade said: 'Switch a couple of the lamps off, will you, Glyn? They're cruel. And hot. We've done pix? She can be moved now. The doc will take his thorough look. A great and wholesome kid, our Olive. I hate handing her over to science.'

Late at night, alone in bed, again, Brade took a call from the station saying shooting had been heard just after 1.30 a.m. on the patch and an armed team were looking. Christ, yet more evil. But he felt pleased to get out, as ever afraid of the empty flat. When the phone rang, he had been trying for a stir out of three porno mags spread across the quilt alongside one another like an orgy, but not enough like. He dressed and put the books back in the filing cabinet under Investments. Out of fidelity to the girls he kept the magazines open ready at the same pages. As Brade left, the Reverend Clifford Hale-Garning came hopefully out on to the landing from his flat directly above. He was dog-collarless, in shirt-sleeves and rugby shorts, and carried a half-full bottle of tonic wine and two glasses. Eternally Hale-Garning searched for a good party, and must have heard movement on the stairs. 'No, Cliff – work,' Brade said.

18

'Poor exploited sod.'

It did not take Brade long, but by the time he arrived they had pulled Sweet Bachelor Percy fully clothed from what used to be Bute East Dock, now a neat, rectangular lake, alongside the hilarious, new, pagoda-style Council offices and a string of dinky marina-style houses. A while ago, Highlife Vernon, another home-grown villain, had been brought dead from the same stretch of water. Bachelor was not dead, though getting there. They had him on the ground beneath a towering, ancient, done-up, coal-loading gantry, unused and boatless for decades, and kept only as a touch of historical atmos. Headlights from two vans made things as clear as was needed.

'Can he talk?' Brade said.

'Mostly water when he opens his mouth,' Seaton Evans replied.

Brade crouched. 'Sweet Bachelor, it's Davey. You'll be grand. A slight wetting, but you've come through worse. A fixture, and you're looking as sharp and bonny as ever. You hearing me? What's it about, Perce?' Sweet Bachelor gave no response but lay poignantly stinking of the dead lake water, his refined, old, big-nosed face very white, except for where the bullet had smashed part of his cheekbone and taken away *in toto* his right eye.

Seaton Evans said: 'We can't try working the pool out of his lungs in case we do more harm. There are another two shells in the chest, point-blank, I'd say.' Sweet Bachelor had a lot of hair still, although he must be over sixty, and it was impressively strung out grey and soaked on the stone like a beached senior mermaid's.

Brade could tell Seaton Evans thought it rough to be hitting Bachelor now with questions. And, fair enough, it *was* hard to badger a face almost all gap. Just the same, Brade said: 'Bachelor, a dead girl, now you, well, somewhat winged. What's it about, friend? Who? Protection? You can tell Dave, can't you? Have I ever let you down? Remember that business with Grenville The Psalmist? Didn't I intercede?'

They had a couple of police greatcoats over Sweet Bachelor but he shivered suddenly and groaned, dragging hard for breath, like a précis message about life in general. Brade heard the ambulance siren. Lights came on in a few marina properties. He saw curtains worriedly twitched back and householders staring across the lake at the lights and at the tense little crowd with their big, throaty dogs. Brade felt ashamed that he could not guarantee these tidy folk a peaceful night and handsome, restful view of the poolside museum stuff.

Bachelor Percy was on his back with his good eye open, as if gazing up appreciatively at the moon and stars through the metal beams of the coal loader. Brade eased his head over to the side, so he might drain more easily from his mouth. Sweet Bachelor would be old enough to remember when this gantry, and fifty like it, worked for their living, not stood as ornamental period pieces in transplanted suburbia. Maybe the sudden foul rush of violence these last couple of days was the final defensive spasms of the lawless crews of whites, blacks and half-and-halfs who had taken what they could from this region for so long, and now knew that big ideas, government-level bullshit, county-level drive, EC-level money and smart new buildings would push them out or under. What used to be called Tiger Bay was converting to Cardiff Bay. There would be casualties. Maybe the battles were to do with getting a slice of the lovely new official riches for themselves: Brade liked sociologising a bit now and then, though he wished it was not so often a smashed body that set him going.

He put his hand under the greatcoats and took hold of Sweet Bachelor's cold fingers. Unlike Maximilian, Bachelor always had plenty of definitely precious metal around his hands, but Brade could get genuine skin contact here and there, and squeezed gently, matily, confidingly, trying to force a little strength through to him, not just because Percy had to get names out before his exit, but because he was Bachelor, and built into the scenery. All right, Brade hated that kind of scenery, wanted it gone, but he did not want Sweet Bachelor gone like this. God, to snuff it drenched in décor water beneath Victoriana. Bachelor was authentic – right-through-rotten, yes, but local-bred, with a record back to Attlee. There would be some squabbles about the jewellery: Sweet Bachelor had his title from being married six or seven times and three or four of them were still about.

'Simeon trying a take-over again?' Brade asked him. 'Bachelor, we all know Si can be unreasonable. Poaching your protection firms? You feel put-upon?'

'Dave?' he whispered, into the stone dockside. 'It's you?

Always to the fore.' Seaton Evans was right and the word came out with a little rush of dark fluid, but intelligible, almost comradely.

Brade went lower, nose to nose, regardless. Communications were the key to so much police work. You had to get to their level. The good eye looked at him, but probably didn't see. 'I knew you'd want to help, Bachelor.'

A couple of the alsatians whined and snarled nearby in their showy way and Brade waved his hand savagely behind him to get them moved.

'Dave,' Sweet Bachelor muttered again.

'I'm here. This is one-to-one.'

'Dave, they still won't give you Top Job down here then?'

'Don't distress yourself about that.'

'And I was upset to hear you had more love trouble,' Bachelor laboriously told him. After the effort he coughed for a time, spraying. 'Sorry, Dave.'

'It's kind of you, as always, to fret about my problems, but you really mustn't concern yourself now, Bachelor. Try to stay comfortable.'

'Yes, comfortable,' Bachelor said, adjusting his body a little on the stone.

'Was this Simeon? Or maybe Les Sendanta and ICE?'

'Your girl, ex-girl, called Julie something?' Bachelor replied.

'Right.'

'Big in one of those new offices in the Square, I hear.'

'Right,' Brade said.

'Gets you to live in a flat up near that fucking Llandaff Cathedral for cohabitation, then leaves you for a one-time super-grass?'

'Right. Don't tire yourself on my behalf, though, Bachelor.'

'You're the one who deserves promotion and affection, Dave, plus real consideration. Women can be so blind. Yes, blind.' He seemed to have a small laugh about that, with more water, and attempted to raise a hand up towards his destroyed eye. He gave up and said: 'Well, I won't keep you.'

Brade had the notion he was dead as they lifted him into the ambulance and decided not to do the bedside trip, not even for Sweet Bachelor. He left Seaton Evans to get on with the basics, again wiped down his clothes and sprayed face as well this time, then drove home making a detour past the house of Olive Rice's parents in Grangetown, on the west bank of the brown, deadbeat Taff. He wondered if they could sleep, following what he had told them earlier, and after Mrs Rice had been to the identification. She was the strong one. The husband had not been able to face it. The husband bothered Brade.

A light burned downstairs, although it was 3.30 a.m. He parked and entered the little front garden, feeling a sort of responsibility to them. Olive had been a delight and took her risks on his ground. Through a small gap in the curtains he saw the television screen, showing what seemed to be an old, black and white *Thin Man* film with William Powell, Myrna Loy and dog, Powell doing his handsome, charming, boozed detective. Brade watched for a couple of minutes, unable to hear the sound, but enjoying it all the same, and thinking about growing one of those sketchy, characterful moustaches like Powell's. When he shifted position, he saw Mrs Rice in a glowing blue and gold dressing-gown was watching the movie, smiling fondly now and then. On a sofa, her husband lay asleep in his clothes.

Brade decided the film was doing a better job for them than anything he might be able to offer, and went back to his car. Sitting there quietly, he realised after a couple of moments that he had been in need of company as much as wanting to give it. He drove on to Llandaff, keeping his eyes off that damn smug cathedral, and climbed into the unmade bed. He disconnected his telephone and cold-shouldered the magazine girls. Around 7.30 a.m. he slept, just after he heard the jogging student priest rubber sole past outside. The way they tried to seem part of normal life was pathetic.

3

'This was a lovely kid, Mr Jenkins, Dave,' Maximilian said. 'I had quite a closeness with her.'

'The bond between a pimp and his girl – often something almost sanctified there,' Jenkins replied.

There was an armed officer on constant guard with Maximilian, and the three of them took chairs around the bed. 'Olive had plans for herself,' Maximilian said. 'This was an ambitious girl. She thought in terms of travel. You could read exciting, distant places in her eyes. She loved an atlas.'

'I know you've got plenty on your plate,' Brade said.

'Well, I'm grateful for the guard, Dave. Twenty-four hours. I feel like that Rushdie.'

Brade said: 'We couldn't leave you strung up and available. Anyone can stroll into a hospital, private room or not. Simeon or Les with God knows what behind a bunch of dahlias. We had the same hazard with Glyndwr himself when he was concussed, and someone might have wanted to stop him coming round and talking about it. Or think of Marlon Brando nearly executed on the ward in *The Godfather*. This position, your nuts are deeply vulnerable. All things taken into account, you're looking pretty good, Max, isn't he, Glyn?'

'Glossy.'

'And you're thinking of me as a witness,' Maximilian said.

'You know about Olive. You were in the Toledo. Well, obviously,' Jenkins told him, running a hand over the leg-sling.

'And then Sweet Bachelor Percy dead, too,' Maximilian replied. 'Dear God, what's happening, Dave? Clearly, the first thing I ask when I hear that on the headphones is where was his muscle, Ivor Lestocque? Ever seen Percy without an attendant, Dave? What was Ivor doing?'

'We've wondered,' Brade said.

'We'd have given you a guard whether Sweet Bachelor was hit or not,' Jenkins said. 'You're a commitment.' The constable went down to the Concourse for teas.

Brade said: 'We wondered about some possible London involvement in the killings.'

'The kind of people Jule Corbett squires around the area now, looking for business chances,' Jenkins said.

'Involvement?'

'In one or both of the deaths,' Jenkins replied. 'What do they signify, Max? What wider picture do they hint at?'

'Tricky stuff, that,' Maximilian said. 'And you're telling me the Toledo unpleasantness was London inspired, too?'

'Maybe. Or maybe just local panic,' Brade said. 'Things are breaking up, Max. Dockland changes. We're seeing mighty

23

destabilisation. This is akin to dismemberment of the Soviet Union. Suddenly, everyone's scrambling for survival, supremacy. Why's Sweet Bachelor out apparently unchaperoned? Answer, because the whole structure of things is shifting. Discipline, loyalties, the protection conventions, time-honoured processes – nothing's as before. Did the radio specify Sweet Bachelor's wound? It was an eye. An *eye*, Max. Would that have happened a couple of years ago, even six months? Totally out of order. This is someone old enough for a train pass. It's true, God made the world from Chaos, and we'll get something great in the Bay eventually, not just the grand billboards advertising it. But what we've got now is the Chaos. Some of it comes from outside. Most developers are the soul of righteousness, but one or two could be as crooked as hell – metropolitan crooked, looking for big gain. Plus, some Chaos is homegrown. And so you're here, a casualty with black grapes.'

'Louise brought them. Well, you'll have heard from the officer. She's considerate. I'm told Erica is really down because of Olive. I mean, Erica's always down, but this is far, far down, poor old walker.'

'So, what's *your* ideas about Olive, Max?' Glyndwr asked.

'Everyone recognises that she had a gem of a ponce and partner in you,' Brade said.

'She came to me looking for warmth and love, a lonely wanderer. What else could I do but cherish her? Olive brought a special, new delight to my life. You, of all people, I don't have to tell, Dave.'

'We don't want you getting stress or weeping, Maximilian,' Jenkins replied. 'Might put your temperature up.'

'I don't know who'd wish her injury,' Maximilian said. The constable came back with a tray and closed the door. They all drank a little. Jenkins brought a bottle of Southern Comfort from his briefcase and topped up the four plastic cups.

'Your own injuries, Max?' Brade asked.

'Healing all right now, thanks, Dave.'

'You didn't see how they happened, of course,' Jenkins said.

'See? This was – well, you mentioned Chaos, Dave. This was absolute Chaos. One minute I'm in the club, swapping tales with placid friends, and then I'm lying full of pain, in the middle of the Square.'

'We're looking for a connection between that night and the Olive thing, and then possibly this wider commercial-political canvas,' Jenkins said.

'Wider canvas. He comes up with real ideas, though, doesn't he, Dave?' Maximilian said. 'Your job, boys. You search for a pattern and if there's not one you manufacture.'

'And we're assuming a trafficking or protection war,' Jenkins replied.

'Last throes among the little locals before they're stifled by world-class competition,' Brade said. 'Did Olive use much stuff herself?'

'To my knowledge, never,' Maximilian replied. 'No need. She had this natural enthusiasm about things. Yes.'

'Listen, Max, I see myself as a custodian of dockland,' Brade said. 'It's to be handed over clean and peaceful, above all peaceful, to the fine forces of change – that is, the good forces of change. Capital has to be attracted. You think the banks and institutions will subsidise gang carnage, and risk protection menace? I see someone like Sweet Bachelor removed and that has its plus side, obviously – yet not an incident to improve the area's profile.'

'Or Sweet Bachelor's,' Jenkins said. 'Where exactly was he in the Toledo events, Max? Did he or any of his people have dealings with Olive?'

'I think you feel like me about Sweet Bachelor, Dave,' Maximilian replied. 'Divided. We can do without his coarse sort, clearly, yet he had character, and nobody could wish him as much harm as that.'

'Was Olive herself in the Toledo that night?' Jenkins said. He brought a large, multi-coloured chart from his briefcase and unfolded it. 'This is the scene in the club, as far as I've been able to get. I've asked about Olive, of course. Fifty-fifty yes and no on whether she was there. Par for the course. Perhaps close to Jule Corbett once or twice – at least twice?' He pointed to a small green circle. 'This is Corbett.' He folded the chart and replaced it in the case. 'We're looking for what's beyond all this, the killings, the street war.'

The door began to open, and the guard constable stood quickly and put a hand under his jacket.

'Erica!' Brade cried. 'Well, you're looking brill, isn't she, Glyndwr?'

'As ever,' Jenkins replied.

Erica had not done any make-up and wore a man's long, grey, belted raincoat and flat-heeled canvas shoes.

'This is fine of you, Erica, love,' Maximilian said, raising his head as much as he could from the pillow to give her a smile of courage. His eyes looked damp again, with gratitude now.

'Oh, I wasn't expecting a party, Dave,' Erica said.

Brade went out into the general ward to find a chair for her. She had brought Maximilian a couple of large, gardening-hints paperbacks and placed them on the bedspread. Jenkins produced the remains of the Southern Comfort and put some into Maximilian's toothbrush glass for her. So that Max would not have to use his damaged arm, Brade turned some pages in one of the gardening books. Maximilian thrilled to the herbaceous border pictures.

Erica said: 'What about the rest of us, Dave? Are we safe – I mean safe working, safe at home? Everyone's wondering.'

'We don't think a Ripper type,' Jenkins replied. 'No abuse of the body.'

'Eight stabs, I heard.'

'You know what I mean,' Jenkins said.

'But obviously we want to know about any of Olive's most recent toms,' Brade told her.

'You said you couldn't help on that, Erica,' Jenkins remarked.

'Olive moved easily between many social types,' Maximilian remarked.

'Like did she have something going with an outsider?' Jenkins asked. 'London businessman – anything like that.'

'Obviously, I wasn't going to talk to these two, Max, before having a word with you. So, I make this journey, even if hospitals turn me sick, plus the fucking out-and-out car vandalising here.'

'Maximilian wouldn't mind you talking toms, Erica,' Brade said.

'Clients, Dave,' Jenkins remarked.

Erica said: 'Well, I . . .' She glanced towards the guard constable.

'Give us ten minutes, Llew, will you?' Brade told him.

The guard said: 'I'm supposed to – '

'I gave the orders for what you're supposed to. Give us ten minutes.' The guard left.

'Do I speak about it, Max?' Erica said. 'This could lead to all sorts, couldn't it? I'm not one of yours, but she was.'

'Well, I can understand your hesitation,' Maximilian replied. Brade heard panic.

'That's what I thought,' Erica replied.

'We can do both of you for withholding evidence,' Jenkins said.

'We'd like some time to think this over, Dave,' Maximilian replied. 'There are implications. Hazards.'

'What I mean – are we safe?' Erica said.

'Christ, a girl's dead,' Jenkins told them. 'You've got to give us – '

'How long to think about it, Max?' Brade asked.

'Say a couple of days? And some private discussion, Erica and me.'

'I can manage that,' Brade said. 'Glyndwr's going to leave you the bottle. Still a fair drop. We'll be thinking of you, Maximilian, praying for a complete recovery and ability to talk – you and Erica.'

'Are you still living up by the cathedral, Dave?' he replied. 'That was her doing, yes – Julie? – the one who preferred the ex-grass? – and now you're stuck with it? Poor sod. Chanting, are they? Can you hear it? But not in Welsh, is it? Surely? You've had a grim deal, Dave.'

4

Yeo picked up a tale that Julian Corbett might know more about the murder of a young whore called Olive Rice than was convenient. At once, Yeo decided to drop him, and drop the project they had code-talked about. From the beginning, Yeo knew Jule meant risk, of course. Yeo had needed a middleman, and a middleman's trade was to be in touch all round and with all sorts. Now, though, the risk was suddenly beyond. All at once, Yeo felt the same instinct against working with Corbett as had stopped him going with Magnificent to that prime slaughter in Manchester. Yeo demanded the simple and the safe. He was a respectable capitalist – in need of more capital, yes, but who wasn't? Just business, you could say. Jule Corbett was now very liable to a visit, visits, from Brade and the clever black, Glyndwr Jenkins – Jenkins, who lived by leverage and digging and the wider view. Yeo feared wider views, when they were taken by police. He might be in one of them. He also feared contact with anyone who was targeted. Another tale said Jule had been in the Toledo that night of the gang turmoil and Cordial Maximilian's injuries. Jule almost always *was* in there. His office. Now, he would probably be on one of Glyndwr Jenkins' gloriously detailed sketch maps. Jule had to be cut adrift, to deal with all that alone.

Corbett came into the Starboard Light one night when Yeo was there with Carol, gave him a small private nod and a small private smile from his demure, kiddy-sweet face, and stood very conspicuously alone at the bar, obviously lusting to talk plans. This had to be hit on the head right now, before any inescapable arrangements were put in hand, so Yeo left Carol briefly and drifted down that way.

'I've had a word here and there, Paul, about what you mentioned. Things look promising,' Corbett said quietly. He was keeping his voice down, but it still came out big and warm, not right for the juvenile appearance at all, more like your loaded Uncle Walter. 'Mention Paul Yeo and people respond. They have faith.'

The sod had been naming names early after all? 'So how you doing, Julian?' he replied. Yeo thought about buying him another burgundy and splash, then decided against. This was not a rerun of the other night but cancellation. 'The heat from this cop frenzy touching you?' Yeo asked.

'Brade and Co? No sweat there, whatsoever, rest assured, Paul.' He gave that a lot of confidence and intensity, and Yeo's worries grew. 'Look, Paul, what we were talking about – I think some movement.' Corbett pursed the dear little mouth, perhaps to show they were allies. Yeo felt almost bad to be mucking him about. 'Potentialities,' Corbett said. 'A couple of lads are on the road now, as it happens.' He glanced about. 'Coming down here. They're very keen for a prelim meeting. These are rare people.'

'Meeting? On what especially, Jule?'

'Opportunities.'

'Educational, business, social?'

Corbett frowned, confused. 'Business, obviously.'

'I'm not looking to do much in that line just now, Jule. As I told you, the *Splott*'s keeping me occupied.'

To clear his head, Yeo had taken this morning off and been measured for a double-breasted all-wool navy blazer with silver buttons at £320 in Jothams, then bought a pair of beautiful black, narrow-fitting fashion boots costing £280, just to let himself know he was not needy. In the tailor's long mirror he looked very fine: tall, between lean and thin, a good head of fairish hair, a thoughtful, more or less trustworthy face. All this was on the way to an identity, wasn't it, for God's sake? You did not get a gold credit card without an identity.

'Diversifying, though, Paul. And possible capital expansion,' Corbett said.

'In principle, yes. Not at the moment. Look, I hope I gave no false impression.'

'As I say, gifted lads. Available, probably. On terms.'

'Can't see much point just now, Jule.'

Corbett went solemn. 'You giving me the run-around, Paul?'

Yeo could not get ratty with an angry, tall doll.

'This was a serious conversation, Paul. Some major job in prospect.'

Bless him, though, Jule had dignity. He looked straight at Yeo, appealing for an honest response. 'Job?' Yeo replied. Now he did call the barman over and offered Corbett a drink, specifying the decent burgundy, even if it got hammered with bubbles.

Corbett said: 'I have to leave. These lads are arriving, I must meet them. They don't know the locality.'

Yeo leaned towards him, friendly. 'They'll probably see all sorts of openings around, anyway. Boom town. At first, they may be disappointed, but . . .'

'I'll look a cunt, Paul. Their travelling time, London, the Midlands. Good boys, but they can get evil if frustrated. I sold them a tale in good faith. They're expecting real propositions.

Your name gave cred. What's got to you suddenly? Scared of Dave Brade?'

'Why should I be, Jule? What have I done?'

Corbett left then, full of rage and dignity. Maybe some fear, too – of what might happen when he told these would-be recruits he had wasted their time. Yeo could not worry about that. He had dodged a crazy mistake. Who the hell except himself cared about his dim worries and obsessions over status, identity, all that eyewash? As long as Carol rated him, he was all right. Plus, he had good status as boat owner/businessman, keeping his tidy little outfit turning over nicely. He could run a reasonable existence based on the *Splott* and what he already had, gradually and unnoticeably over the next months bringing sums out from bank deposit boxes and getting them into decent investments for growth. When Yeo had been angsting about identity one day a West Indian deckhand working for him growled: '*You* feel like Nowhere Man? How about me?' That got through.

Just after returning from the outfitting shops, he had had a call from the estate agent saying that Mrs Clode could not possibly come down to below £520,000 for Highcross Farm and regarded even this price as extremely favourable, special to Mr Yeo as someone of her husband's acquaintance. Sod Highcross. Was it so vital to own acres and gates and a curved gravel drive? He saw what he had been trying to do – match those last-century mansions across the Severn where his great-great-grandfather slaved and fawned. Madness – struggling to obliterate ancient humiliations of a man he had never known.

In the bar, Yeo rejoined Carol at their table. Occasionally, when he had had a day out on the *Splott* and the tides were right she would drive down from their place in Cyncoed and have a drink with him here afterwards, as the vessel unloaded. Not far from them sat a group where fighting over a couple of girls looked imminent.

'So, what's the deep and earnest chat with Julian Corbett, Paul?' Carol asked.

'Oh, you know old Jule. Philosophising.' He could do without a question blitz from Carol. She saw a lot, fast, and her voice would move easily from loving sweetness to the rasp of interrogation. Yeo dreaded losing her. Tall and fair, she had a face that was perhaps just a fraction chubby, but beautiful and gloriously lively, all the same. He would have married Carol, but she did not want it, not yet, at any rate. 'I don't see myself as Mrs Yeo,' she had told him. He was not sure what she meant, but it made him unhappy, jumpy. Who *did* she see herself as, and when?

'We don't need to get involved in his sort of stuff any longer, do we?' she asked.

'Which sort's that, love?' He kept it mild.

She smiled. 'I've watched you grow restless. But you're not suited to that kind of work now.'

Carol spoke considerately and Yeo felt like a goalkeeper who's lost both arms above the elbow. 'Which kind?'

'The kind Julian's in. The dark regions. Darkest.'

'Oh, Jule's all right.' But she had reached him, the way she generally could. 'Not suited how?'

'Darling, don't get touchy. I mean big-time confrontation and risk.'

'I'm thirty-five. I can't handle big-time any longer? That your view, Carol?'

'Please, Paul, I'm only – '

'Could never do big-time? One of nature's corporals?'

'We could be very comfortable now, without all that – the pressure. I'm happy.'

'We're very comfortable and I have to sit here in the kind of pub where law and order don't run and a couple of yobs might catch you any minute in a glassing.'

'What's law and order to you?'

'I like things tidy.'

'And then behaving in quite a fashion, Paul,' she muttered.

'Behaving? What fashion?'

'I'm not sure. But – well, a leadership fashion. The new gear, as if you're auditioning for Mr Mighty – or Mr Magnificent, now Martin Clode's sadly gone. His house. All that scares me. I see you doing profiles in the mirror, searching for *You* again, searching for strength.'

She had a foul way of phrasing. '*Searching* for you.' If it had been 'looking for you' and 'looking for strength' it might mean he could find them, but 'searching' – that said he was frantic, knowing they would never show. Why would she not be Mrs

Yeo? Never mind that dockland future, was his own house built on sand? 'I like what I see in the mirror, as a matter of fact. What scares you, Carol?'

'It's just not you, love,' she told him.

'What just isn't?'

'Leadership. Organising. Lining up people. People like Julian, and those behind him.'

He hated the way she could always get to his doubts. 'You're talking rubbish. Lining people up? What do you know about lining people up? Lining up for what?' Control had more or less gone. 'But suppose it was right, what's so crazy about Paul Yeo and leadership? I can't organise? You're telling me that?'

'Are you putting a project together, then?' She always stuck at it.

'I told you it's rubbish.' *He* could stick at it, too: 'Carol, are you saying I couldn't lead something? I'm the nothing lad, Yeo, not Mr Magnificent? How can you stand living with someone like that?'

This hit her, he was pleased to see. Three of the men at the other table stood suddenly, cursing and swaying, one gripping a pint glass, and a woman started to shriek that she had never been so insulted, the usual pissed forgetfulness. Yeo stood, too, then stepped quickly across and put himself between the men, his hands ready. 'I think you'd all better leave,' he said quietly.

'So who are you?' one of them said. 'You're not the bloody landlord. Get lost. Who are you?'

Yes, indeed. 'Just go,' he replied. He kept his eyes on the eyes of the one who looked most likely to launch something, a kid about twenty-five, no weight or fitness there, though – a street fighter if it was a street of old nuns.

'You're Mr Yeo, yes? That's who,' one of the women asked. 'You the one who knew Magnificent?'

'You're Yeo, himself?' this king of aggravation muttered.

'Yeo,' Yeo said. Speaking the name made him feel suddenly strong. This was the second time tonight it had come out great, full of force, even history. Hadn't Corbett said it pulled volunteers, just the mention? The barman came over to help in case of violence. 'It's all right, Brian,' Yeo told him. 'These good folk are leaving.' The barman returned to serve. In a couple of minutes, the group at the table went.

Yeo returned to Carol. 'You see?' he said.

'What?'

'What? They didn't think they were dealing with some nobody.'

'What I mean, Paul. We've got it made. You're tops now. Why push for more?'

'Because I need to. You need me to.'

'No.'

'I know you do, love.'

He went out to the phone by the Gents and found Corbett's number at the manse from directory inquiries. His wife, that big-voiced, wandering, odd-ball, Henrietta, answered. Another of Jule's problem areas, but never mind. He heard her bellow for him.

'So when can we get a meeting, Jule, me, you and your visiting colleagues?' Yeo asked. 'It's a misunderstanding, yes, but why not see if we can make something of it? I always say opportunities should be grabbed, however they arise. But they understand I'm the Numero Uno in anything we fix, yes? A Yeo project, and far away from this patch, obviously.'

5

'Get here, Dave, like fucking now.' Erica's voice came in a whisper from the phone. It was just after midnight.

He put his book down open on the table and reached for a boot. 'Trouble? Dial 999.' He jammed his foot into the faithful, handmade Charles Laity.

'Just get here. Please, oh, please, Dave. Fast.'

'Someone there?' He found his other boot.

'Trying to get in.'

'Who?'

'Please, Dave.'

Bending forward as though in prayer, he lifted the front of his sweat shirt to wipe his face. When the phone went he had been re-rereading again the end of *The Great White South*, Ponting's account of Scott's South Pole voyage in the *Terra Nova*. These closing chapters always made him weep. Ponting, the expedition's official photographer, did not go on the final, disastrous stage, or there would be no book, because all five men died. But he used extracts from Scott's last journal entries, and the pages had headings Brade found unbearable: 'Death of Petty Officer Evans', 'Bravery of Captain Oates', 'Self-Sacrifice Sublime', 'The Leader's Last Message'.

Then these harsh messages from the real and now. 'How many, Erica, love?' He could hear her breathing, or gasping, but she did not reply. Hardly seeing it now, he stared down at the open book as he waited. Apparently, a recent novel mocked the Scott mission. Cheap. That word – 'sublime' – came from a grander, heroic age. Would it ever be reachable again? He loved to visualise the *Terra Nova* taking free coal aboard in 1910 Cardiff. This town reached out to the whole world, resonated, then. It might again, in a different style.

'Erica? Are you all right?' You gave these working girls your private number – made them take it – because they had perilous lives and in fact would never call Emergency. They feared uniforms. They feared being seen with uniforms – could not face open contact with police, and dreaded blue lamps outside their place, and blue lamp voices giving blue lamp orders. Others ran the law in their streets – claimed they did – perhaps, sod it, really did, off and on – and punished locals who chose outside help, especially and often terribly punished the girls. Her phone went down. He put on an anorak, then dialled Glyndwr Jenkins and got the answer machine, which was better than that noisy piece he lived with. 'Erica's,' he said. It sounded like some chic night-spot and wasn't.

In dockland, witnesses and sources were always scarce. Maximilian could be one and Erica another. Possibly, Maximilian meant to stop Erica being one and might get that message out from his sick-bed to colleagues, despite police presence. Christ, he had practice: his whole life flouted police presence. Alternatively, someone might want to silence both of them, Max and Erica, and Brade would have liked to alert the guard, but no time to negotiate a hospital switchboard. Slipping a small, heavy-headed metal cosh into his pocket he left: wasn't he door-to-door heroism in the here-and-now?

Brade parked far from Erica's house, opposite the theatre that

34

was once a church, and quickly walked the last stretch. There were still plenty of people about – girls, men looking for girls, groups on their way to a club, pimps checking and collecting, a few locals, eyes down, as ever, taxi men on call. Word would go around that he was in the area. *Dave's overtiming. Get lawful.* It could not be helped. Erica had a small, newish house just off Bute Street at the docks end, close to medialand in Mount Stuart Square, right for an intellectual whore. But she said the nearness brought little business, because they were all screwing one another, free.

Her house had a little back yard, with a wooden fence. For a minute he waited outside, listening and giving each window a good stare. The place seemed silent now, and he saw nothing to signal forced entry. The downstairs curtains were closed but he thought he made out a faint light at the edges, possibly a table lamp in her living-room. Upstairs her curtains remained open, so she could not have been expecting to work there tonight.

Walking around to the front, he found nothing wrong here, either. The peacefulness troubled him. Jesus, another dead girl on their ground – a girl who might in due time have coughed a useful tale about Olive, even about Bachelor Percy? Returning to the rear, he opened a gate in the fence and, with his hand on the cosh in his pocket, took the few steps to the house. The yard was concreted over except for a rectangle of soil against a side fence, where Erica seemed to be trying to grow sweet-peas up bamboo canes. Such a grand all-rounder, Erica. When he reached the window, he saw he was right about the light. He could make out nothing inside, though. Putting his ear against the glass, he listened for a while, but there was a lot of noise from cars in Bute Street – joy-riding, kerb-crawling, clubbing, partying – and he picked up no sound from the room. *Erica, have I failed you?*

He gently tried the flimsy rear door of the house and found it locked. Of course it was. Who left doors open around here, even a token thing of varnished cardboard? Then, as he stood there, the traffic noise fell for a moment and he thought he heard a very short, pain-filled scream from somewhere inside, perhaps from behind the drawn curtains. It was as if the sound had been abruptly stifled, forcibly stifled. At once, he shoulder-charged the door. It burst open at the first blow and he almost cart-wheeled into the miniature kitchen. Some light reached there through the part-open door to her living-room. He had the cosh out of his pocket now, and, holding it down at his side, made quickly for the lighted room. Briefly, he considered shouting who he was, and dropped the idea. Down here bright people could do instant translation, and 'Police' came out 'Target'.

He saw Erica in the middle of the room with another woman. It took him a couple of seconds to recognise her as Olive's mother. The two of them stared at Brade, terrified. Erica held a framed picture in her hand, though he could not see of what. 'Put that nasty little thing away, Dave,' she said.

'I thought trouble.'

'It was just from seeing this photograph,' Mrs Rice said. She put a hand apologetically over her mouth for a second, had probably silenced her scream like that just now.

'I hope you're going to fix that bloody door, Dave.'

He slipped the cosh back into his pocket. Going closer, he saw the picture was of Erica, Louise and Olive, arms around one another's shoulders, at the seaside somewhere, maybe Coney Beach, Porthcawl: there seemed to be the top of a fairground ferris wheel far behind them. Olive, in a simple, flower-printed dress, and lit up by the sun and a great grin, looked like a child on a day out, and that might have been about right.

'Am I causing problems all round?' Mrs Rice said. 'Forgive me. I wanted to ask some questions, that's all.'

'Dave, why I rang, she didn't just knock the door, but was moving about in the yard.'

'I was – hesitant,' Mrs Rice said.

'She thought I might have a client in.'

'In the house,' Mrs Rice explained.

'That as well,' Erica said.

'It's the first time I've ever been to this area, although I live so near. Olive never wanted us to come.'

Erica put the photograph back on her ginger sideboard and went out to inspect the door damage. 'You leave me exposed to the wolves, Dave,' she called. 'Olive's not the only girl who's been cut to death on this manor, you know.'

'I was away on a course then,' he said. Thank God. Big, big legal troubles and police career troubles over that one.

'I think you'll understand,' Mrs Rice told him. 'I had to speak to somebody my daughter knew – liked. These are people who might have an idea how it could happen.'

'Where did you get the address?' Brade said.

'I asked around.'

Appalled, Brade said: 'Mrs Rice, in this district most people are law-abiding and lovely but one thing they don't do is give out addresses.'

'Somebody did. Perhaps I didn't seem usual.'

'Well, drifting about alone down here at night – '

'People like Dave always say "down" when they're talking about dockland,' Erica remarked, coming back from the kitchen. 'It makes them feel heroic, as if only they know how to cope – in a spot where the rest of us survive as routine. It's for their image – so crucial to police. Like undaunted? No no-go areas. Also, they feel superior, because they can leave when they want and go back "up" to wherever. Dave lives by the cathedral – yes, still, Dave? – so wholesome, and leafy. Take the dog out for a shit you hear anthems.'

They sat down. Erica made tea. The room and kitchen were brilliantly clean, the furniture all rubbish, like in Brade's own place, and maybe the same discount warehouse. A serious detective was identified by shoe quality, not chattels. Erica unscrambled a nest of little genuine oak veneer tables and allocated them one each, with a circular piece of padded paper on it in case hot cups scorched right through to the carpet.

Brade said: 'I need to know if she had any recent special – '

'Contacts,' Mrs Rice replied.

'Perhaps some more important relationship,' he replied. 'Meaningful.'

'Jesus,' Erica replied, 'I never thought I'd hear anyone sane use that word, especially fuzz.'

'The kind of relationship that might have, yes, meant something to Olive – that she'd want to talk over with you and your husband. These things happen.'

'With her ponce?' Mrs Rice replied. It obviously took something for her to get that out, but she smiled marginally, to show she could face up.

'No, a relationship – a real relationship,' he said.

'Something real enough to earn eight, ten knife wounds?' Mrs

37

Rice asked. 'She was quite small. How did he find the space?' She stayed impassive. Brade had not come across many like this. 'Or it could be a she, I suppose.'

He said: It's the kind of crime where we're in difficulties, because of the victim's many, as you say, contacts, and the – '

'Unfettered life-style,' Erica remarked.

'Absence of pattern,' Brade said. 'Also, as ever, the evil silence tradition among some in this community, affecting not just Olive's death, but another you may have heard of – quite an old man, a feature here – and further pieces of violence. We're not offered information. Erica's a good, caring friend, Mrs Rice, and will chat away about anything, except what counts.'

She had brought out some sponge cake with the tea and they sat eating and drinking from the yellow-trimmed china, her room momentarily quiet except for occasional banging of the ruptured door. Mrs Rice was thin and small, like Olive, and cheerful-looking like her, even now, though not as pretty, and probably never as pretty. There had been wonderful refinement in Olive's features, still ungnawed by the job when she died. Mrs Rice's face missed that.

Now and then, her eyes went to the picture on the sideboard and dwelt there as she chewed. Strange it could move her so much. She would have others of Olive at home, surely. Perhaps it was the effect of seeing her so evidently happy in the company of the two girls, as if enraptured by this new life and these new friends: gone for keeps. Jealousy? What Mrs Rice's face lacked above all was the delicacy of her daughter's lovely short, slim nose, and the smooth line of her jaw and chin. Mrs Rice's nose was a bit too beaky, her jaw and chin too thrusting, too male.

'If it was only a casual contact, all the girls would be worried, Mrs Rice,' Brade said, 'because they could be next. Some maniac. That's why I'm wondering about a relationship.'

'We're worried all right,' Erica replied. 'I keep telling Simeon. He does nothing.'

Brade said: 'Olive was the sort who would have – '

Erica began to yell: 'I couldn't have a what-you-call – relationship, if I wanted one? Is that what you're telling us, Dave Brade? Or Louise? We're somewhere to shove it, and that's all? We can't love – be loved?' Agony tugged at her heavy face and bristled in her voice.

Brade said gently, respectfully: 'Erica, you know I don't think that, didn't mean that. I've seen you, both of you, in fine and solid relationships. History Man, for instance. All – '

'Well, I suppose Olive did give a hint or two,' Mrs Rice said.

Erica turned towards her, the anger with Brade suddenly forgotten. 'Now, careful, Mrs Rice. You need to know prevailing conditions.'

'This was a hint about someone special, Mrs Rice? Really, a love matter?'

Glyn Jenkins came in via the broken door, looking ready for trouble and boozed up to his hair-line. Brade gave him the smile that said he should sit down and stay mute. Erica brought another cup and saucer and cut him some cake. If his brain could do anything now, he would wonder why he had been dragooned into a tea party in the middle of the night. 'And now Mr Hard has arrived to help out Mr Soft, yes?' Erica said.

'How special, Mrs Rice?' Brade asked.

'Someone from London?' Mrs Rice replied. 'Would that make sense?'

'Would it?' Brade said.

'A man from London connected with the redevelopment – the Bay. In a position.'

'A lot of London firms are involved, sure,' Brade replied. 'We're a hub now. Someone – well, professional?'

'She did seem to think a lot of him.'

'Name, perhaps?' Jenkins asked, as he would, slewed or not. 'Age? *Which* profession?'

'Just spoken of in a very, well, sideways fashion by Olive. Do you know what I mean?'

'Of course,' Brade said, before Glyn could get in again. 'But someone who gave her a genuine glow?'

'It's the best I can do, I'm afraid,' Mrs Rice told them.

Brade saw Erica relax. 'We get all types around here now, it's a fact,' he said.

'A picture?' Glyn asked.

Mrs Rice's eyes went automatically to the photograph on the sideboard. 'A picture?'

'To show you what he looked like,' Glyn said. 'Girls do that.'

'Oh, no, nothing so definite.'

'Some fond description? Again, age? Colour? Married?'

'No details. Just this impression.'

'That's right,' Erica said. 'We had that impression, too. Some-one nice, kind.'

'Oh, well that really narrows it down,' Jenkins grunted, breathing something hearty and expensive into the room. 'We'll ask TV *Crimewatch* to help us find someone nice and kind who stabs.'

'We didn't like to press, Mr Brade. One thing we've learned with Olive – not to push too hard.'

'So right,' Brade replied. 'The man – visiting here off and on, or down here for a long spell, say with a firm?'

'We thought occasionally. We supposed maybe an executive who would come to inspect – to see things were all right at certain stages, then back to headquarters. She'd talk about him being here again in a few days, and would be quite excited. That kind of thing. Olive really did have feelings, Mr Brade.'

'Certainly.'

'Did she say executive, actually say that?' Jenkins asked.

'How it seemed.'

'Perhaps you wanted to think he was an executive?' Jenkins said. 'Someone with class, not your ordinary, cheap-jack punter.'

Mrs Rice looked troubled, then beaten. She nodded slowly. 'Yes, I suppose it might have been wishful thinking.'

'Your reading of things sounds very reasonable, Mrs Rice,' Brade said. 'Erica, look, between us Glyndwr and I should be able to patch up the door. We'll have something at the station for that. Then I'll get workmen around first thing tomorrow – none of our people, don't worry.'

'Did Olive ever go to London to see him?' Jenkins asked. 'Where in London? A district? The City? But, no, she was part of his scene here, that would be all, I suppose. He'd have another legit life at home.'

Mrs Rice stood up. 'I came to ask questions, but seem to have been answering them instead.'

'Erica doesn't answer questions, Mrs Rice,' Brade said. 'She's the loveliest of girls, but under the influence of her proprietor, Simeon, and very into enigma. Her name's as near to that as her parents could get. I'd rather you didn't walk from here now. Glyn and I will drive you home. Well, *I'll* drive.'

'Watch them,' Erica said. 'Oh, probably nothing body-wise.

40

They're very lack-lust. Or possibly only go for each other. They'll dredge your mind, though.'

'I wish, really wish, there was something to be dredged.'

'I'm joking about them,' Erica replied. 'Dave's fine. He'd fuck anything.'

By the time they had taken Mrs Rice home and then repaired Erica's door after a fashion it was 4.30 a.m. Brade dropped Jenkins and went to call on Maximilian at the hospital. You had to be caring. The guard was good – heard Brade's approach from yards away. There had been no trouble, he said, which meant *Why the hell am I here, minding this old, broken worm?* Brade sat at the end of the bed, while the guard took a break. Maximilian looked winsome: he had one of those faces that in sleep gave out a dignity and calm not always possible with consciousness. After ten minutes, he groaned mildly, then opened an eye and gazed through the leg sling at Brade. It was like glimpsing an animal's hellish eye at the end of a burrow.

'Davey? Here's a treat to wake up to. Better than weak tea.'

'Erica thinks someone from a London interest did Olive – at least Olive,' Brade said. 'Possibly Bachelor. Important that, Max. We have to wonder if they're on the edge of something massive. The sort of big-boy, metropolitan take-over we all fear.'

'You're fretting about me re the funerals, I expect,' Maximilian replied. 'Personal attendance is probably out. They'd think he was after the limelight if Maximilian went, wheelchaired and ward-pale. But I'll want to send some flowers, in both instances, obviously. Although I could phone from here, I'd love it if someone I trust went to the shop to make sure of quality, freshness, Dave. Irises, basically, for Olive. These have youth. Bachelor Percy? Carnations, do you think? They carry weight nowadays. Off-white. Any info yet on why Ivor Lestocque was missing on the night?'

Brade wrote the flower details on the back of his chequebook. 'Inscriptions?'

'Here.'

Brade stood and went around the bed to read the pencilled messages on his arm cast and record them: *Olive – a sweet child, gone too soon from all who loved and cherished her. God bless. Maximilian.* The other: *Percival. Ever genuine, ever cheerful, ever esteemed by his many friends, M.*

'Heartfelt, Max.' Brade sat down again. 'London?'

'Dave, you come here, sponge cake in your teeth at 5 a.m. and roll me a cracked tale about Erica talking unilaterally. The oldest trick – a bad hour and when I'm low. Making out it's to do with floral tributes. Shame.'

'Was Olive into some quite serious, continuing relationship, Max? She might need something like that, I mean, something beyond what even you could provide.'

'They'll feature these funerals – give a garish prominence on local TV,' Maximilian replied. 'Grief's not public property.'

'Some smart operator a regular with her lately, Max? Possibly top job, but gang-related – London gang. Big office car and so on. Chauffeur, perhaps. Suit.'

'Socially, we get almost the whole spectrum in dockland now, true,' Maximilian replied. 'They come late. Thank God, people like you and me always had faith in that square mile, Dave. Our lives invested there. Souls.'

'Would it have bothered you if she developed a steady thing with a loaded businessman? Someone able to dwarf you. Place in Chelsea or Hampstead. String of nags. All kinds of big, shady power.'

'You're floating the enraged jealousy option? I'd harm Olive? I was in here and helpless when she went under. There's no dispute about the time. Forensic have fixed that.'

'You have friends, Max.'

'Among whom I know I number you, Dave, without prejudice to either of our professions.'

Brade stood: 'No, Erica didn't grass anything. Nothing beyond confirming what came from elsewhere.'

Maximilian smiled. 'Erica? You don't have to worry about me and Erica. Am I likely to plan harm for her, someone run by dear old Simeon? This isn't just a girl with legs we're discussing. Her parents lived in Stoke Poges, where a sad poem known world-wide came from. Do you think I'm some sort of jungle thing, Dave?'

6

Jubilation always set in with Paul Yeo once a job was hatching, and it fizzed now as he walked slowly past this noble bank, savouring the wide, accessible swing doors and the three side-street turnings for getaway. Revolving doors could be a tangle. At moment like this, he knew it was not just money that drew him so hard to these outings. If you already had nearly half a million, most possible hauls looked minor. But Yeo adored being in a team – this time, leading. A job could wrap around him, warm him, place him, build him. His worries about Corbett he could shelve. It was the kind of team that had to hold together when the rough moments came or they would all sink, and that gave him a brilliant sense of security. He was bound into something. Even with Jule part of it, this group *would* hold together. They'd make a killing. Rephrase, rephrase; they'd clean up. The price for Highcross Farm was sliding sweetly. These big places were still hard to sell. A fair haul here would give him a bit more spare if he did buy.

Corbett had found a couple of great lads. One of them was in the bank with Jule at this moment – with him, but not actually *with* him – memorising layout, counting the staff, sizing up security guards, spotting cameras. What Jule, with his background, called prep. These lads were as professional as you could get in this sort of operation. There would always be risks and a thousand uncertainties, but you tried to minimise – keep them to the bare thousand. These boys knew that, accepted that, and were ready to work and work again at the preliminaries. The other partner was walking towards Yeo in the street, taking his own look at the geography. They crossed on the pavement not far from the bank, without meeting each other's eyes or speaking. This was the bright South London lad, Tommy Samson. He would be noticing things, storing them, yet nobody could spot it. Yeo and he would also go inside the bank soon, while the other two came out and did the exterior. That way, you had four slabs of all-round knowledge to pool. Yeo's word would be the main word, but everyone could speak.

Reconnaissance was a hazard, especially inside. Security cameras did more than put faces on a screen somewhere upstairs. They filmed. If a bank was hit, police ran recent tapes and itemised unfamiliar customers, especially unfamiliar customers who weren't customers. Casing, you picked up brochures offering investment offers or small company advice, but that looked obvious with hindsight, and hindsight was what a raid and a tape gave no end of.

Just the same, you had to familiarise. For Yeo until now, this was an unknown building with an unknown doorway, surrounded by unknown streets in a distant town. You did not just arrive with masks and pistols on the day and hope flair would do it. Flair filled jails. If you demanded a raid right off home ground, and Yeo did, you needed a good gape in advance. It was Blackpool, in season, so the streets and the bank had plenty of strangers about. That helped. The four had dressed casual, like trippers – T-shirts, sandals. Burn the stuff tomorrow.

The four of them met afterwards in a cavernous, Formica fish and chip bar just off the sea front, dolphins and manta rays and marlins muralled in jokey colours on the bright yellow walls, plus a couple of décor lifebelts and a harpoon, but you did not expect the Savoy. This place was crowded, too, and noisy, so they could talk. Yeo loved what he saw of this town. His first visit, yet he sensed at once it rated. Blackpool knew just what it wasn't and was, and he could respond – felt the same, for now. Nobody but the British did resorts like this – the confusion of stately, beautiful, old and flashy, crummy, new, the crazy, gleaming tower, a gale eating at the beach even in July and flinging sand around, the smell everywhere of low cooking – especially in here – the noiserama fun palaces. Plus the gangs of hoarse, cheery, holidaying girls and boys screwing everything they could out of their week or fortnight here, yes, screwing, screwing.

Blackpool was part Yeo's idea and part Tommy Samson's. When they all first met a week ago at a pub in Swindon, as sort of half-way point, Yeo mentioned he had read holiday-makers spent over £400 million at Blackpool in a good summer. This had been a conference just to try notions and get sight of one another.

44

Tommy was on to Blackpool fast. He laughed and looked amazed, saying that as a matter of fact he had short-listed Blackpool himself. Yeo thought he was being buttered. But then Tommy made his case. He had actually stayed in Blackpool with some bird and what he had noticed was people spent and spent, and – the great bit – most used cash. Mainly, this was a working-class spot and you did not see cheques or credit cards. Visitors forked out notes to their landladies and in the caravanners' Spar shops and off-licences, all of which would end up raw and ready and untraceable in local banks, especially at weekends, because people did not want heavy amounts lying vulnerable on the premises over Saturday and Sunday. That meant a hefty collection by security firms on Monday mornings. Tommy had checked it, seen it happen. This would be the time. That Monday morning feeling, he called it. Getting behind a bank counter these days was not on unless you did hostages, what with armoured glass and fat, ceiling-high bars. But inner doors were opened for the boys in cosh helmets taking money sacks to the van.

Yeo had felt the leadership leaving before it arrived, this know-all kid had it all so practical and parcelled up. In fact, he had been ready to drop the Blackpool idea then, to keep Tommy down. Jule must have seen it and said in his quick, fixer's way: 'Well, I suspect Paul's got a whole list of possibles, Tommy. He'll want to weigh up.'

And this thinking, creative kid, Tommy, had accepted that straight off, no pushing at all. 'It's your project, Paul. Yours right through. I shouldn't run ahead.' He was a mixture, this lad, Tommy. There was all the push, but also the politeness. And then a strange sadness in him, too, now and then – or beyond sadness: grief. Yeo had noticed it when Tommy spoke about taking the girl to Blackpool.

Anyway, the meeting was better mannered than a boardroom, and Yeo had said Blackpool did sound pretty good, so here they were with plaice and chips, plus optimism, plus workable recollections of the bank and street. Whenever he found a job that looked a goer, Yeo could shed some of that crippling gloom, which he supposed came from the Jerry in him – twilight of the gods stuff.

'Jule will get the necessary?' Graham Flanders asked across his plateful. He'd do the driving and provide cars. Forty-odd, a bit tubby but according to Jule almost track standard behind a wheel and almost clean – only very minor stuff.

Corbett said: 'Modelo A-90s. Nine millimetre automatics. One each.'

'New?' Flanders asked. Apart from the weightiness, he looked useful – small-featured, sharp-eyed behind big-rim glasses, a smile and a voice full of cockiness, but you needed that. In any case, anyone could put it on in a fish and chip caff. The day could be different.

'Of course new,' Corbett said.

'Of course,' Samson said.

'Spanish? These will cost,' Flanders replied.

'A bit,' Corbett said. 'It's a good stopper at this calibre.'

'But for show,' Yeo said. 'Frighteners.'

'We hope,' Flanders replied. 'How much each?'

'Don't worry,' Yeo said. 'I'll see to it, at this stage.'

'Paying yourself back from the collection?'

'That seem reasonable?' Yeo asked.

'Of course, Paul,' Samson replied. He did not eat much of the fish and chips. 'Make an investment for the team, you get it returned.' This lad was tall, also a bit heavy, but able to carry it, with hard-cropped hair, hefty, black eyelashes and a minor moustache. All of it liable to stand out on film? The moustache could go afterwards.

'Ammo?' Flanders asked.

'They'll be loaded,' Corbett replied. 'Fifteen rounds. That's a lot of fire-power, from four.'

'Spare ammo?' Flanders asked.

'It's not the fucking Gulf War,' Corbett said.

'Something go wrong so we're in a siege, we'd need reserves. Or it could be just one of us, cut off. Things get chaotic.'

'They won't,' Yeo said. 'I don't want them used at all, if it can be done.'

'Obviously,' Flanders replied. 'But in case.'

Thorough or jittery? Yeo could not tell.

'Relax, Graham,' Samson said. Perhaps he could.

'It's you boys I'm thinking of,' Flanders replied. 'I'm behind the wheel – the dolly bit.'

'But you'll take one?' Corbett asked.

'Of course I'll take one. Basic protection.'

'We all lose the weapons straight away after,' Yeo said.

'Skim them over the waves?' Flanders asked. 'I'll pull in on the front and we'll dawdle down to the beach.'

Yeo smiled. 'Give them to me at the last switch. I'll get them into the sea.'

'That's easy for Paul,' Corbett said.

'Get rid even if they're not used?' Flanders asked. 'We're talking what – £750, possibly a grand each gun?'

'Chickenfeed. We get rid,' Yeo replied.

'Basic,' Samson said.

'Routine,' Corbett said.

'So I'm outvoted.' For a second, Flanders held up his hands and knife and fork, with strands of battered fish on it. Surrender. 'What's the worry, though? The source dodgy? A gossip?'

'The source is perfect,' Corbett replied.

'Basic to ditch weapons,' Samson said.

'We can't know how much available,' Yeo said. 'That's a grief.'

'End of July. Almost full season. It will be rich, Paul,' Samson replied.

'Four-way equal split, except for the overheads,' Yeo said.

'You take no premium?' Samson asked. 'Leader's fee?'

'None of that,' Yeo said.

'This is generous, Paul,' Samson said.

'How I work. It's a team.'

'Right,' Flanders said. 'Jule thinks more than a hundred grand. This is right? That figure pulled me in.'

'What we'd hope,' Yeo replied.

'But no real estimates?' Flanders asked.

'We can't.'

'Could be a lot more,' Corbett said.

'Definitely,' Samson said.

'Disperse right after,' Yeo told them. 'Four different ways. Not even Jule and I travel together.'

'Basic,' Samson said.

In the car on the way home to Cardiff with Corbett, Yeo said: 'The London boy, Tommy – don't tell me how you found him, but what I can't have at any price, Jule, is linkage.'

47

'With?'

'I hear Brade thinks a London end to his problems – Olive Rice, Bachelor.'

'I heard, too.'

'You see what I'm getting at?'

'Tommy?'

'I don't mean he did them. Not at all. Did he? But, look, you go-between for London interests wanting their piece of the Bay, which is totally fair enough – your profession. But people like that would know the general scene up there, and I worry in case one of these outfits pointed you to Tommy, Jule – gave you the name. Grapevine. So, some digging in London and Brade could be on to us by accident. *That* linkage.'

Corbett laughed: 'Would I, Paul? I mean, knowing the way you work? The care. Mixing two kinds of business? Never. That would be like – oh, I don't know – that would be like bringing you weaponry already job-used. Christ, utterly slack and – slack and criminal.' He laughed again. It sounded all right, not too loud.

Yeo laughed, too. 'The story is Brade and Glyndwr see these deaths as more than – more than just dockland deaths. Symbolic. The start of something very big. They think the Bay's bringing in top-flight London villainy. Have Dave and Jenkins been getting at you at all, Jule? You'd be short-listed.'

'Oh, they'll reach me eventually, no question, but formal inquiries, absolutely nothing more. They work through the Toledo membership. It's pathetic. They'll tire. Or something else will take over.'

'It had better not be us.'

They would not risk driving into Cardiff together and had left Jule's car at Newport station.

'So, no probs, Paul,' Corbett said as they split.

'None I can see.'

'That's good enough for me.'

'Now you sound like Tommy Samson, but I can handle a bit of flattery.'

7

Brade went with Glyndwr to see Julian Corbett at Bethel Baptist Chapel in the Square. Jule deserved attention. He and his wife Henrietta lived with her widowed father, the Reverend Floyd Llewellyn, in the Bethel manse. But this evening, Floyd was giving pensioners tea and conversation in the house and asked Brade and Jenkins to use the chapel itself for their talk. The three of them were seated in a front pew, Glyn's Toledo club chart spread on the floor at their feet. Above them, on the wall, a painted text said *Without shedding of blood is no remission*. Religions could be damn blunt.

'This is you, Jule, the green J in the green circle,' Jenkins told Corbett, pointing at the diagram. 'Olive's O is in different coloured inks to show where she was at three visits – around 10 p.m., just after 12, and then 1.30-ish. Here, here and here.' Again Glyn pointed to his chart. A couple of days later, she and Sweet Bachelor were dead. Probe the Toledo battle and you probed both killings: this was Glyn's thesis, and he could be right. Working on Corbett might be a way in. Corbett lived in two worlds. Maybe more than two, though Brade knew only about the manse and the Toledo. Plus whatever went with the Toledo, which could be infinity – and might be all sorts of London involvements. Apparently, Jule had a college background, but seemed to make no use of it. Brade grieved over that. It should have given Jule access, yet here he was, still unsubstantial and grey area.

'Floyd's terribly upset, obviously, Dave,' Corbett said. 'He can remember Sweet Bachelor Percy when he'd occasionally attend Bethel. Sometimes I've heard Floyd shout despairingly in his bedroom, "Lord, what woulds't thou have me to do?" '

'Now and then He'll answer,' Brade said. 'That's the grisly part. Did you talk to Olive at all that night, Jule? She's quite close to you twice, if Glyn's got it right.' Brade pointed to the J and a red and a yellow O.

'A few words. Anything material, I'd have come to see you, obviously. In view of what happened, then and later.'

'You didn't go outside with her one of the times?' Jenkins asked, raising an erect half-arm.

'With Olive? Come on.'

'Was the talk with her about clients? We need names,' Jenkins said. 'Some visitor you might have introduced her to?'

'She wanted to have a go at the Karaoke. I said, why not? She thought the manager wouldn't like it.'

Where did Corbett's cash come from? He drew no Social Security, and that wouldn't have kept him in his style, anyway. Of course, there were a score of people in dockland with incomes and cars and clothes and jewellery and shoes that stayed mysterious. About most of them Brade could make a guess, though: permutate pimping, burglary, pushing, protection. And now and then he nailed them for one, two, three or four of these. With Jule it was trickier. He seemed to waltz his tall, wispy self around between all sorts, like the Liberal Democrats, mostly on the edge, tied to nobody, except with nauseating devotion to that strange, intemperate wife with the crazy name, and through her to Bethel and her father.

Glyn Jenkins said: 'No mention of where she'd been, who with?'

'They don't, do they? The job has its protocol. Any talking and they've got peril.'

'Arsehole,' Jenkins replied. 'Haven't you noticed, she *did* get peril.'

Brade wanted to say something about the coarseness in a church, but let it go.

Corbett had hardly looked at the chart when Glyn pointed, but seemed troubled by private thoughts. He fascinated Brade – that free-floating, freelancing, on-spec life; so different from the fenced-in career Brade had picked. Jule would know by feel how to cash in on the Bay. Local knowledge, local savvy. He might earn commissions by putting one big, outside businessman in touch with the other, spotting opportunities and potentials and hazards, smoothing paths. Maybe education did come into that, after all. These days, they had university business schools teaching instant profits, not *Great Expectations*. Jule could be Our Man in the Bay.

So, had Percy been bothering one of Corbett's mighty clients – Sweet Bachelor trying some cheeky, crude, old-style protection ploys on one of the big contractors, for instance? Had Olive been bothering one of Jule's mighty clients – refusing to accept love had ended? Would Corbett be able to handle those kinds of bloody clear-ups himself? He had no form to judge by. But if they were beyond him, he would know a few lads who could and would take them on. In some ways, Jule was like those creative business go-betweens who soared in the eighties. They might still soar where bold expansion was under way in the Bay. Was Corbett an emblem of triumphant Western capitalism?

'I'll go to the funerals,' Corbett remarked. 'To Olive's at least, Floyd's doing both, of course.'

Brade said: 'Will your City business contacts like you tear-stained at a working girl's obsequies, maybe on TV, plus father-in-law doing the show? Good public relations? Who you middle-manning for these days, Jule?'

Corbett turned the long, gentle face stern. 'They can make what they wish of it, David. The community aspect overrides. Oh, yes, of course, I hear these sudden tales of someone unrun-of-the-mill in her little life. There did seem to be a gleam of special tension about her that night. I heard a girl telling her, really going on, that she looked great, and good enough for anyone.'

'This was Louise?' Jenkins asked. 'Did she sound as if she knew the man?'

'Possibly Louise, yes. I gather she's disappeared. You heard that, Dave?'

'Oh?'

'Gone to lie low somewhere, I'd think.'

'We needed to talk to Louise again,' Brade said.

'And again,' Jenkins said. 'Erica wasn't in that night, was she? I haven't got her on the chart. But Louise is here, sitting.'

'But we didn't get an indication of which "anyone" Louise was talking about – what sort of "anyone", or where from?' Brade asked.

'Choosy, I should think, by the fuss the other girl was making. Straightening out Olive's clothes and rubbing tart-flash off her make-up.'

'Choosy to mean what, Jule? Real class?' Brade said.

'Real class to them's a pre-fuck payer,' Corbett replied.

Again Brade recoiled at the profanity, especially beneath a text

51

and from the minister's son-in-law. This was why he jibbed at religious buildings: they seemed to set up conditions, and real life had enough. Spires he detested most – the towering useless-ness and corny wish to dwarf. Bethel didn't run to one of those, thank, well, God.

'And did Olive talk to any other people, Jule?' Jenkins asked. 'Present in that section I've got Carl Minter, Bachelor for some of the time, Ivor – '

Floyd came in with one of the nice old age pensioner women wearing a grand cerise hat. She had a grievance about the neighbour's cat howling at night in her front garden despite written objections sent Recorded Delivery. 'I suggested she talk to you, since it might easily become a police matter, Dave,' Floyd remarked.

'Glyndwr deals with that facet of Operations,' Brade replied. 'He's been on the special two-year miaou course.' Jenkins made a show of asking some questions and pretended to write a few notes in his book. Then, when Glyn had taken the pensioner to the door, Brade asked: 'So, what do you hear, Floyd?'

'I hear a people, my people, crying out for peace and safety and wholesomeness.' Tall, with artfully cut white hair, Floyd had the knack of making himself look ravaged by distinguished worry.

'*Our* people. Wonderful folk here, for the most part. Don't consider yourself isolated. I hear it, too,' Brade said. 'You, me, Glyn – we're all working to achieve wholesomeness. It's why we're here talking to Jule.'

'He climbs nightly aboard my lovely daughter, and she wanted him, no question, but whether he can be believed – '

'Thanks, Floyd,' Corbett said. 'Yes, it is indeed one of my pieces of wonderful good fortune that Henrietta wants me.'

It was spoken like an exit line, as if Corbett had decided not to take this kind of reflection from Floyd. And, in a moment, Jule, too, left.

'We talk to many, Floyd,' Jenkins told him, 'measuring one story against another.'

Floyd pointed: 'And weekly I put *my* story forward from that pulpit, God's story, but who listens? The world goes its dark way.'

'You *do* have influence, Floyd,' Brade said. 'Floyd and Bethel –

so much part of things here. These deaths could be the last, grim kicks of a dying, foul regime. The new Bay's the future.'

Floyd's real names, and those on the chapel's Events board outside, were Rhys Gareth – Rev. Dr Rhys Gareth Llewellyn, Pastor – but to get multicultural he insisted on being called Floyd, after the black, former heavyweight world champion, and first man ever to regain the title, Floyd Patterson. Llewellyn idolised Patterson – kept bout pictures of him in the manse hall and spent a lot of doomed time trying to get his thin body to what Patterson's was at his peak. Floyd had his hair shaped Patterson's way, the prow bit in front. 'Some people desert your fine church yes,' Brade said, 'but, for instance, there was good in Sweet Bachelor, something he might have learned here. He could still win the love of women.'

'Oh, that,' Floyd replied. 'Them.' The door of the chapel opened. Floyd turned quickly, then whispered ecstatically, like someone recounting a vision, 'But surely, surely, here they in truth *are*.' He raised his hands, as if blessing or thanking the building for its magic influence. 'Wondrous moments of aptness are vouchsafed within these beloved walls, which Bachelor once knew so well.'

Two women and a well-dressed man came briskly in, one of the women beaming, the man doing mock-up solidity by smoking a curled amber pipe. 'Dave,' she trilled, 'we've been searching all over for you. Someone at the nick said you were here.'

'And the pipe? Does the pipe bother you, Rev?' the man asked in a rich, badgering voice. 'In a church, I mean.'

'God's house is big enough for you and your tiny fire.' Floyd beamed. 'Don't tell me, don't tell me,' he cried excitedly, pointing shyly, 'you two ladies – do I associate the faces with – seen around the area, passenger-seating in his vehicle with the late Perce? Am I right? Say former wife, current widow? Yes?'

The woman who had already spoken said: 'Intrusive? But just to see Dave.' She was about forty, with a broad, sly, comfortable face, quite decent skin, what looked to be still genuinely fair hair worn short, and a body standing up to things. She wore a classy, three-quarter length, greenish-brown, all-wool coat, the buttons terrific.

'Why, Fiona,' Brade said standing in his pew, 'you haven't aged a bit, dearest. And Miriam. It's grand to see you two

53

friendly. I'm terribly sorry about Percival, Miriam. Perhaps you heard, I was with him when he died. He spoke of you – a loving farewell. I was going to be in touch.'

'Kindly as ever, Dave. I've never understood why there should be animosity between Miriam and me,' Fiona replied. 'Bachelor and I had our day, and it was good, but it finished. Then it was Miriam. Does that mean we should shun each other? Dave, I'd like you to meet my current – Harvey. And, Harvey, here's Dave's colleague, Mr Jenkins. Gifted. Plus God's personal rep in dockland, Floyd.'

Harvey remarked: 'I'm not sure this is the place – rather public and hushed – but, as I understand it, Mr Brade, Fiona put her own personal capital into several of Percival's projects, and this might well give, almost certainly would give, a valid claim on the estate in law. As you probably know, Fiona's in the will for a quarter, but we're not at all sure this is fair. We would prefer an agreed sum, out of court, avoiding costs.'

'Bachelor had a finger in so many pies,' Floyd answered fondly, chuckling. 'There'll be some tricky untangling to do. He was evil right through, but not in a simple, easily definable way.' Harvey put the pipe in his pocket and gave some businesslike smiles. Dark-haired, slightly pasty, he might have been a year or two younger than Fiona.

'Dave, I had to come with her,' Miriam said, 'or she'd have turned up, anyway, wriggling in, getting my role, proxying next-of-kin.' The visitors took a pew now, too.

'Did Bachelor say anything about feeling threatened lately, Miriam?' Brade asked. 'Obviously, in his game – games – he would always feel threatened, and you, too, but any notable darkening these last couple of weeks?'

'Bachelor was never one to show tremors,' Fiona replied. 'Harvey will not take it amiss if I say Bachelor Percy was the calmest man I've ever met, except hormonally, of course.'

'Miriam?' Brade said. 'Did you notice anything, love?'

'Bachelor had stresses, obviously. He feared getting squeezed.'

'By the Bay machine? They all do,' Jenkins said.

'I think it was making him feel small-time, already,' Miriam explained.

'That's one thing Bachelor could never be,' Fiona cried. 'Oh, he would resist, resist. Or inveigle.'

54

'But specific worries?' Brade asked. 'Scared one of the other local outfits was better placed? Say ICE? Or Simeon?'

'I've heard one or two quite decent remarks about Simeon de Courville,' Harvey stated.

'Simeon's rubbish,' Floyd replied.

'Simeon was always something of a *bête noire* with Bachelor, it's true,' Fiona said. 'There's a coarseness present, a flashiness. White Merc, those Eyetie suits.'

'But Bachelor wasn't scared of him. No.' Miriam, in a denim jacket and worn jeans, would be about thirty-four, spare, narrow-faced, her mousy hair frizzed out in small wings at the side, going for the youthful dimension to match her gear, and doing a fair job, all told.

'Someone new, some stranger? An outsider?' Brade asked.

'The area's swarming with them, I gather,' Fiona said. 'Scenting a buck. I despair. Why wasn't Ivor with him?'

'Maybe someone new, yes,' Miriam replied.

'From?' Brade said.

'Harvey's not exactly a solicitor, not in full, but he has a notably legal background,' Fiona said. 'Many up-to-date volumes at home. I'm really intent on keeping everything amicable, and decorous. For example, I'm not saying anything about Bachelor's jewellery, although in June 1989 I did give him a ring of very great value, which he prized, and which I understand was definitely on the body when arriving at Casualty.'

'I'm not the one to speak to about the estate,' Brade said. 'The lawyers.'

'But you sort of run this area, that's the fact of it, as I recall. "My place" you call it, yes? A word from you to whoever would be of point.'

Miriam remarked: 'Obviously it's bloody rot for them to try muscling in now, Dave. Fiona took Percy for a bucketful when they split, as you'd expect. And she'd been bedding Harvey *inter alia* for months before that. Percy owes her nothing, dead or alive, and she's damn lucky to be in for a quarter. She can have the fucking ring.'

'Balm is what the church can so often offer in these tricky situations,' Floyd said. 'I think of varous contradictory parables.'

Miriam said: 'Bachelor believed everyone would be swept aside. An era ruptured.'

'Looking for an alliance, then?' Jenkins asked.

Harvey said: 'Mr Brade, we'd like to be kept in the picture with relation to Percival's affairs. I mean, Fiona would, and has a right.'

'A will's a will,' Jenkins said.

'She has to stand up for what she believes,' Harvey replied.

When they had gone, Brade said: 'Glyndwr's going to show me the spots outside where the street battling took place, Floyd. I feel ashamed – well, we both do – that this barbarism could occur so near to Bethel, a serene place of worship.'

Floyd said: 'Well, I don't know that makes sense. Bethel, the place in Second Kings, was where Elisha called up a couple of she bears to maul forty-two little children for calling him baldhead. This is a front-line church.'

Floyd went back to the manse, and Jenkins and Brade did their tour. Near the James Street edge of Mount Stuart Square, Glyndwr said: 'This is where Maximilian got his first wounds. We think we can do three of Les's ICE lot for that but not him himself, sod it. He was looking after his mother, still in the club, feeding her pork scratchings and Guinness throughout.'

'It amazes me Bethel's been able to keep going,' Brade said. 'Great spot for a night-club.'

'The Rev would never surrender.'

'And to think of Jule Corbett living here. Ours is a wonderful, cheek-by-jowl patch, Glyn. I'll miss that aspect, when it goes.'

Jenkins studied notes. 'Maximilian had only his arm broken here, and the ear damage. He tottered on into the Square a bit further before someone did his leg with a car near the Exchange.'

'Christ, once intended as the Welsh Parliament building, and now a mere locale for this foulness.'

'Two runs at him. Forward, then reverse. A Renault. Well, it could have been worse.'

In the morning, on his way to work, Brade stopped at a florist's and ordered Maximilian's flowers. There would be no official police tributes, and certainly not for Sweet Bachelor, but Brade also chose a small spray of roses to accompany Olive, from Jenkins and him personally. He put their names in full on the card and the message, *In memory of a lovely, lost child whom we all failed.*

Glyndwr probably would not mind, nor the hierarchy. Too bad, anyway. Brade paid and asked the woman not to send anything until he telephoned: the post-mortem people were holding the bodies and he had no funeral dates. As Max said, things were bad enough for Olive without faded flowers.

Brade wanted to see Leslie Sendanta today, founder of International Corporate Enterprises, the biggest protection outfit south of London, which had been bulkily represented in the Toledo on the fight night. Brade walked down from his office in Bute Street to Rat Island, where Les and the family lived in a couple of big old houses knocked into one. Sendanta could be hostile and spitting dangerous – rubbish, but, like Bachelor, indigenous rubbish, and Brade loved visiting his place, except when pulling him in. That had happened two or three times. Three, but twice the bugger's lawyers worked acquittals.

Brade dawdled for a while, leaning over the sea wall. He watched a couple of boats motor out on the tide towards the Flat Holm sand banks, one a big British Dredging vessel, the other Paul Yeo's smart, neat middle-sized craft, the *Splott*. Difficult, unknowable man, Yeo. Had there been some money-bright link with Magnificent Martin? Glyn Jenkins said so, but no proof. Glyndwr saw dark networks everywhere, a natural, mightily gifted cop. The story went that Yeo had been sniffing around Highcross, Martin's ex-house and farm in the vale. He could raise that sort of money? Brade walked on.

In Sendanta's big front room, full of very decent Victorian stuff, Brade said: 'Olive, Bachelor, Max. What's happening, dear Leslie – the start of Armageddon on the streets? I'll take you apart first.'

'Dave, did anyone see you come into my house? This is a good street – decent new families looking for a foothold in the Bay. They spot Brade calling here, and what's my reputation?' Sendanta had the kind of round, heavy-featured face and wide mouth that could occasionally give him a sweet-tempered, generous appearance, but he fought that.

'I'm supposed to use the fucking tradesmen's entrance?'

Sendanta was about fifty, heavy in the shoulders, arms and

57

fingers, too, eyes quick, skin unmarked anywhere in sight even after thirty years of local battles and his times inside. Calling on Les, you immediately got the sense of a really boisterous, cheerful, crowded household. White capitals on a Welsh slate tablet fixed outside told you the double-fronted property was called Chatsworth, after the stately home in Derbyshire, which apparently Les visited once. Brade said: 'Some animals, Leslie, if you give them pressure – if you squeeze their usual habitat – they turn wild in panic, tearing at one another and anything near.'

'This is rats? I've heard that re rats. You calling me a rat, Dave? *You* listen. Don't think you can't be reached. Your address by some priceless cathedral – it's been noted.'

'Stop shouting. Think of the neighbours.'

'Throughout that bloodshed in the Toledo and around, I'm with my mother, comforting her, that's established. This was a wholesome family occasion.' Sendanta had a lot of skill, plus, at the times he got his Not Guilties, a set of poisonously gifted solicitors. Luckily, Glyndwr had since managed to discredit this partnership and smash it. An outfit like that soured the patch, and you had to do what you could. Les also had standard flair at terror-silencing witnesses.

'To them you're nothing, Les.'

'To who I'm nothing?'

'The Bay money bags. The City of London lot et cetera. You, Simeon, Maximilian, the late Bachelor – nothings in their book. For years you were little princes, dirty little princes. Now, sod all. So you claw at one another, or even one another's girls, like Olive, trying to pull yourself out of the pit in time? Yes?'

Les stood up from the wide, brown leather fireside chair and stepped towards Brade, his big hands ready. Brade sat still, busy on an unfriendly smile. The door opened and Leslie's mother came in, a baby cradled in one arm, and holding the hand of another child, about a year old. 'I've been earholing, my boy,' she said. 'Can't you see he's here to provoke and get you blurting, jerk.'

Brade rose and gave one of his nice, full bows from the waist. 'Mrs Sendanta. And whose are these two fine additions? Glyn Jenkins is talking to Simeon today, so I get Les. There's no justice.'

'You said it.' Like her son, she was heavily made and almost as tall, grey hair piled high and majestic, her chin out towards Brade like a weapon. 'Yes, we're being squeezed,' she said. 'Well, we've been squeezed before. You and your lot try it non-stop. Other buggers. We see you off. We're still here.' She stared proudly at the children. 'There's a future for little Ferdinand, and Imogen. We hold our domain.'

'I'm trying to work out who they're like,' Brade said. 'It's someone worthwhile, not Goering. What's happened to Louise?'

'Who?' Sendanta said.

'Louise. Erica, the thinking man's tart's colleague. Has she been silenced?'

'Now, what the hell you talking about?' Leslie replied.

Mrs Sendanta came further into the room and sat down. Brade resumed his place on the long sofa and Leslie went back to his chair.

'What nauseates me, Dave,' she said, 'is you've got the nerve to come here alone, no back-up. You think a charmed life? Holding us in contempt, Dave. Unwise.'

Brade said: 'Was Sweet Bachelor getting ahead somehow, Les? He's made himself a corner with the new, metropolitan biggies? You moved him aside?'

'Percy! This family's got a name going right back,' Mrs Sendanta replied. 'Sweet Bachelor had no history at all. Common.'

In the evening, he stayed on at the station looking at statements until after 11.00, and then suddenly found himself fretting hard about Louise. He drove to her flat in one of the smaller blocks behind Bute Street. It was shut and dark, curtains closed. For a few minutes he thought about having it opened officially or opening it unofficially himself now, but decided he lacked enough to go on, yet.

Instead, on foot he made his way to Erica's beat further up Bute Street. She looked pretty good in a white alpaca jacket. 'Sod off, Dave. It scares the clients. You don't look my class.'

'These boots cost three hundred quid, for God's sake,' he said.

'Disappear and I'll fix you up free one afternoon.'

'Louise?'

'She's told you or yours everything she knows.'

'Where is she?'

'Now and then she travels. We don't have to punch a clock.'

'Where?'

'Worry somewhere else,' she said. A blue Carlton pulled in about twenty yards away.

'Don't panic. I could be your pimp.'

'You're getting above yourself.' She walked towards the car and, moving out into the road, began talking terms through the driver's window. At one point she turned to glance at Brade and laughed aloud. Perhaps the tom had asked if she was already committed. Then she moved back around the car and, without glancing at Brade now, climbed in on the passenger side. As they pulled away, he memorised the number and wondered how many times her mother had told Erica in the dear family home at Stoke Poges not to take lifts from strangers.

In the mail at his flat Brade received a picture postcard signed *Louise*. It said: *Dave, I heard you were worried about me. No need. I'm fine, just spreading my wings and lower.* It showed a small, river-trip vessel on the Thames and had a London postmark. A couple of girlie subscription mags came by the same delivery and he needed to see at once whether these could extend his horizons, so postponed studying the postcard.

A while later, when he did come to reconsider it, his anxieties grew. Postcards needed no sender's address: no door to knock and check she really was 'fine'. A bit of geography in the picture might have something to do with the sender's location, or not. And was the sender Louise? Louise's handwriting? He couldn't remember ever seeing any. Although it did look like a woman's, that meant nothing. This could be a card saying, 'Stop looking for *me*, Dave.' Or, 'Stop looking for *her*, Dave.' Why? Because she was 'fine'? Because she was not 'fine'? Because she knew too much and did not want to tell it? Because she knew too much and would not be allowed to tell it? Or, to put that worse, because she knew too much and could no longer tell it?

Why send it to his flat and not the nick? Louise had his address as well as home phone number in case of bother, and might prefer the personal touch. Or, was it someone saying, 'Lay off,

Dave, and we know where to find you if you don't' – the sort of hint Sendanta had given? Brade would hate any sort of violence so near that bloody cathedral. He put the magazines into his Investment file, then gave the postcard even more study. The picture was of a frail-looking motor boat, with a few passengers on deck. The Palace of Westminster filled the background. Louise had turned to working river excursions? Louise had landed an MP? A lord? Louise was weighted and water-logged? Brade checked he was carrying his strip of plastic and went straight to her flat and let himself in. He could hear breakfast TV through the wall from the next flat, and that would cover any noise he might make. The curtains were drawn, but enough daylight penetrated. He stood for a second inside the flat, his back against the front door, while he scanned the geography and took a long sniff. How long since she disappeared? A week? Things probably wouldn't be too bad yet, although it was summer. In any case, all the inner doors visible were shut, except at the end of the little hallway, and this one seemed to lead to the kitchen. From there came the odour of fairly recent basic cooking – chip fat, maybe, and cauliflower – and, almost suppressed by it, traces of some quite decent perfume. He had not brought the metal-headed cosh with him today. It would have seemed despondent to carry that in daylight, sign of a miserable disbelief in Bay progress.

Gingerly, he moved forward and opened a door – the required swift, sudden push while standing to the side, uncentred by the frame. It was a cupboard for hanging clothes and storing the vacuum cleaner and mops and looked harmless.

Horrified, he realised now that despite those token frets over Louise, some fraction of him wanted to find her dead. Christ, he sickened himself. Brade saw where the foul thought had come from. Taken with Olive's murder, Louise dead, here, might mean he was dealing only with a standard, nut-case, Ripper-type, tart killer, and he could manage this. It would still be vile and alarming, but the feeling that big, organised, calculating and careless outside powers were somehow involved would disap-pear. He feared those, and doubted he was in their league. If you were kept low level for years you had to believe you *were* low level. Brade had a clear notion of his range, and his range was Cardiff dockland and its usual, grubby, hard, limited evil.

Suddenly he realised that when he told Sendanta he would be nothing once the major lads moved in, Brade was talking about himself, too. He had grown used to dealing with down-market, off-Broadway villains like Leslie, or Sweet Bachelor, or Maximilian or Simeon, and doubted he could move up. Did he want to? He preferred the minor devils he knew. Their crimes and trials could be expertly dealt with, and then he would return home to the South Pole readings and other paper thrills.

Edging forward he stood still again for a second, at the second closed door on his right. Of course it could not be just a Ripper killer, for God's sake. Rippers did not send soothing postcards. And a Ripper would not do Sweet Bachelor. Brade shook with shame at the brutality he had dreamed. His job was to look after people, save them, not offer up a girl as sacrifice to keep him comfortable. He shoved the door open and stood square in the gap, a kind of daft daring, supposed to wipe out that callousness.

It was her living-room and had no body in it and nobody. His eyes went first to a large, sketched head of a man fixed to a board on the wall and pitted with holes. Three darts with red, white and blue flights formed a tight cluster on the mouth, but the holes were everywhere on the face and forehead. When he approached he saw the drawing was a very good, ungenial likeness in pencil of By-a-nose-Albert, her one-time pimp and partner, and that the nose had also in fact taken an exceptional number of hits. It had begun to break up, the way syphilitics used to go, as his father repeatedly warned him. He crossed the passageway to the door opposite, which would be the bedroom. Again he paused, again he sniffed hard. The perfume trace might be stronger, but that was all, wasn't it? What he dreaded was to open this door and find her dead-as-mutton face looking at him with condemnation for letting it happen, even wanting it to happen, and then for taking so long to find her.

This was her bedroom, the bed unmade and not too spruce-looking, a large picture of Yves Montand in that trucking movie hanging alongside her dressing-table without dart holes. Brade had seen a few tarts' bedrooms in the course of work and release, and Louise's seemed remarkably plain. Usually they had some fluffy toy on the bed, to signal childlikeness, but there was none here. Louise might be too young. Perhaps it was only the older girls who needed a teddy to deny time, and those seemed to be the sort whose bedrooms Brade had been in, one way or the other. She had no mirrors either, except on the dressing-table, no cupid statues, no fancy bed linen, just run-of-the-mill white cotton – well, whitish. She was not here, nor in the kitchen. He went back to the living-room, wanting to find anything that showed her handwriting, and began pulling open sideboard drawers. As he was crouched over trying to sort through the jumble of stuff in one of them, he heard a tiny sound behind him and turned as fast as he could, knowing it was not fast enough, and half raising an arm to protect his head.

'What the fuck you doing in here, Dave?' Louise said. 'Did you get my card?' She looked a bit worn but nothing worse, wearing a bright, cerise cotton suit.

'Why you back, Louise? This is great. You want to talk to us, love?'

'For Olive's funeral. I ask you, could I miss that, Dave?'

'Nice of you, Louise. She was a great kid.'

'And there'll be a hell of a lot of business around – press, TV, sightseers.'

'We still need to know who she was meeting. Please.'

'I didn't make the bed, did I? Christ, you ought to say when you're going to call. Just upped and went. I'd had enough.'

'I'm getting nowhere, Louise.'

'But we're all sure you're doing your best for her. And for Bachelor, the grey swine.'

'Do you know why Ivor Lestocque wasn't with him on the night?'

'Look, I don't want you to stay, Dave. My only rule is I don't screw tinkers or police, knowingly. Well, Glyndwr that once, but I was depressed then, and he can turn a phrase. One day I might change, but now I'm tired and sweaty in all the wrong areas.'

8

Paul Yeo said: 'When you get down to it, bank jobs are about where you can park.'

'So's life,' Jule Corbett said.

They managed a bit of a giggle. Three of them managed a bit of a giggle, Yeo, Corbett and Tommy Samson. Flanders, who would have to get this big car to the due spot and then out of it, muttered something Yeo missed – not something serene, not something he wanted repeated. From the Senator they could see the bank, but were waiting well back. Yeo, Jule and Samson would walk fast from here when the moment came, balaclavaing just before the door, now you see me, now you don't. Flanders had to give them five minutes inside, then mask himself, put the car close, on the pavement if need be, and wait, nicely on view, motor running, so they could topple into it with the loot and be away to the first switch, no hanging about. Flanders had called it a dolly role. It wasn't, and he knew now. What took him so long, if he had done this kind of work before?

The three would carry two empty sacks each into the bank. Filled, that was plenty of bulk and weight and not for carting far by hand. But never park right outside a bank until the end. Four tense men in a vehicle, especially on double yellows, were neon. Someone might press the alarm or do 999 on a car phone before things even started.

Corbett had another glance at his watch, nothing too jumpy, but jumpy. 'Late.' So far, Jule had been pretty sound. Yeo had definitely seen worse.

'They mess about with the timetable,' Tommy Samson said. 'To fool raiders, would you believe! But never more than half an hour in it.'

Samson seemed all right, too, but Yeo would still have liked to know more about how Jule had found him, where he came from.

'Well, I've got to be back for a funeral tomorrow,' Corbett replied.

'Funeral?' Samson said. 'Girl funeral? I heard about that.'

'Yes?' Yeo replied.

'Sad, sad, sad,' Samson said. He seemed able to give it real sorrow. Then he picked up: 'Me, I'm due at an Elvis fan club do tonight, never mind about tomorrow.'

'You'll be able to buy cokes all round,' Yeo said.

'You should hear me do my Elvis, Paul.' He pretended to bang a guitar and sang a bit of 'Blue Suede Shoes' in a warm voice that came quite close, though with some sadness there still, even despair.

'Christ, shut up and watch, will you?' Flanders bellowed, staring dead ahead like someone in shock.

They went silent. The windows were shut, but yelling in a main street had to be stupid. What happened to all that Flanders cockiness? Doing leadership, Yeo said: 'Talk can ease the strain, Graham, that's all.'

'Absolutely nil strain,' he answered, not moving his head, as though in a plaster collar, still shouting.

'We're all edgy,' Yeo told him. 'We cope in different ways.'

Flanders said: 'Just some work to do. Concentration.' Now, he did turn to Yeo, alongside him in the front. 'Oh, Christ, rabbit away if that's how you operate. Makes no odds.'

But they stayed quiet for a while, gazing ahead themselves, searching traffic for the cash van. Then Corbett said: 'Highcross Farm coming your way, Paul? The whisper's out.'

'Looks like it. Suddenly they want a quick sale. Enid's short of readies.'

Conversation shut down again. Yeo found it hard to frame his words with a dry mouth, but he loved the Britishness of chit-chat when tension put the squeeze on. Gossip proclaimed guts – offhand valour, like David Niven. Not everyone reacted the same, though. Some went totally self-contained and that could be just fine. The yell might not mean panic, and Flanders would be all right. The Senator was sure to be there, nearside doors open, engine alive when they came out, all as scheduled, and Graham ready to drive like Monte Carlo. His hands were relaxed on the wheel now, not kneading or clawing. As for hands, Yeo fought the urge to touch the Modelo A-90 in its shoulder holster, craving communion with the gun's smooth bulk. He had an idea Tommy Samson would notice that and see it as a twitch. So right. Tommy kept civil, but did he wonder now and then if he was with a Mickey Mouse gang?

The three of them left the car. A gaudy armoured van had stopped at the bank and two of the crew made their way in, red and white crash helmets, long truncheons hanging from their belts. A third stayed in the cab. They had to forget him. Of course, he'd see what was happening as soon as they reached the

bank and get maydaying. The clock would start ticking then –
then at the latest. Why they had five minutes maximum.

Corbett left the car first, second, Tommy, Yeo last. The order
did not really matter, but this was as planned. The other two
seemed to think Yeo would want it – need to see them on their
way, no backing down. That made him proud because they
never doubted he would follow. 'You'll do it great, Paul,'
Flanders whispered, as Yeo left.

'See you soon.'

'Richer.' He looked all right, sounded all right now, eyes
steady, greedy and sane, ready to meet Yeo's. Jule would not
pick someone who broke apart.

The three walked line ahead, keeping a six or seven yard gap,
again not with one another, though this time they *would* be with
one another as soon as Jule reached the doors. Tommy and Yeo
would sprint to join him and they'd go in as a screaming trio,
the automatics visible and ready, forty-five rounds on tap. This
job could have taken four at the bank, even five, so you had to
use what there was full-out. They would all have pulled the
balaclavas on by then, but not until then, as this was a busy
street. There were risks. Some of these pedestrians might remember a face, or all three. Leadership was choices. If Corbett had it
right, no face but Flanders' had been dossiered, and he was in
the car.

Jule had reached the door and was masking. Yeo saw Tommy
do his too, and then sprint. Yeo fixed the navy balaclava and ran.
A woman walking ahead heard his footsteps and turned to look.
She was oldish, wearing a light dress and straw hat, and for a
second seemed about to laugh – laugh at the absurdity of
someone in a wool helmet on a hot summer's morning. Then, as
he went past her, she seemed to realise. She did not scream, but
turned her gaze sharply from him, looking the way she was
going, and lowering her head, pretending she had seen nothing
and would never be a danger. As he joined Jule and Tommy
they all brought out the automatics and threesomed loud and
quelling through the doors.

This was always going to be the crux minute, maybe the
disaster minute. The timing had to be lucky, and the counter
door open to let the van men in and out. Plus, the terror factor
had to hit right away, or there might be resistance, even heroism.

That could come from anyone, not just the van lads. Yeo had done the street map and reckoned it would be ten, maybe twelve, minutes before the police could issue weapons and get here, supposing Blackpool had none of those fucking cruise cars already tooled up. And supposing they had no intelligence. How could they? Had Tommy Samson been obvious on his holidays and later when casing this job to log time variations? Flanders, yelling just now – had he known how to keep silent in the planning weeks? If they did have ten or twelve minutes, Yeo meant to be far from here by then and into the first car switch. As makeweight in a couple of teams he had done two bank jobs and learned speed counted more than anything. Without speed you could be shoved into using the armament, and then things might be truly unmanageable. Things might go unmanageable, anyway.

They had it beautifully right and the counter door was wide open. Yeo led in, roaring at the clerks and van pair to lie on the floor and stay there, roaring it over and over. Noise was another weapon. Fright sweat and heat sweat stung his eyes and soaked the navy wool, but mainly fright sweat. Tommy had to look after the customer side of the counter, customers there already, customers who came in, and a security guard who prowled, too bloody young and game and fit-looking.

Yes, the timing was sweet. They caught the van men bringing out their cash load, so this much was bagged. Yeo watched them think of fighting back, both young middle-aged, both tubby and soft and fatherly. These boys were trained to calculate their chances, and they looked at the Modelo A-90s and the fingers nursing the triggers and calculated there were no chances, thank God. They carried the sacks with one hand, the other free for the truncheon, strictly as per drill, probably, but made no move.

'Get flat and give it or you're dead,' Samson said, not shouting now, but very sincere and Cockney and intelligible. So the two folded down to the quality parquet floor as they were told, four burly green canvas sacks on the ground between them, like camp gear.

Corbett stood on a desk, kicking papers all ways, swinging the pistol in a great, ferocious arc, and shouting: 'Get flat we said, didn't we? Do it. Fucking do it.'

A few of them had been slow, but they stretched out now.

There was absolutely no panic, the manager would no doubt tell the media. Just surrender. Yeo lugged the four bags to near the counter door, ready for exit, then handcuffed the two van men together. He pulled their helmets off and threw them across the big room. He loathed touching their face flesh.

The strongroom stood open among the desks. A male clerk, lying in its doorway now, gazed up at Yeo. He must have been checking the money freighting. 'Get up,' Yeo said, and gave him the two empty sacks. 'Fill these.' The man lay there, maybe too scared to move, maybe resistant. His little blond moustache flickered like a score board. Yeo bent and jabbed the gun into his ear. The man rolled on to his knees, then stood. 'Good lad,' Yeo said. 'I knew you could do it. Twenties and fifties.'

He filled the sacks with notes and Yeo dragged them to the door. 'OK,' he called to Jule and Corbett jumped off the desk, his eyes bright and triumphant in the balaclava gap, and he and Yeo started slowly backing out. Each lifted two bags of money in one hand, like the van boys, but able to do better than the van boys with the other and keep the pistols moving in big sweeps to screw the jinx hard on.

Tommy joined them when they came out from behind the counter and took the last two of the bags. The three backed towards the main doors, Corbett yelling that it wasn't over yet and nobody move. It was noise, but now nothing more. Once Yeo and Jule went through the counter door, armoured glass was between them and the staff again and threats could not work. Yeo left the building first and, for a second, was too scared to turn and look for the Senator. By now, he had trouble seeing through the sweat film, anyway – wanted to wipe his eyes, but had no free hand. The wet wool of the balaclava stank and sat on his forehead like a poultice. There it was, though, the car, not quite perfect placing but near enough, with both doors open in welcome and smoke from the exhaust sending ready signals. It had been sick and cruel to think Flanders would chicken. Yeo brought his head around to look for pursuit from the bank if there was any.

'Let's get there,' Corbett said. His voice had gone high and wild. It looked and sounded like he would turn and scamper to the car.

'Keep backing,' Yeo told him, 'keep covering.' The young

security guard had appeared in the door, ignoring the orders, risking the pistols. He was talking non-stop into a handset clipped to his shirt, giving the descriptions, counting the people, reading the registration, guessing at the exit route – altogether a gutsy and brilliant asset to any bank, the sod. You'd have to be good to hit him at that range with a handgun. He came on. Tommy stopped and sniper-crouched, arm full out, classic. He took slow aim and fired twice, missed twice. Yeo saw one bullet lift a big masonry chip beside the door.

It was stupid. The boy liked violence? Was that his speciality? But if it was, he did not seem good at it. There was a kind of foolhardiness to him, as though he did not much care about his life. Despair? The notion pushed into Yeo's head again. 'Leave it,' he called. 'We're clear. Come on.' He thought he heard police sirens, but he often heard those in evil dreams. You couldn't use names. Did Tommy know he meant him?

And when Yeo tried to get into the passenger seat of the Senator, the fat sacks ahead of him, he found Flanders had moved there, must just have moved there and was staring frozen again through the windscreen, the balaclava on, his glasses in the eye space.

'Get over,' Yeo said. 'Drive. When we're all here, drive.'

Corbett was into the back seat clutching his sacks and gasping.

'Can't,' Flanders whispered.

'Write him off. Fucking drive,' Corbett howled at Yeo.

'Him?' Yeo nodded towards Tommy, still crouched, apparently careless.

'Drive. They'll blast us.' Corbett was stretched out on the rear seat, keeping low, the money under him. It could be he had fouled himself.

Leaving the bags on Flanders' lap, Yeo ran around to the driver's door. Flanders did not even seem to notice the cash.

9

Of course, they filmed him in the street on his way to Bethel and Olive's funeral. Brade knew how it would look on the evening news: here's the girl's coffin, here's the cop supposed to be finding who did her, ho, ho. He was walking on his own and for a couple of minutes felt the job weight grow almost unbearable – not the first time this had happened: his *High Noon* complex, he called it. *I could be at home with a couple of good, aided fantasies.*

Both outfits, BBC and HTV, wanted to talk to him, with Bethel's doorway in the background for a flavoursome shot. He would not have it. At no time would he have posed with a church. He had nothing to say, except how sad he was, and that would come over as creepy, police PR. Viewers could not know Olive's brightness and zest, the lovely good cheer, unsquashable until now.

Because the girl was a tart, Sweet Bachelor a villain, and the setting dockland, the public would assume a half-committed investigation, if that. In jungles jungle things happened. They'd regard a token show at the funeral as the biggest effort Brade was going to make, and many would think this enough: people like Olive and Percy went looking for pain and danger, and they'd got them. Perhaps. Brade's job, though, was still to look for whoever went looking for Olive and Percy and he gave it the lot. This place, the docks, was policed like everywhere else, and he policed it, with some help from above and below. Well, plenty from below.

In the porch, Floyd stood awaiting the body – that crazy haircut and his terrible, shagged-out shoes, manse shoes. Sometimes, Brade wondered whether those who stood in for God did well by Him. 'I learn humility from such occasions, Dave,' Floyd said. 'One feels simply part of a caring circle of local folk. Bethel is almost full, though many inside would never approve the way she abused her body.'

'Used it, Floyd, used it.'

'Some of the new office people, talented men and women. Several of the most solid local residents. My own daughter and Jule, her hubbie. And two schoolteachers. On such days, Bethel reaches out, reaches out and finds itself.'

'Press in there?'

'Here comes the wood kimono,' Floyd replied. The hearse approached, bulging with wreaths. Brade went in and found a seat at the back, well clear of that blood text. Maximilian, in a wheelchair, with his plastered leg out in front and supported on a 40 doz. Mars Bars cardboard box, was across the chapel from Brade in the left aisle. A message came yesterday that Max had changed his mind and felt an obligation to attend, despite injuries. Brade agreed at once. Max had a small, decent segment that ought to be encouraged and he was not under arrest. A couple of Brade's lads accompanied him now, in dark suits and black ties. Brade had insisted. This was an authentic occasion. There had been talk of arming them, but he overruled. Walthers at a funeral seemed wrong.

Floyd came in behind Brade speaking those New Testament words about resurrection and light as he led the coffin gang to the front. He had a fine, loud, deep, nearly believable voice, and for a couple of minutes Brade could see why people might find consolation in a church. Floyd watched fondly while they set Olive down and then briefly put his hand on the casket before going up the few steps to his pulpit, a kind of communication, a kind of possessiveness. Although he looked like a busy ashtray Floyd had core. When he went, Bethel might go with him, part of the changes. Where would the new Bay keep its soul? St Mary's up the road would stay, and the new mosque in Alice Street, and the United Reform, but Bethel might be missed.

Louise and Erica were in a pew with what could be husband and wife neighbours of the Rices, a squat couple with dull clothes, who kept their eyes on the wall ahead, trying to forget the rest of the congregation. Yet there were honest folk here. Louise had a scarf over her head and was in black leather for as far as Brade could see – a long, very superior-looking, big-shouldered, unglossy coat, which must have been hellishly warm for a summer's day but which scored in colour. Erica had not covered her head and wore a dark blue, almost matronly, loose-cut, silk-style dress, with a flowery cravat, also basically dark blue or black, around her neck. These two did gaze about, noting who had come, watching closely the progress of Floyd and the coffin party when they paraded, staring hard at the box, and then towards Olive's parents at the front. At one point, Erica turned right around, as though searching for someone. That interested Brade, and he watched to note where her gaze would settle. He learned nothing. When Erica's eyes reached him she gave a good, fat smile and seemed satisfied. Brade sent a good, unofficial smile back and she resumed facing the front and grew

71

very still. She was paying attention to Floyd, who read out the words of the first hymn. It was one Brade always thought loved being a dirge.

> *The Lord's my shepherd. I'll not want.*
> *He makes me down to lie;*
> *In pastures green he leadeth me,*
> *The quiet waters by.*

Bachelor had lain by the quiet waters of a dock turned amenity, but had not been led there, or not by anyone helpful. Yes, where *had* Ivor the minder been that night? There was a trace out for him, but no luck, so far.

The organist had a bonny touch, and Floyd gave a very strong, baritone lead, eyes closed some of the time and at others staring at the coffin or at his daughter, Henrietta, and Jule Corbett, in the third row. Floyd adored that jumpy, sombre girl and made the best of Jule.

> *Goodness and mercy all my life,*
> *Will surely follow me.*

If goodness and mercy followed Olive, at least one of them failed to get close enough.

Floyd's little sermon had gorgeous splashes of humanity. 'This torn child – we think of her agony and of the waste. And if she and we were alone in our petty lives we might despair. But she was not and is not, and nor are we.' He began to sing, unaccompanied, leaning out from the pulpit, moving an arm now and then in a wide, consoling, confiding half-circle. It was a blues number that Brade loved, 'His eye is on the sparrow'. This Southern States number would be right up Floyd's street. After a few bars, his daughter joined in, then, a few seconds later, Erica, then Brade, then a pew full of youngish people in smart, casual gear – the crew mentioned by Floyd from the new offices, here for a squint at low-life and the folk who moved in at night. The organist picked up the melody.

Maximilian seemed to be crying, hunched forward in his wheelchair, shoulders heaving slowly now and then. Maybe a

72

broken groan came from him. 'Weep?' Floyd continued from the pulpit. 'Yes. But our weeping will have an end, and our resolve to clean and save and refashion this society with the help of God will triumph.' Preachers were under foul pressure to manage a thumbs-up. At the next funeral, would Floyd have any chance of squeezing this sort of dream from Bachelor's doused corpse, ex-member of his congregation or not?

The final hymn was a rouser, its chorus a sort of fighting shout:

> *Up from the grave He arose,*
> *With a mighty triumph o'er his foes,*

– a message that death did not rate. Brade would have liked to believe that, too.

It was Mrs Rice who arose here, though, and, wearing mourning mauve, no hat, suddenly left the front pew, shoving her way fiercely past her husband, her tough little face blank, and began to punch Maximilian, first kicking the Mars Bars box away, so his plastered leg crashed to the floor. Max gave a grand yell of pain audible even above the exultant song.

Maximilian's keepers seemed slow. There were definitely no instructions, not even on nod and wink frequency, to leave Max exposed to whatever came, and Brade's decision against weapons had nothing to do with that. The officers must have thought the service had grown too much for Olive's mother and that she was simply leaving the chapel in distress. Also above the words of the hymn, Brade heard most of those used by Mrs Rice as she hammered at Maximilian's face, head and damaged ear and now repeatedly put the boot into his broken leg. 'Corrupter. Baby cunt purveyor. Child destroyer, girl alienator. Habit-maker, coke briber, pox donator, knifeman.'

The hymn had finished and people sat down. 'No,' Max cried, 'I was in bed at the time.'

'Before, you sod. She was already scarred inside and out. Seduced. Taken away from me. Punished for something by you. Abused.' Suddenly she moderated, grew regretful. 'Oh, Christ, this stupid storm of rage. I brought a knife myself to slit you, but it's in my bag.' Mrs Rice, almost lovely in her weeds, held out a hand urgently for her husband to pass the bag, like the collection-plate. Floyd had his eyes wide, nodding occasionally, getting the tempo, noting the community aspect.

Now, the two detectives did move, to Brade's relief and regret. One grabbed Mrs Rice in an arms-all-round, smothering tackle. The other went for the bag and knife. Someone from an adjacent pew tried to ease the box back under Maximilian's leg, but he could not bear it to be raised again, so some worthwhile damage must have been done, redone, perhaps permanent. Was there anything slimier than a limping ponce? The officer took Mrs Rice out and Floyd coughed briefly to signal the interlude's end. In his final prayer, he mentioned the outburst to God, as 'not, perhaps, beyond understanding – a mother's grief, a mother's rage, fruits of those feelings which thou, Lord, in Thy wisdom, hast conferred upon us as an unarguable boon.' Off the cuff, he was telling God that He had to share blame for the brutalities and the 'cunt' reference, more taboo than anything Jenkins had uttered in the church. Floyd might lack as theologian, but his heart was right.

The undertaker's men came down the aisle and picked up Olive. Louise turned as the coffin passed her again, watching it hard, then looked across to Brade. She mouthed a word: 'Wait.' Outside, when the hearse had pulled away for the crematorium, he stood among the congregation as they chatted before following or leaving. The cameras and blatant newspaper people loitered. Henrietta and Julian Corbett approached: 'You still into solitary, finger pleasures, Dave?' she asked.

They had transferred Maximilian to a stretcher and brought him out very gingerly to the ambulance now. With the church in the background, it looked like faith healing that hadn't. Max seemed to have fainted from pain. It would not be death. The cameras swarmed around him. This was going to be a tricky one for Mrs Rice: wounding with intent? Doing it to a cripple in church might offend a court, whatever the provocation. Brade would have to work on this for her.

'How's middleman life, Jule?' he asked.

'No business commitment would have kept me from here today, Dave. How could one fail to support Floyd, to support Olive, to support one's neighbours, new and old?'

'Making any money?' Brade replied.

'I know Floyd will be for ever grateful you showed, Dave,' he said. 'He wanted a spectrum.'

Brade crossed the road to Louise. 'That poor, poor woman,' she sobbed.

'Mrs Rice?'

'It got to me. Well, you see. After all, I'll talk. Fuck them. Erica says no. But.'

Brade began to move off. She would not wish to be seen with him for long. 'Where? The flat?'

'Mine? You in and out of there? Not on.'

'My place?'

'Time you had a woman in.'

'Thought you didn't with police.'

'I need to ply a bit here first. You don't mind being subsequent, do you?'

'To?'

'As it comes, Dave. I need to speak.'

'You'll find me all ears.'

'We'll find something to do with them.'

'And clean your face up,' he replied. 'You've got rivulets.'

At 3 a.m., after he had read again all the early preparations of the *Terra Nova* for Scott's voyage, he telephoned Louise. Before he had spoken she said: 'Bugger off, Dave.'

'I'm expecting you.'

'Don't.'

'You wanted to talk.'

'I had a rethink.'

'Louise –'

'I'm busy.'

'Afterwards? Don't worry it's unsocial hours.'

'Never.'

Part 2

10

'I don't know whether the hospital switched him off or what,'
Julian Corbett said. 'After all, it's more than six months, Carol.
He might just have slipped away at last. Some would say a
release.'

'Not his family? Well, obviously.'

'No frenzy, but I think Paul ought to be careful for a while
now. Frankly, both of you.'

'They still blame Paul?'

'Crazy. Not fair. But these people – Tommy's father, brother, a
cousin, his mother, even, and friends, they're part of a community, you know. Part of a culture up there. Death of a relative,
their first idea is, fix the blame. It's The Procedure. That's their
quaint term.'

'God, it sounds like Sicily,' she said.

'No, New Cross. South London.' Corbett gazed about the long
living-room of Highcross Farm. 'It's great here. You've done a
wonderful job in the time, Carol. So serene and beautiful. It
seems all wrong to be talking violence. Possible violence. It
might be nothing. I love all this real stone and wood.'

'We save on wallpaper.' She looked about the living-room,
too, and then out of the window again over the wintry fields, the
paddocks and little patches of wood, and ultimately to the Bristol
Channel. There was a tremendous sense of space, yet she felt
incarcerated. 'Bosky, I believe is the word. We're almost fully
settled now.' There were times when Carol Hobbes wanted to be
out of it and away, permanently away. They came more often
lately, these urges. Today, hearing Jule's news, she felt them
tugging at her. She could not help it. Paul really thought this
place would work the magic, settle her, soothe her, make her
want to be Mrs Yeo – Mrs Yeo of Highcross. Sad. For Paul, that
would be another step in the non-stop mission to establish
himself: husband and wife, maybe kids, in a big, handsome, old,
Vale house. Its age was crucial. Here beginneth a dynasty. But
she felt shut out from so much of him, and shut in by this damn

property: Paul had taken to calling Highcross that, not a house. Carol found it all unbearable. Well, bearable, just about, so far.

How did Jule Corbett know so much about this dead London boy's background? She said: 'Paul talks about it all endlessly – Tommy Samson. Usually a bad sign, Jule.'

'It's the old man – Don. He can be a hazard.'

Gazing towards the sea again, she said: 'Paul's about due. He's been out on the dredger.'

'Yes, I know. I didn't want to break something like this shore-to-ship.'

'He's been waiting for it. How can they blame him, Jule?'

Corbett did not answer right away, as if wanting to be tender. When he did speak he sounded sick. 'Paul was driving. It's mad but they deal in simplicities.'

'But he shouldn't have been.'

'Of course not. Oh, Jesus, that's down to me. In all these months there's been no day when I've forgotten. I pick Graham Flanders and he breaks up. If Paul hadn't – If Paul had crumpled, too, we could all have been blasted. The police had six marksmen there a minute after we cleared. Body armour, the works. Paul was brilliant. A leader.'

She had heard all the recollections, all the arguments, all the rationalising, a thousand times before. Did they sound feebler the more they were repeated – more frantic, more cloudy, less true?

They gave her pretty much the same story each time, Paul and Jule, except that Paul's version had stuff about Jule that Jule never mentioned. Maybe Jule could tell stuff about Paul that Paul never mentioned. But for now at any rate she was Paul's and had to see things his way, wanted to see things his way. And he did not trust Corbett – never had, in full. So Carol didn't, either. Even today – now – Jule looked so neat and mild and sensitive. She could not believe in him.

'Here he is,' she said. Yeo's blue Rover passed the window, crackling along the drive: best quality gravel, pumped from the Channel bed by the *Splott* herself, of course. For a moment she glimpsed him in profile and decided he had probably picked up the news. Either that or, seeing Corbett's car already parked outside, he guessed things were dark. Although glimpsed for only that second and sideways on, his face showed misery and regret, even dread. Carol could not recall him ever looking afraid before. He was in that bloody navy blazer with the silver buttons, like a tennis umpire. Once stopped, he turned to give her a small wave, then sat in the stationary car for a while, obviously getting himself together. He'd be OK. Given time, Paul was always OK.

When she left the window and sat down, Corbett said: 'Tommy wouldn't have talked, even if he'd surfaced. And the family won't. That's Procedure, too. They handle these things for themselves.'

'God.'

By the time Paul came into the room, he wore that serene, victorious smile he had picked as right for leadership, and for the new laird of Highcross. She wished he would work less hard on his roles. He strode towards Corbett, hand out in greeting, buttons flashing, eyes manic with confidence. She could see no dread in him now and had to admit it was a hell of a perform-ance: the sort of effort that made him pitiful and so lovable.

'I don't think we've got anything to worry about, Jule,' he said, shaking Corbett's hand. 'But it's good of you to come out. I'd heard, though no details.'

'Obviously, we can't send named wreaths because cops always get to that sort of villain funeral. They'll be looking for the leads he didn't give. But a coded job, and I'll tell the Samsons off the record who it's from. Something simple, though definitely not cheap. Sincere. It's vital we make our gesture.'

Paul said: 'Well, they've had time to come to terms with it, I'd have thought – the family and so on.' He sounded brave, almost offhand, and then spoiled it. 'Haven't they, Jule?' It was a plea for the right, comfortable answer. Carol wished she could do something to help but felt lost. Corbett did not reply.

'How can they blame Paul?' Corbett had already told her the answer, but she still had to ask. They sat down and she poured some drinks.

Corbett said: 'Look, it's envy as much as anything. The Samsons hear Paul's moved to a new place since the outing, at over half a Big One, smarter car, even thinking of a new vessel. And they've got a dead son/brother/cousin/mate.'

'None of that caused Tommy's death – our house or the bloody car or ship,' she muttered.

'They're not logicians, love,' Paul said.

81

'For God's sake, don't sympathise with them. They got their cut, didn't they?'

'Of course. Everything was dead right,' Corbett said. She saw him wince. 'Everything was exactly right. Knowing Paul, what else? I personally delivered that and gave the sincerest regrets, obviously.'

'They're bound to hate us,' Yeo said. 'Me.'

'It might still all blow over,' Corbett replied. He went into a flat-voiced, lecturing tone. 'There's Billy – that's Tommy's brother – and Don, and Tommy's cousin, known as Amiable. Hard to tell how they'll jump now. The culture lays down the way you act when kin's betrayed – as they see it, I mean. They understand only brutality, even before this. So, I worry. On top of hearing about this house and the possible new boat, they're sure to get a wrong idea of the actual job and of what happened.'

'Well, we hit him with the escape car – no getting away from that,' Paul said. Once he did face some trouble he faced it head on, another of the things in him Carol loved.

'But they're liable to have a crazy, poisoned account,' Corbett replied, 'which they believe because they want to – an escape from grief. Maybe they've even been fed lies by the Blackpool police, so they'll turn angry, do a vengeance trip and put the finger on the rest of us. That's standard. The law want everyone who was in the Senator. They don't give a shit who killed Tommy Samson. Good riddance.'

Paul sat crouched on a chesterfield. 'Honestly, I offered him every chance to reach the car.'

Over and over she had heard this. It came out now as if he repeated it to himself even oftener. She couldn't tell whether he believed it, and had not been able to tell when he first said it.

'Even too much,' Corbett replied.

Paul had hinted, half hinted to her in that slippery way of his, that Corbett helped mess up the Blackpool thing, not in the Flanders class, but sufficient. 'Jule, you go to London and see the family? You've told them Tommy had his chance?' she asked.

'Again and again. I've drawn it for them, Carol.'

'Of course he has,' Yeo said. 'For his own sake, not just mine. I trust Jule to do his best for me.'

And it sounded good. It sounded true. 'Jule, do you ask them what sort of version they've got, and where it came from?' Carol said. 'This distortion.'

'I can't pressurise. Not too much. Tommy's people start looking evil at me, too, for backing Paul. I'm from his manor, so just as much a foreigner – seen as in some dirty conspiracy against their kid. And, of course, I was aboard the Senator when we hit, and I recruited him.'

'Mad to think of you like that.'

'How they are,' Corbett said. 'Programmed minds.'

He sounded and looked like a gold medal middleman, someone who would always see himself safe, regardless. The more he talked loyalty the more she heard the only survivor somehow on the raft. In her eyes it pulled Paul down that he worked with such people, made him grubby. 'How the hell Tommy's lot know Paul was on this job, I still don't understand,' she said. 'You didn't tell them, Jule?'

'Would I?' he replied. 'No, I enlist Tommy and, clearly, he boasts to them about who he was working with. Paul's a name, even in South London.'

'People tell their parents and friends something like that?'

'Don Samson's not like any parent, is he, Carol? He's in the trade. Paul asked me to put some feelers out, so I go to folk I know – the Samsons in New Cross, bloody Flanders from the Midlands.'

Paul stared out of the window, and when he spoke it was as if reciting. 'I was slowing, expecting Tommy Samson to get in after firing. Why he fired, who knows – stupid. This was a kid who right up till then acted like a good soldier, the best, fitting in, being sensible. Some strange, inner darkness and sorrow but always entirely constructive and a real help. Then, suddenly, he can't stop himself blazing off. So I wonder now if he knew more about hit jobs than robbery.'

At once and very firmly Corbett said: 'Oh, no, Paul. Am I likely to bring someone like that in, an animal?'

The little-boy face pleaded for reasonableness and understanding. Carol saw he was scared. He'd fucked up on both people he supplied?

'If he was a hit-man he wasn't much of a one, anyway,' Paul replied. 'Not with an automatic, at least. Maybe knives and

83

closer range?' She did not understand that. What was being said? Paul remained bent over, not looking at Jule. Carol did look, and saw him working hard to hold his face impassive. Paul said: 'Almost as if he didn't care what happened to him – overwhelmed by this mysterious gloom. By now the security man has come right out of the bank. This was one hell of a bloody hero, Carol. He grapples with Tommy, who's struggling to hold on to the bags of loot. I'm moving the Senator up towards Tommy, no speed, I swear, no speed, but we're not parked where we should have been, so I want to make it easy for him.'

'Certainly,' Corbett said.

'And then suddenly he's somehow right in front of the car and under us. He could have been shoved by the guard, you know, deliberately.'

'How I've always read it,' Corbett said.

'No speed, but I know we went over him.' Paul took a drink and coughed, some of the scotch dribbling down the gorgeous blazer in a thin line. 'I can feel it now,' he said, 'the body. Knocking into someone like that who's sideways and on all fours – there's bulk, like a big dog, and the car jumped and lurched. I lost my grip on the wheel for a second. He's still holding the sacks and he looked up at me from the road with his dark eyes, maybe even a proud little smile because he had managed to keep the money.'

'Stop,' Carol shouted.

'Yes, I could have. Stopped. I looked in the mirror and Tommy was not too great on the tarmac, one bag oozing notes by his side.'

'Please, Paul. You're hurting yourself.'

'Myself?'

All this was new to her. How slow was slow? Why couldn't he have touched the brakes, then? How was Samson so 'suddenly' right in front of the car and under it? 'You're saying the guard's the one they should go after.'

'He got out of it with no scratch,' Corbett replied.

'He deserved a medal,' Paul said.

They were all quiet for a while. She saw the two men running that day's doings through their minds yet again, shaping and reshaping and suppressing things to fit the version they needed, perhaps the version they believed. But in New Cross Tommy Samson's clan would be playing the sequence in their own heads, and seeing it *their* way.

'What exactly do they think, Paul – that you were in such a rush to get clear you abandoned him?' Carol asked. 'Belting out of the scene without Tommy, and then not stopping to pick him up when he was hit?'

Paul stretched out on the chesterfield now, apparently relaxed, his blazer undone. Perhaps he had decided to get back some poise. Confession had done him good? 'Tommy should have dropped the sacks and used both hands on that guard. This was just insane greed. Well, we're all into greed, so I won't be harsh with Tommy.' He had a short laugh. 'Harsh with him? Nice! I ran the poor sod down. But Jule can't say to the family it was the boy's own fault, can he? Too agonising for them.'

Briefly, he looked full of agony himself, then remembered he was at ease. 'Even without Tommy's haul we had plenty. He'd have done all right. Well, his family *have* done all right. We lost all his load, anyway. Absolutely no need for him to get battered like that, head and chest crushed.' He drifted into silence for a few seconds, then sat up and crouched over again in misery. 'Oh, God, what a mess, Jule. A kid's life. However you see it, it was committed to me.'

Corbett said: 'I could hear the two-tones. You had a duty to the rest of us.'

'The family won't swallow that. I don't blame them.'

'I'll fix you up with some weaponry, just in case, Paul,' Corbett replied. 'You got rid of the other after the job?'

'Of course.'

'These aftermaths,' Carol murmured.

Yeo said: 'Carol didn't want me to have anything to do with that job.'

'Dim to bring it up now,' she replied. It was not true, anyway. She had objected at first, yes, but what he said that night in the Starboard Light had troubled her and eventually changed her mind. She did not fancy being known as a nobody's long-time girl. She could not have cared less about Highcross or the Rover or a new dredger, but she did want Paul freed from all those mad, belittling worries of his. And now he had some extra. She knew Paul had hoped the long wait for Tommy's death would make family anger fade. Instead, hate festered. Now, they might come looking.

'How soon can you get Paul some armament, Julian?'

'Very.'

'The dockland police – Jenkins and Brade – do they wonder about your life, Jule, your income?'

'Glyndwr and David are no worry.'

'And the Samsons – what are they capable of?' she said.

'It would have been better if you were still in the other house, really. There'd be people around. Easier to defend. It's remote here, and a lot of open ground.'

Paul stood up and went and gazed out of the window, across the larger paddock, as if expecting to see invaders right away. 'Yes, quite a bit of no man's land,' he said, and laughed again. 'Mind you, people like Samson – I mean London people – they don't much fancy coming off their home patch.'

'You've got prowler lights outside?' Corbett asked.

'Of course. Magnificent had those put up,' Paul replied. 'And the alarms.'

'We could be worrying about nothing,' Corbett said. 'I'll get my ear to the ground again.'

'If it seems bad, maybe you could move in for a time, Jule,' Carol suggested. 'Double the fire-power.'

'That's certainly an option,' Corbett replied. She saw him thinking of ways to dodge that one, if the time did come. This lad lived on contacts, and who shot their suppliers?

When he had gone she said: 'What was that about using a knife, then?'

'So hopeless with a pistol. The lad must have had something going for him.'

11

At home, towards midnight, Dave Brade had a couple of visitors. He had been watching *Prisoner: Cell Block H* on TV, one of his favourite programmes for conversation, human interest and fashion, but when they came in Erica wanted it switched over to something on the arts show about a writer called Joyce, who turned out to be male, and Irish. Brade did not fight too much. 'You'll be missing the party,' he said.

'We were worried about you,' Louise replied across the noise of the books panel. They were chewing over a cheery item called *The Dead* and the significance of a horse in it. 'Not tarts-with-hearts-of-gold worried, but scared you might get thrown off the patch now. Dave, we can't face that. We've got a proposal. This will save you, keep your job. Information, Dave. What you've been craving.'

They had their work gear on, but with any luck nobody in the building would have seen them at his door. What with the time and so on, they would not pass as Jehovah's Witnesses. Louise's gear was not too bad, in fact, except for the boa. Erica had to give her legs every chance and the denim skirt did.

'All-round acquittals today for the Toledo mayhem. Your chiefs are going to be pissed, yes?' she remarked, half turning from the discussion, now about snow on a grave. She pointed with her thumb at the screen. 'Fucking Hampstead plonkers, this gang.'

'Jury wouldn't believe us,' Brade said.

'I've heard of that sort of thing,' Louise remarked.

'And Maximilian's evidence – deliberately useless. He knows who did it to him, but – '

'You really expected him to spell that out in the box?' Louise asked. 'Even now he's keen on life, Dave.'

Brade said: 'He could have got us such sympathy – all that obvious damage and pain. I'm disappointed in Max.'

'This is a filthy place, Dave,' Erica said, looking around. 'You'll catch something from it. Nice area, too. Whited sepulchre.'

'What information?' Brade asked.

'So, we thought you'd be depressed and we ought to come out,' Louise explained. 'We left them celebrating the Not Guilties in the Toledo and around, but it will last a couple of days and nights at least, so we won't miss anything.'

'Yes, feeling all-through sick,' Brade replied. 'Listen to this, will you, Louise – one of their damn QCs said I couldn't get any progress on Olive and Bachelor so was trying to fit people up for the Toledo thing – rough justicing.'

'He must know you, Dave,' Erica said.

87

'She. Glyndwr's hurt beyond – his great battle charts laughed out.'

'Dave, it changes things. We're still terrified – even more – but we have to cough now,' Louise replied. 'Why we're here.'

'I've heard this before.'

'I told you, things have changed.'

'And we thought a nice prolonged threesome, to buck you up,' Erica said. The author's portrait had come up on the screen and she was giving attention to this squinting Joyce, speaking over her shoulder. 'You've got some scotch or grass? We felt it only decent to offer aid, in view of your annihilation, Dave.'

Brade said: 'But, Louise, you – '

'Don't with police? I'll stretch a point. This will be medicinal. You can have your mags out as well if you like. You're keen on a crowd.'

'Pussy to the right of you, pussy to the left of you,' Erica said.

'I'm a bit into buttocks, as a matter of fact.'

'Louise goes for that. Me, no. Why we both came, to give scope. One of us could have brought the information.' Erica switched off the programme.

'What information?' Brade asked. He went to his filing cabinet and produced some whisky and wine.

Louise had picked up a framed photograph from under a chair. 'Pretty, and with willpower, I'd say. This a picture of Julie, the bird who walked out on you?'

'Ran. I should get rid of that photo. But – I still set a place for her sometimes at table.'

Erica remarked: 'If you cleaned the place a bit, I mean, just the basics, jemmying off one or two levels of shit, not lunatic house-pride, she might come back. You want that, though? Dave, you've got to stay on the patch. These people above you – hard, unforgiving. You'll catch the flak for those acquittals. And they'll hear what the cow brief said about six months of getting nowhere on Olive and Percy.'

'They'd already noticed I'd got nowhere,' Brade remarked.

'But uttered in public now, making monkeys of you and yours.'

'Do they shag at all or like blow jobs – on the house – any of those higher-ups?' Louise inquired. 'So we could apply a kindly influence for you.'

'Who the hell would we get in your place, Dave? Some new broom.'

'Besides which, if you go, dockland gets bloody ungovernable – Simeon, Sendanta, Max, the whole poison cocktail. You could feel that new power in their champers-and-chilli party tonight. The rats are up out of the sewers, smiling, Dave. Who's going to contain them? Nobody but you can do that.'

Erica said: 'Mind, Glyndwr's not bad and the right shade, but not on his own, nor with someone new who hasn't got the knowledge, and the disposition. Things could get rough for us. Rougher. Unprotected entirely.'

'What information?' Brade replied.

Louise asked: 'If you show some progress, they'll leave you alone, let you stay, Dave. Tell them the case is cracking, slowly.'

'They know the slowly bit.'

Erica remarked: 'Well, I'll strip, shall I, Dave? I forget. Do you like doing that for a girl? Gusset fetishist? I need a kinks card index.'

'Pull the curtains, for God's sake, Erica,' Louise remarked. 'There's a church out there with a sculptured Christ.'

'What information?'

'Olive's special lad, obviously,' Erica replied, quickly naked.

'Yes?' Brade said.

'It's a bit vague,' Louise replied, 'but the computer might turn up something.' She slipped out of her clothes, too, and began ceremonially to undress Brade, humming some requiem.

'A name?' he asked.

'A first name,' Erica replied.

'A first name he gave Olive,' Louise said.

'So it might be right, might be make-believe – a cover,' Erica said.

'Do people use their real name with us?' Louise remarked. 'But it's something, Dave – something for you to show the hierarchy. You'll tell them, from a confidential tip, very confidential. You wouldn't want it around that you're banging two *poulets* at once in your home. Not at your rank.'

'Take care how you use it altogether, won't you, Dave? Where could the name come from, but her chums?'

'That's true,' Brade said.

'Thanks for being such a comfort,' Erica replied.

'Please, Dave, no comebacks.' Louise moved towards the bedroom, holding his hand.

'I know how to be delicate,' he said.

'Of course you do,' Louise replied, her kid-face old and terrified, though, for a couple of seconds.

'Are you going to get the porn, Dave?' Erica asked.

'Well, yes. It's that bit extra.'

'Right,' Louise said. She and Brade paused.

'This is a lad about twenty-five, South London somewhere,' Erica told him. 'And called Tommy. Smart, tall, dark-haired, nice-looking, thin moustache, and he does Elvis impersonations – good ones, with guitar, of course.'

'Is it useless, Dave? Of course, "Tommy" could be just a joke – I mean, a tom.'

'Tommy? I wish it could have been Jasper or Ivo – a trifle rarer in South London. We can try,' Brade replied. 'Did you ever see him?'

'God, look at him. It's obvious you're deprived,' Erica said. 'Doing it to yourself never answers, you know. We do have a saintly role, you see.'

'He wouldn't meet us,' Louise replied. 'Or maybe it was Olive – wanting to keep him strictly to herself. That does happen. But she described him – like that.'

'I'll get Glyn to check with the Yard's computer to see if they've got anything on a lad called Tom, about twenty-five, into attacking working girls. And I can talk to Jule Corbett at this end,' Brade said. 'He's in touch with a lot of London connections. No luck with him earlier, but if I can give him a name – it's possible.'

'Jule?' Louise grew anxious. 'Well, be especially vague about sources,' Louise said.

'Jule? He's all right, isn't he?'

'Is he?' Louise replied.

'So get the picture reinforcements, and mind you don't jam that in the file drawer,' Erica said.

12

At home in Highcross Yeo had a chirpy call from Jule Corbett saying some London contacts were very eager to meet '"the great Paul Yeo" – their words, Paul, though I wouldn't argue"' – and happened to be in the neighbourhood. 'They've got a proposal I'm not privy to. For direct discussion between principals. As ever, I'm go-betweening, that's all. The Bay really is putting us on the map again.'

What sort of map? This did not seem the kind of stuff Yeo wanted talked about on the phone. It did not seem the sort of stuff he wanted anything to do with at all. He preferred good distance between himself and Jule's London acquaintances. Tommy Samson had been a London acquaintance. Were the ripples of big-time dirt edging his way?

'Absolute fans, Paul. Absolutely nothing unpleasant. Well, would I?'

It sounded a bit too absolutely all right. 'Meet where?' He would not let these people into Highcross. That was home now, a decent, established, Vale atmosphere. Carol could get happy here and serene, despite the threats. She was bound to learn to love it. He could have said the Starboard Light but gossip sprouted fast from there. He could have said the owner's cabin on the *Splott*, but never mixed different sides of his life. Jule did not offer the manse, where Floyd and pushy Henrietta prowled, so they picked a back-street café in a district of Cardiff called Pontcanna, wherever they got a name like that. The area was a mix of tall and small old housing, and was growing chic because the two television outfits had settled nearby and many of their staff lived round about, sounding off to each other in shops and bars about their great programmes. You could call the district smart, as long as you had not been anywhere.

Over cappuccinos now, Drinkwater, the giggly one, said: 'Well, we've heard tell of you, of course, from way back. The name Paul Yeo, it's always been golden. But when we got a whisper and it was confirmed that you managed that Blackpool outing – well! And when I say a whisper and confirmed, I don't mean from Jule in either case. Rest assured of that. If there is one thing Jule Corbett does not do it's leak. Why he's in demand.'

Jule nodded acknowledgement.

'The Blackpool visit was style, Paul. We said, "This boy we must have with us."'

You would think he was picking a cricket team.

Hamer, his bald, big-eyed friend, went for modesty and quietness, at least at this stage. 'Look, this is going to sound strange, Paul, but running down Tommy Samson, regardless of your definite feelings for him, when he didn't stick to the rules and was putting the whole team in trouble – that was classic getaway motoring – moment of truth material. It's the sort of flair and hardness we're searching for Paul, to complete our squad. And so we're here now, having asked Jule to put us in touch. And let me also stress – we went to Jule, not Jule coming to us.'

Maybe Corbett saw they were hammering it too hard. 'Thanks, lads. But I know Paul would never think I'd spill.'

'That escape, so total, so profitable from out of possible disaster – work of an ace operator.' Drinkwater chuckled noisily for a while, high-pitched, in spurts. He did like a laugh. Soft soap and it seemed all wrong. They were talking about a boy's life and a family in pain, however crude. 'We know the Samson people from a long way back,' Drinkwater added.

'We appreciate you felt bad about it, Paul,' Hamer said, those dish-aerial eyes suddenly laced with double-measure pity. 'Tommy Samson had real points. The whole family's got points. Don's first wife, Norah, a sweetheart and large-hearted in many ways – Tommy's mother – and now Eloise, and her swimming. But you did what had to be done.'

Jule had taken off his coat and jacket and hung them on the back of his chair to prove relaxation. He said: 'The thing about Paul, lads – is these days *he's* the one who actually puts jobs together. He organises. He leads. What you're suggesting is only to handle the car? Paul can talk for himself, naturally, but I'm not sure at this moment in his career he wants to be just Wheels.' He sounded like a personal agent, which Yeo could have objected to. But let it go. That was the sort of job Jule always did.

Drinkwater nodded hard a couple of times. When he spoke

now it was in the slow, clear style for someone deaf or stupid. 'Paul, we know that. Why we're offering some special help, you see.'

'This is a deal you'll really see the merits of, Paul,' Lance Hamer said.

Lance, bollocks. Probably his real name was Sid or Arthur. Yeo was hot on names.

'In a nutshell, we'll help you see off Don Samson,' Drinkwater declared. 'You can't handle that family alone, not even you, Paul, although accomplished. You don't want them invading and fucking up your legit business, do you – the *Splott* et cetera. What I hear, you're thinking of expansion, another boat. You can do without distractions from New Cross. And that's the least they'd do. You personally are a target, naturally.'

'Don Samson?' Yeo replied. 'Wipe him out? Oh, look, I don't want – '

'You're right: Don's definitely the one to worry about. Billy, younger, stronger-looking, and a genius with armament, but no real stature,' Drinkwater said. 'He'll back Don in whatever, though, and there's another, a cousin, Jason Young, the one they call Amiable.'

'I don't worry about Don,' Yeo replied. 'From what I hear he's experienced. He'll understand it was inevitable – Tommy, I mean.'

'What he understands doesn't come into it, Paul. The Procedure rules him.' Hamer had an old briefcase with him, a really distinguished article, reddish in soft leather, and he brought from it two big pieces of paper. He glanced about the café, almost empty in mid-afternoon, then passed the documents over, still looking very considerate, almost as if he wanted to say sorry for what they showed. At once Yeo saw they were foully thorough plans of Highcross and the grounds, every door and window marked in, every security light, every alarm, the house done from the side and front. 'Only copies,' Hamer said.

'Of what?'

'This is something Don Samson had specially prepared last week,' Drinkwater replied. 'They were done for him by a talented group of researchers we know, so in a roundabout way and at a price we got access.'

'They've been down here?' Yeo said.

'Wouldn't you say?' Hamer replied.

'After all, it's only what we expected, Paul, isn't it?' Corbett told him.

'You'll see your bed's marked in,' Drinkwater said.

Yeo muttered: 'But how the hell...?' He had so carefully excluded these two from Highcross, but others had already been around there, sniffing and sketching. That unnerved him. The whole notion of being sucked into London business unnerved him, revolted him. It brought a new scale, and he might look small. He felt what he had built here and was still building could be smashed. Suddenly, his breathing grew fast and jerky.

'You wouldn't see someone's face pressed against the window at Highcross while they did the drawings,' Drinkwater said. He had a giggle about that and even Jule gave a laugh but stopped it. Despite the schoolkid ways, Drinkwater could be fifty, maybe a little more, with all his hair, but grey, and a doughy, grey to beige face and very heavy, rough-cut moustache, mostly still black, the grey just starting to get in there. Grey would soon be his general theme visually. He was careful about his clothes, and had on a very white shirt, with a dotted tie in a bright but not rowdy mix of colours. Looking at him, you might have said a head waiter off duty or owner of a shaky sweet shop. Probably he and Hamer were a settled couple. That did not matter at all, everyone to his special ways, though it was worth knowing.

'Yes, Don understands about Tommy,' Hamer added, 'but not the sense you mean, Paul. Or he thinks he understands. What he thinks is this was no accident – and thinking it is as bad as fact.' Hamer's voice stayed pretty low. He had that take-it-or-leave-it way of talking, like doctors.

Yeo said: 'If he really wants I can tell Don the full tale on Tommy, really go over it yard by yard. There's nothing to hide.'

'Not a fucking thing,' Corbett added, striking the table.

'Could I guess what that security guard would do?' Yeo asked.

'Don thinks his thoughts,' Hamer replied, 'and the thoughts are stuck on him by a culture. What experience and his brain tell him doesn't matter.'

Yeo found he longed to rip the plans to pieces and scatter them, as if that would make him and his house and his place in things safe again. Whenever the door to the café kitchen opened, the paper rustled mildly, like someone or something creeping up on him. Now and then he felt Highcross was a curse, supposed to bring solidity but making him weak, a terrible pride error.

'What we don't know is the kind of group he's putting together to visit you, Paul,' Drinkwater said. 'Himself, Billy and Amiable, for sure, yes. How many others, though? They'd come mob handed.'

'But one thing's certain: take out Don and the lot falls to pieces,' Hamer remarked. 'That's the beauty of it.'

Drinkwater said: 'The Procedure very definitely fixes the duty on Don. Billy wouldn't have the impetus, and Amiable – a cousin, he's only on the edge of it, really. He'd wait for orders. Most of the time, Amiable's amiable. Not when he's been pointed at some target, though. You've got to dig him out of the betting shop in New Cross Road.'

Hamer stood and walked to the window. Yeo watched, Hamer glanced back and saw his interest, gave a little frown and immediately sat at the table again. 'Sorry, Paul. Just getting the circulation going. Not to alarm you. I see nobody out here. We're totally incognito in the area. No tails.'

Drinkwater said: 'I look at those plans, and Lance and I have been out to take a glance at Highcross itself, from a distance. Beautiful spread. A lot of fine landscape. Undefendable. I gather Jule mentioned that. Hence, hit first. Pre-emptive the word, Jule?'

'Exactly,' Hamer declared from behind his cup. 'We can point you to where Don will be, at a particular time and very exposed. And we can also make sure there's no interference. That's our personal commitment. These are very unusual circumstances. Don doesn't often go unprotected and hardly ever acts to a timetable.'

'We're determined to make things easier for you,' Drinkwater said.

'On the other hand, we do appreciate this is not at all your sort of thing, Paul, seeing off someone from cold, as it were. We're not saying it's easy, only necessary – for the sake of your own protection.' Hamer took that very slowly, getting the words right, so all of them could see the interesting difference between easy and necessary. The last bits of winter sun shone in behind him, giving a real golden gleam to his scalp. He waved his hands a little, to emphasise things, helping out the gentle voice. He might be a drinker or big eater, his neck creeping up to take over part of his face, and his breathing was obviously hard going – always, not just in a crisis like Yeo's. Hamer was younger than Drinkwater, probably a good ten years, but more worn. He would have been better without so much light, even when it was pale and came from behind, like now.

Julian Corbett remarked: 'You boys make a case, I wouldn't argue, but you have to realise Paul's a businessman. He's got standing in this area, the *Splott* and so on. Prospects as the Bay expands. It's a fair shock to have people come at him with those plans and start talking about . . . well – '

'An execution,' Drinkwater said. 'Certainly it's a shock.'

Of course, with a middleman like Jule, you never knew. His job was to set something up, not pull it to pieces. This could all be pre-planned between the three, including Jule's objections, and the showy catering for Yeo's point of view. That might be so Hamer and Drinkwater could deal with the doubts and seem reasonable.

'Don't we know Paul's value!' Drinkwater cried, beaming about the obviousness of it. 'Look at Highcross!'

'It's just Don will blast you *in situ* if you give him a tenth of a chance,' Hamer remarked, 'and that means if you let him live. You don't realise how heavy the pressure will be on him to do you.'

'We'll set him up a treat, Paul,' Drinkwater said, 'and as part of the package you handle the driving in our later enterprise. I can promise you you won't need to run any of us down!' That gave him a subdued cackle for a while. 'We're disciplined, we're thinkers, we're street-sound. This is a job just over the Severn Bridge from your area, a realm we're not familiar with, so knowledge of the roads et cetera will be another plus, on top of your skills.'

Did these two know somehow that he longed to do damage across the bridge for an ancestor's sake?

'Oh, and there'll be a useful gain for us all,' Hamer added.

'Yes, we might as well mention the bloody object of the exercise!' Drinkwater said, through another small guffaw.

'Maybe not in the supreme league by your Blackpool standards, Paul, but chances like that come rarely.'

'It will be adequate and we hope untraceable,' Drinkwater

said. 'You'll have some big expenses now, living up to your image at Highcross, and this will be a contribution, Paul. You're going to need true hunter nags and clobber soon, surely. Integration at the right, county level. You can't lose. Don out of the way, plus a juicy pay day.' Drinkwater leaned over and took the plans back, folded them and handed the papers to Hamer.

Jesus, how could you know if they lied? How could you know if Jule had put those drawings together for them, a dark, insistent bargaining ploy? Jule had education and versatility. Could outside people do a survey like that and nobody spot them? These two might want Don Samson wasted for their own reasons, and had looked around for a candidate to edge into doing it. They'd set Samson up, yes, but for somebody else to do the actual gunning.

'I'll have to weigh all this up,' Yeo said.

'Of course,' Drinkwater replied.

'But, listen, Paul, we've put it in front of you, utterly open, from true respect, so we wouldn't want to think you might chicken out,' Hamer remarked.

'Not a question of chicken out, for God's sake. Options. I've got all sorts of commitments, developers to supply, a diary to consult.'

'I don't see how you *can* chicken out, given our frankness, and given the menace from Don,' Hamer said. He was facing Yeo, eyes popping and breathing like a steam train.

'I don't usually work in my own area, or even near,' Yeo replied. 'The police here – they're sharp. They're good at spotting signs.'

'Brade?' Hamer said. 'The skids are under him. He fucks up all round – wanking, tarting, crossing the neighbours, dreaming.'

'Jule's been briefing you?' Yeo asked.

'There won't be anything for police to spot. We know you've got a stake in this town, Paul, and always avoid local trouble,' Drinkwater said. 'That's why the special extras – the co-operation offered re Don. Would Lance and I want to get involved in a hit on the Samson family otherwise? A fierce tribe. We're really putting ourselves out in your interests.'

Jule leaned forward, smiling, like a spokesperson. 'I think Paul sees it's an offer worth considering. He can't commit himself at this stage.'

'Right,' Drinkwater declared.

'But the opportunity to snuff Don imposes a timetable,' Hamer said. 'This opening comes very soon, Thursday week. His second missus, Eloise, is in a women's water polo final. Rare item, women's water polo. He'd got to be there, giving support.'

'After that, he and his boys might be down here in the Vale or around the Starboard Light looking for you and yours, anyway, Paul,' Drinkwater said. 'He'll have Carol listed, naturally. That's a lovely relationship and needs cherishing. And from our selfish point of view, we don't want any damage to our driver, do we? You're an investment.'

'Say an answer in a few days?' Hamer remarked. 'A yes answer?'

'Oh, Lance gives pressure, in his own quiet way,' Drinkwater said with another loving chuckle.

13

Brade was summoned to divisional headquarters in Cathays Park to see Raging Bullfinch. There had been a brief fall of snow and the grass areas around the park's glossy, pillared war memorial glinted like confectionery under a light cover in morning sun. He took a short walk near the soaring stonework, getting his defence together beneath the angel of death and his sword, footprints mucking up the white sheet. This could be final. They had been very patient with him.

Until now he had carefully not disclosed upwards the name given him by Louise and Erica, and especially not to Bullfinch. As tips went it was hopelessly thin, a tiny starting point, almost laughable. Anyway, he wanted control of how the information was used. Bullfinch could be hasty, shrill, liable to flutter about all over, like a bird trapped in a room, oblivious of where excitement shit might fall. And so the nickname. Any noise or unsubtlety in the search for 'Tommy' gave the girls peril – more than they already had. This morning, though, Brade realised that if R. B. took him off the patch, or off the cases, the girls would be exposed, anyway, and Glyndwr Jenkins' job might grow shaky, linked to a has-been. Brade had obligations. He prepared to offer optimism.

In his fat-faced, slit-eyed, pert-nosed, whizz-kid, jumpy-calm way, Bullfinch looked troubled. Stacked on his desk were what appeared to be about a dozen porno mags, and Brade thought he recognised the top cover's comforting, assertive bare female behind, though it had been besmirched by some liquid, possibly oil or Worcester sauce. The magazines seemed to be giving off an old sprout odour.

'Dave, by mail I've had a round robin complaint from good people in your flat block,' R. B. said. 'This is up near the cathedral?'

'Oh? Yes, lovely folk.'

'Do you recognise these magazines?' He spread a few of them on his desk, so that more covers and grand thigh regions were visible, some of these also unpleasantly stained. Good recollections nudged at Brade. The sprout smell strengthened.

'I?' he replied.

'They came in with a letter signed by the occupants of seven flats in your block, Dave, alleging that you "systematically" – their term – dispose of these articles in other people's waste sacks, not your own, spreading them around.'

'Amusing,' Brade replied. Christ, what sort of people went snooping in waste? Never did he place the books on top, determined to avoid offence. Having taken the trouble to lift their bloody old cat food tins and veg and chop bones and God knew what else to shove the things right under, he received this sort of thanks. 'May I see the signatures?'

Bullfinch retained the letter. 'Think of it as a confidential whisper to me, Dave. Neighbours don't like taking grievances direct to a police officer – those foolish, traditional fears of us. And particularly this sort of grievance, possibly. I don't see this behaviour as standard for a promising detective. Couldn't you burn them, on completion, Dave?'

'There are no open fires – I mean, sir, supposing I had such stuff.'

'You can see their point of view? One of these bags gets ripped open by dogs and the collector carrying it from their door to his vehicle finds the pictures and associates them for ever with number seven or nine or fifteen in the block. Which are you?'

'Eight.'

'There you are, then. This is high-quality accommodation, I believe, Dave, and the signatories could well be decent old people or, in that location, vicars, even prebendaries, possibly gay vicars and prebendaries. None of those folk might wish to be shackled in the minds of the refuse collector to this open-leg art, made butts of coarse humour at Cleansing. Besides which, some, including myself, would regard this material as anti-woman.' Right-on thinking had helped zoom Bullfinch up the greasy pole. He struck one of the magazines with the back of his hand, and a little waft of Hoover dust reached Brade. 'You do share them out in the bags, which gives an element of fairness, yes. But even so.' He flicked some pages. 'Have you thought of moving?'

'Shall I take them away, sir?'

'But not to repeat the problem, Dave.' He piled up the magazines and pushed them across the desk to Brade. 'And the second part of their letter speaks angrily of what they call "an orgy din" coming from your place three nights ago. You had girls in? Along those lines?'

'The noise would be something on TV. One of those worth-while programmes about rites in India. I must have accidentally knocked the sound up.'

'This was "flesh sounds" – again their term – Dave. They say they checked all channels and there were no comparable effects. Beating? You them or they you? Obviously, this is entirely a matter of taste, but have you thought if you were in some fracas such as the Toledo brutalities, were hospitalised, and doctors see whip scarring on a senior detective? The Chief would be disappointed. *Do* you have girls in there? Aren't the magazines enough? That's what I understood, since Julie.'

'I'll move the TV off that wall, sir.'

'They bring you anything?'

'Who?'

'The girls. Inside stuff about the patch?'

'Well, sir, I'm happy you asked that and do think we might – '

R. B.'s voice grew thoughtful. 'Look, Dave, as a matter of fact, I don't mind these cases drifting on the way they are, and wouldn't care to think you delight a couple of tarts to a degree where they start pushing irresistible bits of new evidence to you.

Now, I'm not in charge here, nor anywhere near, of course, and mustn't speak for those who are, but as I see it, we don't want this whole untidy business reactivated by a sordid court case – perhaps more than one. Is that going to do the patch any good, a patch dear to both of us, Dave? I served there, too, for a while, before Traffic. Now, vile headlines? *More* vile headlines? Didn't we have enough over the Toledo fracas? We're looking for resurrection, remember. Will rehashed details of low-life killings encourage people to move into the Bay, or move their money into the Bay? I'm no politician, Dave, but one discovers political issues are unavoidable in high police work. I talk to top folk in the Bay apparatus, many of them ninnies in their own right, but with power now, prospective knighthoods. Do you think they need that kind of publicity – the appalling murders of a baby tart and a poncing, violent pusher? You'll say they were also people, and of course they *were* people, Bachelor included. Their deaths are as significant as any other and diminish us as much as any other. But are they people we want to make an endless or recurrent fuss about? If we'd had early arrests, trials would have been inescapable, clearly. We didn't, through absolutely no fault of yours, Dave. Look, we're six months away from all that, and it's slipped out of public consciousness and, crucially, out of media consciousness. Good. Naturally, you still have your job to do and I would not inhibit you in any way. However, I do believe we should note these other factors.'

Brade gathered the magazines.

'That sort of stuff leaves me desperately cold, Dave.'

'Sorry. As porn goes, it *is* fairly soft, sir.'

'Do you want me to ring for a Scene of Crime bag, or a cape to cover them?'

'They'll go under my coat.'

'Dave, I don't want them slipping – on the stairs or in front of the building. They are a foul insult to womanhood. The wind might take them. This reminds me of Billy Liar and the calendars.'

'Don't know him. I'll do a fire on waste ground.'

'It's furtive, Dave.'

'Ours is a furtive game, sir.'

Brade went back to his office in Bute Street and Glyn flourished a sheet of notes. 'Criminal Records computer can't do anything with just a first name, approximate age and knifing skills. I'm told we'd get hundreds, maybe thousands. Vice are no help, either. But you mentioned the Elvis take-off. I thought I'd try that.'

'I wondered about it.'

'Yes?'

'Yes.'

'OK. A couple of London shops specialise in his records and memorabilia. I gave them a ring and got the numbers of the secretaries of four Elvis fan clubs. Did any of them know a boy called Tommy who does an imitation of the King? Three said straight off, Tommy Samson, New Cross. Apparently, a famous villain family, Dave.'

'Great.'

'Yes, but he's dead. Took a bump on a bank raid in Blackpool and survived six months in a coma. But he would have been fit and well and available when Olive and Bachelor happened.'

'We talk to the family?'

'The local nick say they'll brick-wall for ever, and have already been heavily worked on, of course, in case any were at Blackpool.'

'People change when someone's dead.'

'The nick says no.'

'Nobody captured on the raid?'

'There were three other men, masked up. One or two sketchy descriptions from passers-by, and bank personnel gave stuff on physiques. Nothing much use. One had glasses. They're still free. The haul was £340,000 among three, which should have been four, though they might have done the decent thing and seen the family all right. R. B. bearable?'

'These won't do the trick for him.' Brade stacked the magazines on a chair, ready for burning on a Bay rebuilding site.

'Tommy was hit by their exit car,' Jenkins said.

'Might the family be looking for an accounting then, one way or the other – unless they were in the vehicle?'

'Pretty definitely not, apparently. They're all well alibied.'

'A traveller,' Brade said. 'Lives New Cross, works Blackpool. He might have done trips here, as well.'

'How I see it, too. Did he sing to Olive? It's great to think Elvis can still reach out to a new generation of kids.'

'I preferred Victor Sylvester's strict ballroom tempo, myself –
slow, slow, quick, quick, slow. Real civilisation.'

Brade drove to see Olive's mother near the Taff. It was a tired
old area, Grangetown, but he felt a fondness. Mrs Rice lived near
what had once been a mansion, stuck down among ordinary
terraced houses for some builder, now a jazz pub. 'My husband's
gone, Dave,' she said. 'I don't know what I feel.'

'Gone for good? Oh, I'm sorry.'

They were in Mrs Rice's front room, an upright piano in one
corner, with sheet music for 'Elmer's Tune' on the rack. Over the
hedge the drab Taff oozed, very near its wide, mud-flat mouth
here. 'You had someone walk out, didn't you, Dave? The sight
of their back moving away becomes so heavy for the moment,
yes? It was always on the cards he'd go. Alec couldn't take it.
Well, who can? I think he blamed me, though he never said.'

'Spouses can be sods.'

'Blame for Olive's way of life, her kind of death. Then my little
breakdown at the funeral, the court, the front paging – "Mur-
dered girl's angry mum bound over for church attack". Not nice,
as we say around here. Too much for Alec. I suppose that's
understandable.'

'So was the outburst,' Brade told her. 'The court said so.'

'You were good there, Dave. Beautifully worded extenuation
and it came over so sincere. Alec? Oh, stuff about work colleagues as well as the neighbours. Olive was always very special
to him.'

'Fathers, daughters.'

'Yes.'

Brade waited.

In a while she went on: 'Alec was always a bit flaky. We keep
in touch.' She gave a microscopic sob, turned away for a moment,
then recovered and faced Brade again, impassive, her jaw set
hard once more. How old were people who liked 'Elmer's
Tune'?

'I wonder whether Alec would come back if I could pull in
someone for Olive's death,' he said. 'People sometimes feel an
arrest completes things – puts life back to normal.' And to hell
with Bullfinch. To hell with Bullfinch even before Brade came
here, but to hell with him faster and by the shortest route now.
Was R. B. in quiet receipt, as the phrase went – in quiet receipt

from somewhere, someone, for trying to put a brake on the inquiry? Bullfinch, a bird in a gilded cage?

'They do?' Mrs Rice said. She sat on the piano stool. Brade chose a moquette armchair away from the bay window.

'What?'

'See an arrest as putting things right.'

'But we're not even close,' Brade replied. 'The alibis all stand up – Max, Simeon, Sendanta, Sendanta's ICE swarm. Glyndwr Jenkins has done everything to smash their tales, and he's abnormally gifted. No. They'll grow unmanageable.'

Three-fingered, she picked out what might be a piece of 'Elmer's Tune'. 'There's something new?' she asked, but without any real sign of interest.

'Did you ever hear the name Tommy Samson from Olive?'

She remained blank-looking. 'This comes from one of the girls – Erica or Louise? What made them talk at last?'

'Not one of the girls, believe me, love, absolutely not.'

'Who else?' She struck a rasping discord. 'I told you, Dave, Olive never mentioned anyone specific here, true or false. She said she had something nice going, something steady, and that was all. No detail.'

'You didn't ask about him?'

'Would this be some crook? And you think my Olive would be drawn to that sort?' Then her voice fell: 'Yes, you have to be right.'

'She wouldn't know. These people put on the charm. I'm fooled all the time.'

'Anyway, maybe she was lost – could no longer tell good from bad.'

'A rare skill. Think of the electorate or the Oscar judges. And I'd be much higher if I always had it. Might she have said anything to Alec – when you were not around?'

She shook her head and gave up the tune, thank God. 'He didn't like talking to her – latterly. It hurt too much. Alec's sensitive. Alec's a mess. But I suppose it's possible. He was such a pious prat Olive might have longed to win him back, and the only way would be to describe this bit of hope in her life.'

'What I thought.'

'If he listened. Once he told me he felt he could actually smell her clients when she came into the room. Smell them, Dave. He sat there with his nose in the air when he said it, like a dog. It showed that for him there was nothing of her left, just the whiff of business.'

'A kind of jealousy?' he replied.

She stared at him, said nothing, then closed the piano lid. The session was over. Brade let himself out and drifted off to see Julian Corbett. He found him having tea with Floyd and Henrietta at the manse. It was a lovely, square, light room, with no sign of anything churchy, not even embroidered texts or religious books on the shelves. He could see what looked like a couple of boxing volumes, a biography of Sugar Ray Robinson and *Who Killed Freddie Mills?* plus some political stuff – *Seize the Time* by Bobby Seale and a biography of Malcolm X. There were a couple of big, amateur water-colours showing Flat and Steep Holm, Steep Holm haloed by scores of gulls, and a framed photograph of Patterson in a crouch winning back the heavyweight title from Johansson in June 1960.

Floyd went to bring Brade a cup. 'This is nice, Jule, Henrietta,' Brade remarked.

She was dark, unpretty, grave, voluptuous, probably brighter than Jule. It pissed Brade off to think it, but probably brighter than himself. He liked her. She did not fit in.

'Is it something we can listen to, Daddy and I?' she asked.

'Oh, general matters,' Brade said. 'Jule hears so much.'

'He grasses?' Henrietta stood to get more tea. She was in a mottled brown and white, monk-style robe which reached the ground in a wide skirt, and looked ardently medieval. Despite her features, Corbett was probably lucky to have her. Brade thought most men were probably lucky to have the women they did. 'Such a lovely girl as Olive, yes, Dave?' Henrietta said. 'It has to be either a nut or she somehow got to know more than she should.'

'I certainly never heard of her failing to gratify,' Floyd replied.

He and Henrietta left soon afterwards to do the washing up. 'You've got something, Dave?' Corbett asked.

'The name, Tommy. This is something Glyn Jenkins turned up. From a petrol station attendant. Apparently, Olive and an unidentified man about twenty-five called there in a car and she spoke the name.'

'Which petrol station would this be, Dave?'

'Glyn's sitting on that, for the moment. You know how detectives are with their bits.'

'Won't even tell *you*?'

'Especially me, Jule. I wondered – any Tommy commuting from London on business to these parts? Not someone you've middlemanned for?'

'No surname?'

'Well, there wouldn't be. This is just Olive speaking to him casually.'

Corbett asked: 'Is a client going to give a girl his right name?'

'We've nothing else.'

'A petrol station? You know the vehicle then?'

'Stolen. Dead end there.'

Corbett assembled his delicate collection of features. 'I'm running all the London people I know through my head and I can't think of a Tommy, and certainly not a Tommy of the age you want. This didn't come from one of the girls?'

'Olive told them nothing – a kind of possessiveness?'

'Because if it came from one of the tarts, Dave – oh, they'd say any bloody thing, wouldn't they, to get you off their backs? Louise actually did a runner for a time, didn't she? This comes from Louise, Dave?'

'A petrol station, Jule. Louise, nothing. She would never speak, even if she could. Nor Erica.' Brade turned his voice flinty: 'I don't want them given the spotlight, Jule.'

'What's that mean? Which petrol station would it be, Dave? An assistant? Around here, aren't they self-serve?'

'Henrietta's looking a real picture.'

'Perhaps she's wasted.'

'There's a future here, Jule.'

'Be part of it, Dave. We'd all miss you.'

14

Corbett had a call from Don Samson, asking him up to London right away 'for a general fucking chinwag, Jule, old son'. It was the kind of message he did get now and then, and was probably

106

safe enough. Nobody would tap a manse phone. Of course, they might tap at Don's end. The words were typical Don, even now, in his bereavement – offhand, hail-fellow, but with something big lurking. Well, of course something big. He had lost a son.

Corbett felt troubled. Too many sides – Yeo, Hamer, Drinkwater, Samson, Dave Brade, Brade trying to intuit like a detective, and all of a sudden equipped with dangerous insights. All right, if you worked in the middle, you expected complications, your cream came from complications, but he feared he was losing his hold. On the other hand, if Don Samson wanted to see you you went. Corbett would have liked to take Henrietta, but she could not get off work at the bank. It would have been a true comfort to travel with her, have his meeting with Don, then link up again somewhere. He felt weak without her.

'It's safe, Jule?' Always she would spot when he had special stress.

'For heaven's sake, I don't go out to his territory. This will be the middle of London, darling.' He gave no names, no places.

Samson would make a reservation at some restaurant a couple of hours before arrival, no time for anybody to line up trouble. On Thursday week, wherever he was going then, Samson might be more at risk, if Hamer had things right, and Hamer probably had. Those two looked crude, even comical, but had subtlety. You could not get subtler than the way they were sucking Paul Yeo in. Corbett regarded the help he had provided as minor, not worth half the five hundred they paid. The strategy had been all theirs, and he had scarcely understood its shape when they first made contact. Almost anyone could have turned out those scare drawings.

Samson said a fish restaurant in Soho. In most of the best bits of London, Corbett found a fizzing sense of liveliness, something he missed at home, despite the changes. True, the bloody beggars and cardboard shacks darkened things. Did they *have* to live like that?

Although Don Samson sounded pretty basic he knew his way around and had picked up many insights on white wines. Don would be a loss. He was used by several very large-scale, quite spruce London people, and some of that work trickled Corbett's way. 'Tommy's funeral, a nightmare, Jule,' he said, 'an agony.'

'Well, yes. Yet I longed to come, but impossible, Don. The

police want Blackpool pointers. Our flowers, Yeo's and mine – I explained, we had to code the card.'

Samson gazed past Corbett. 'This is someone who kills my son through panic, or couldn't-care-less, or hate – I can't say – and then sends carnations marked what was it, Ronald Stapleton?'

'We wanted a solid name with class.'

'Tommy was a great kid, you know. Of course you do.' For a second, Corbett thought that long, bumpy, bony face might break down into weeping. Samson still stared at some spot beyond Corbett, his eyes blank, but very near to melting. A restaurant like this would be chilly about sobs from a male. 'I still can't get away from what I thought first – Yeo banged into Tommy and didn't give a sod. He was going to get clear refuckinggardless. Smashed through him. Well, you were in the car, Jule. You know I'm telling true.'

'Something like that,' Corbett replied.

'A kid of twenty-five.' His eyes blanked again. 'He could be wild, but he'd handled some important things for me and my contacts. Some things via yourself, down there in Wales. Neat work. No comeback, or am I wrong?'

He could be, but Corbett did not mention the tea and seed cake visit by Brade. Corbett was supposed to prevent leaks. That cow Louise, or that cow Erica. Brade might have more than he showed. They did not always put everything on the table right off, waiting for you to respond. 'It's hard, Don.'

There were a couple of families eating near them, people giving their children a treat, and Corbett approved that – a restaurant that was part of the community, like places on the Continent. Don suggested a mixture of smoked fish to start. Corbett liked it when someone in the know picked from the menu and wine list. Making choices troubled him. He liked options open, a habit through living in three or four or six camps. The Muscadet Don ordered he found a bit dry and said so. At once, Samson sent for a Chablis instead. What did this ugly, hurt, sad, targeted bastard want? 'If I know you, Jule, you'd be screaming at Yeo to stop for Tommy.'

'Yes. To be fair, maybe Paul decided he couldn't risk it for the sake of the rest of us.'

'Tommy's fighting to hold on to that sack of gains, not for himself, but because a team puts everything in a common pot.

This was duty is how Tommy would see it. How he's been brought up. But the one in charge thinks entirely personal, entirely how-do-I-finance-a-new-boat or a new house? If this means squash a kid, squash him.'

'I don't know, Don.'

'You can't say. I understand – loyalty. That's good in you, Jule, but, we all know it, yet he keeps going.' Don took a little of the sadness from his face, though much more hung on. 'I didn't bring you up here to listen to grieving. We've said all this before.'

Corbett went for the sea bass. Don took haddock. He leaned across the table to whisper confidentially: 'You were right about that Muscadet, Jule. I'll bring you again for advice.' He sent for another Chablis. Upping the flattery must mean they were near the important bit. Corbett went easy on the wine. He needed his mind sharp. 'Why I had to see you, Jule – I should be into vengeance. You know that thing, The Procedure? A local bloom.'

'It's – '

'But I'm not, Jule, not into vengeance.' He shook that rough old head. One of the kids in the family party watched him, scared. 'There's room for an arrangement here.'

'What kind of – '

'You could handle it. I hope you will.'

'This is kind, Don. All round kind – to me and Yeo.'

'Tommy was too long dying. The heat goes. Exhaustion, almost a sickness.'

'So understandable.'

'Vengeance, anyway – how would it work? Thought of the problems? Oh, the bleeding Procedure says its piece, but Yeo's a long way away. I hate operating off my ground – call it superstition. A lot of us like that. And then again, I don't know his habits. Nor the first idea about the geography of this item, the Vale of Glamorgan, or the layout of the place he lives in. Hopeless trying to find out, bound to get spotted. If I had plans of the house or a map of his grounds it would be different. I haven't. No way it can be done. How do I get to him?'

'I could certainly handle any deal you wanted to make, Don.'

'I don't know nobody better. You and your missus, a great combination. She's an investment adviser, yes?'

'Worried stiff that investment's going from shortage to drought.'

'Funny to have someone in a bank when you're – Well, you know.' Samson ate like a gourmet, picking out bits that looked special, not filling up. He showed delicacy. It seemed a pity that Drinkwater and Hamer had this fierce down on him, but not something you could ask them about, just wait until they told you why, if ever. Samson leaned over his plate and did a whisper: 'What it seems to me, Jule, is we deserve more of the Blackpool profits. We had our slice, I'm not disputing – well, you couriered it yourself, and many thanks – but Yeo did better. Yeo always does, I hear. Jule, you satisfied with what you drew?'

'I took the basic.'

'Yes, well the basic's all right but we don't see it as enough. Tommy's mother, Norah, feels it very deeply. We're not together, but all the same. Even Eloise, who I'm with now, is very hurt. She got on famous with Tommy. All above board, Jule, I stress that, though of an age. This is not just we lost a boy – it's we had a boy pulped so Yeo could turn squire and Onassis. Plus the divorce here and Norah's new place really gave me deep costs. Fucking Chislehurst. Don't tell me prices haven't recovered.'

'Drop vengeance? It's a serious proposal?'

Samson fell sombre. 'If you're part of a culture, it takes a lot of breaking from. Almost a sort of treason.' He hunted a few choice bits off the skeleton. 'But The Procedure – antique, daft, trying to be the Mafia, and I'm not going to act like that. I'm by nature reasonable, Jule. They say savage, but I know what works. Would we be lunching here now if I didn't? I've got police quizzing, day in, day out, trying to put me or Billy or Amiable or all of us in that Blackpool car with Tommy. They heard of family bonds. Don't worry, Jule, they get nothing. But you see the point? They'll be watching me for some get-even spasm. It would be curtains.'

Corbett glanced about, examined the other customers more closely.

'No, I've kept an eye, Jule. They're not behind me today. And Norah – nearly demented by the zonk-out and then death, yet opposes more violence. The damage is done, and nothing can put it right. She's had enough suffering and risk, and wants what remains of the family intact.'

'Adult.'

'This sounds calculating, I suppose, Jule, setting a figure on Tommy's suffering though, again, I'd rather term it reasonable. I'm thinking of around fifty grand on top of what's already come, to put everything square and waive the blame. Some of this going to Norah, obviously. Eloise agrees to that. She's a sporting girl. It would be once for all.' He took a large mouthful of the wine and topped Corbett's glass. 'But to you, because I trust you, Jule, I'll say I'm not inflexible even on fifty. Negotiable. Although it's the life of a sweet boy, this is still for discussion, and I want you to make that clear to Paul – but without selling me or Tommy cheap or too early, of course. Your skills, Jule.'

'No violence?'

'No violence, no stalking party. Give Don Samson's word on this. Yeo can lie back and enjoy it on his bleeding estate, just fifty lighter. He's going to think a lot of you for bringing this kind of offer to him, Jule, so you'll be in profit, maybe, from that end, too. I'm eager to help you – show some gratitude. Yeo can find that much, dead easy. All I hear says so.'

'This was a worthwhile trip, Don.'

'I see you as a real colleague of Tommy.'

'Thanks, Don. I hope so, sincerely.'

Samson did not stay for sweet or coffee. 'But you linger. I'll pay now. I don't like being anywhere for more than an hour and a half, even a friendly spot like this. Another superstition. The word can get out and people mobilise fast. Be in touch, will you? Obviously, a good percent in it for you, plus rail fare – first class, naturally. You've got status to keep up. Straight back home or girling here?'

Corbett took in an exhibition of Victorian painting – not the kind of thing you'd tell Samson. Tissot, above all, Corbett went for. One day he would have enough to own one.

He arrived home very late but found Henrietta still up. She was like that – needing to see him safe, and to talk about his day and her own. It was lovely of her. He had bought her an ochre silk cravat, something that would put a little colour on that subfusc capuchin thing she had.

'Productive day, darling?' she asked.

'Passable. Rather long-term and general.'

'Sounds big-wheel – above the detail and everyday. You

111

progress. I've had some excitement myself, Jule. I was picked up – and by *two* men, at once. Darling, it's all right, they know you, had been trying to reach you at the manse, but Daddy was out, too, so no answer. They waited for me near the bank. Lance Hamer? Drinkwater?'

'They what? How did they know where you worked, for God's sake?'

'I thought you must have told them. I think that was what they said.'

'Well, yes, I must have.'

'You didn't? They've been researching? Why? Does it matter, Jule? They seemed nice enough. Possibly a pair? We talked in their car, that's the sum total.'

'About?'

'They seemed to know you were due to go to London soon on business, and wanted to catch you before.'

'They knew how?'

'Darling, don't ask me.'

'You didn't tell them who I was seeing?'

'Could I? I wouldn't, naturally. But I don't think you said – just an impression of hazard.'

'You didn't say that?'

'What?'

'Hazard?'

'I said nothing, except London, Jule. And that they appeared to know anyway. They're going to ring. Let's go up, yes?'

In bed, she wore the cravat, nothing else. 'It's sort of racy, Jule.' She was giving out thorough passion, legs locked around him, nails in his buttocks, biting, head threshing – the kind of tumult he found nowhere else, ever, and not always here. It made him wonder whether she had been turned on by someone earlier.

At just after 6 a.m. they were woken by Floyd, who was in that old, purple track suit and had his Bullworker in one hand. 'Phone, Jule,' he said. 'An Otis Drinkwater?'

Corbett pulled on trousers and a shirt and went downstairs to the hall telephone. Floyd continued on to his study to complete the forlorn work-out.

'Jule,' Drinkwater said, 'we heard you were seeing Don. This is not from Henrietta, let me assure you, who was the soul of discretion on your behalf. You've got a winner there. Lovely girl.'

'Yes, well, I was going to tell you about Don. Just a routine get-together.'

'What I thought,' Drinkwater replied. 'Don's always good value. That face. We heard he's prepared to settle with Yeo. Likewise from sources.'

'Well, yes. He did float that as a possibility among wide discussions. Nothing final or definite, though, at this stage.'

'Clearly, that's something it would be better Paul Yeo did not know. In the circumstances. Very destructive. We'd prefer he stuck to the arrangement we have already, as a matter of fact, and I believe I speak for you there, also, Jule.' He had a gentle laugh. 'We'd like to save Paul a few grand, wouldn't we? Lance boy is nodding a hundred a minute here, Jule. He's with me in the public booth. We're very comfortably fixed up for living quarters, by the way, thanks to you. Wild Wales. We gather Don might be prepared to come as low as fifty grand, or even less.'

'No figure mentioned, only the general idea. Otis, Yeo was never going to hear from me about that offer, clearly.'

'Right.'

'I see no profit there.'

'Right. And, obviously, you would never mention to Don our plans for him – Thursday week, the water polo. No, obviously not.'

'Oh, come on, Otis, would I?' Corbett declared.

'I'm just putting the question as a formality, Jule. I told Lance you wouldn't, even inadvertently. Confidentiality.'

'The core of my trade.'

'A quality for which you are justly famed, Jule. We've got to get Don knocked out of the way.'

'Otis, there are extensions here.'

'A lot of other things depend on that, which I won't elaborate now. We felt we'd been lucky to find a chance through Yeo and would prefer nothing disturbed that. We rang last night to see if you'd heard how he's thinking about the package, not knowing you were going to London so soon.'

'Nothing yet,' Corbett told them. 'Paul's the sort to give it very thorough consideration.'

'Stuff him. It's useful you still have contact with Don, and only

113

natural in your kind of work, but there are obvious perils. I pretend only Lance worries, because I'm supposed to be the ever creative, jolly one, but I fret, too, Jule.'

'Don't. Everything's fine.'

'Great. Your Henrietta's exceptionally – well – vibrant, I'd put it. And a real brain, I imagine. We don't want to be seen too much around that area, Jule, but it seemed important to make contact with her.'

'How did you know where she worked, Otis?'

'Didn't you tell us that? Oh, somehow, anyway. Exceptionally vibrant.'

'Well, yes,' Corbett replied. 'And yes to a brain, as well. Plus, she's very sensitive.'

'I love that in a woman. It's written all over her, Jule.'

15

Brade grew anxious again about Louise and Erica and decided they must move into his flat for a while. Since the Toledo verdicts, dockland villainy thought it could do what it liked, and someone might want to silence a talking tart. The girls could go on working, but drive back to Llandaff when they clocked off. It made no real sense: anybody wanting to harm a tart had a thousand choices. He needed to do something, though, and this was the best available. Terrifying that Mrs Rice and Jule Corbett guessed right off who gave the Tommy name.

Mrs Rice probably would not talk about it – probably did not talk at all about Olive's death, except to him. He had the impression of an immense and secret bond between her and Olive, something beyond a mother's feelings for her daughter, and beyond death. Possibly, Mrs Rice even accepted Brade's denial that it was the girls who had spoken. But Corbett might be different.

Of course, people in the other flats would probably not care for these special neighbours, even temporarily, and might be in touch with Raging Bullfinch again. Brade considered asking Jenkins whether he would take one or both of the girls into his house. But Glyndwr had something settled going now with that bossy, divorced, live-in, large-chinned, Welsh-speaking departmental head from the Wales Tourist Board, and possibly she would not want a docks whore commuting from their home and talking confidences to Glyn, especially Erica. Glyn's partner might see that as two blacks excluding her. In Brade's flat block Erica's colour could be an advantage: several of the neighbours were sweet old progressives and would hate to look racist.

The girls said, all right, they would give Brade's place a try, but not pay rent nor 'obligatorily' provide services in lieu, because they had been pressured to move there. At once he accepted this.

'Don't be so quick at ditching the chance to screw us, for God's sake,' Louise replied. 'Are we suddenly repulsive?'

While the girls settled in during their slack time before the evening rush hour, he went with Glyn to see Olive's father at his workplace. Jenkins had previously talked to him there. Rice sold touring caravans and the three of them sat in one now. He made tea on the stove. 'You're very shrewd, returning after so long,' he said. 'Yes, perhaps one's attitudes change.'

'We might have new information, Mr Rice,' Jenkins answered. 'I was distressed to find you and your wife have split.'

'Nothing left for us.' He turned silent for half a minute. 'I've another daughter, you know. Why should one girl go like Olive while the other marries, has children, creates a fine home?'

'You confronted Olive on that?' Brade asked.

'I had to know whether she thought it was I or her mother who conferred this fierce lust upon her.' He poured.

'Not many street girls are moved by lust, Mr Rice,' Brade replied.

'How else would it begin?'

'This must have been an agonising conversation with her,' Jenkins said. When he tried, Glyndwr could be useful in this kind of sensitive interview.

'I needed to tell her – absolutely needed to, a compulsion – that I loathed every man she ever went with. Loathed them top to toe, could somehow visualise them, see them at her, this appalling graphicness, and especially her taking it in her mouth. While she talked, I was looking at her lips and tongue and I was enduring those visions.'

His voice went up towards a howl and the gleaming little caravan boomed. It was hooked to the electricity supply and, as well as the stove, they had light and a powerful two-bar fire. All the same, Rice kept a full-length, fleece-lined sheepskin coat on and buttoned. He would be in his late forties, sad-faced, lined more than his age, dull-eyed even now when he was moved, going to fat, breathing loudly, as though half smothered by his recollections and imaginings.

Rice said: 'I needed to learn it in full, explicitly.' He winced. 'Oh, I know, you're going to ask, was this a kind of jealousy – I mean, concealed, sexual jealousy. Police! That's occurred to me, of course.'

Jenkins said: 'You're tough on yourself, Mr Rice.'

'Now you might understand why I could not stay with my wife.'

'Would you say yourself it was sexual jealousy?' Brade asked.

'Motive? Absurd, isn't it? One's daughter.'

They were seated around a table on upholstered benches that probably could compose a bed. These comfortable vans were designed for carefree travel and here they were, drinking thick tea from stained mugs, talking about the murder of a girl, skirting incest. Almost.

'We've got a name,' Brade replied.

'Yes? Well, it's possible. When I had spoken to her, put my aversions, she was desperate to convince me parts of her life were still worthwhile. She talked about a man she was seeing regularly. That word "regularly".' He whined it, mocking. 'In a way it was touching. Nauseating.'

'This conversation – you and she were alone in the house, presumably,' Brade asked.

'From far back she distrusted Naomi, my wife. Olive knew my feelings and wished to, well, plead her case, I suppose you'd call it.'

Jenkins said: 'Yes, we thought she might want to make a point to you. Often there's something mysterious and unique between father and daughter.'

'To prove this "regular" man's distinction, she tells me he's a Londoner – big deal – and has business interests all over – here, in the North, you name it.'

'Where in the North?'

116

'Oh, he'd taken her to a top-class hotel in Blackpool. That was really supposed to wow me, "top-class". She meant the kind I'd never been able to afford for family holidays.'

'You've got the vans. Did she say which hotel?' Brade asked.

'It's important?'

'Or how many stars?' Brade replied.

'I wasn't interested.'

'She craved your approval, Mr Rice,' Brade said. 'Your forgiveness.'

'But how could I?'

'We've got the name Tommy Samson,' Jenkins answered.

'No name.'

'Not even the Tommy bit?'

'I'd have told you previously.'

Brade said: 'We didn't hear about this long talk previously.'

'Perhaps it was all too close in time,' Jenkins remarked. 'Too much of a wound.'

'She didn't say anything about his business contacts here?' Brade asked. 'Did you pick up any sign she knew them?'

'How would she in that life?'

'I wonder why he came to the docks, you see,' Brade replied.

'Because he wanted a girl.'

'Could be,' Brade said. He stood. The caravan rocked. 'We'd prefer if you did not put this name around.'

'It came from one of the whores at last?' Rice said.

'No, indeed,' Brade replied.

'Where else?'

'No, not from them,' Brade said.

Two days later, near midnight when the girls were out at work, Brade had a visit at home from Simeon de Courville, proposing a deal. Despite the cold, he was in one of those silk Italian suits that looked mottled yet filmy. It was double-breasted, mauve-grey, and cut with a lavish curve from the tip of the lapels down. Simeon sported all his usual finger and wrist gold and what could be Gucci shoes, also in the mauve-grey region. Probably, he drove the white Mercedes, so he would have made an impression on anyone who saw him arrive. He was round-faced, round-headed, with astonishingly narrow hips that were his

117

pride, as much as the Mercedes. Although Brade had put him away for some spells of time, Simeon took frequent foreign holidays in the sun and had no trace of cell-drag on his face skin. He believed he had charm, yet never pushed this too hard if you showed you doubted it. About forty-five, Simeon was probably near the peak of his earnings, shitty charisma and luck. For ponces and pushers this would be the optimum age. It must be seven or eight years since he was last locked up. He had a great smile, full of good, mild teeth, and he kept his hands exceptionally well, possibly manicured professionally. His hair had gone, except segments over the ears and on his neck, yet, as could happen, the baldness seemed to give a boyishness to his face, and helped him pass off what were outcrops of more or less genuine evil as mischief and *joie de vivre*.

'Dave, what worries me – Louise could be falling for you, you know that?' Always at the start of a conversation Brade was surprised by Simeon's voice, magnificently deep for such a frame.

'No way.'

'What she talks about is weaning you off them mags. Yes, weaning, at your age. I tell her a man's leisure he can use how he likes. But I'm going to lose her from the streets, Dave.' Solemnly, he shook that glowing head.

'And you can't lean on her too hard because I'd see the marks when she came here.'

'Not my style. But what I do gather is there's not much of her kept covered when she's here. And then Erica – she's begun seriously saying she loves your mind.'

'Jesus.'

'Well, exactly, Dave. Of course, this is typical Erica, no Italian way and prizing intellect.'

'That lets me out.'

'Don't misunderstand, but I've told her that over and over. You did pass the eleven-plus, I hear, though. What's more, you read. Hardbacks, not just the magazines.' He gave one of the smiles to signal no intent to insult.

'Only *The Great White South*.'

'Erica says you're what she calls "stimulating on heroism" and have theories about "the hero figure as type through the ages".'

'*In* type – the Scott book.'

As pimps went, Simeon, like Max, was not especially violent and Brade could recall no tales of really lasting damage done by him to any tart, though he had run some very headstrong ones over the years. He had ideal ponce build: smallish, but not physically negligible, nimble for quick in-and-out of the Merc to collect, and slim-limbed and thin-necked, increasing the impression of youth, so a judge might go that little bit more easily, especially a judge into men. Simeon managed Erica and lately had some sort of unexplained stake in Louise, Louise always claiming to Brade that she functioned unponced since By-a-nose.

'They've cleaned up the place a bit for you, have they, Dave? Look. I'll tell you what it looks like, if you don't mind me saying – it looks like spite, that's all. We win that Toledo trial, you get your face rubbed in it, so you search for ways to mess us up. show you still run the patch regardless, can still call it "my place". You take my girls and screw one of them into treachery and talk the other into it. Well, you screw both, obviously, legs like Erica's, but this is how it's working out. These are damn cheap tactics, Dave. I have to say that.'

'The girls are in danger.'

'What I can propose is a deal. This would be an arrangement where I come up with something for you, this being information. I-bloody-e, Dave, I'm offering a deep degree of fink. That's not Simeon by nature, I hope you'll agree. On your side, you'd promise to let the girls return home, and if they don't want to, kick them out. Plus, from you, a promise not to approach them later with the object of casting further influence. By which I mean, I don't mind you making contact with them now and then and having it off with Louise, pay or not, prime times or not, but not in a loving, special style, Dave Brade. Just basic sex, no avowing or, above all, empathy. She's a sucker for empathy.'

Simeon had refused to sit down and was striding about in his bantam way, making these declarations and holding a tumbler of rum and coke that Brade had given him. The great voice fluted.

'This information is about what, Sim?'

'You'll do it, Dave?'

'I never meant them to stay here more than a few weeks. I tire.'

'Now, is this really right? They talk like they think for ever. Louise has been to the cathedral.'

'I suspected that.'

'She bought a hat. So you see my problem. Not Erica. That's the intellectual thing again – atheist, or the other.'

'Agnostic?'

'Probably. When I first met that girl, Dave, she had no idea, none at all. Frankly, I felt sorry for her. Learning, education, yes, and legs, but no kind of notion what her physique might be worth if well presented. I feel I've built an entitlement.'

'Is this information about Olive?'

'No, Sweet Bachelor. We were close. Well, I don't have to tell you, the eternally twisting jerk. Look, I'll send personnel to help you get the girls out, if they won't leave.'

'I can't have noise here, or breakages.'

'And you'll return her if one of them comes back – Louise, probably. Supposed to be going to the church, and sneaking over to you on the quiet.'

'You're talking about interests Sweet Bachelor was in touch with? You'll name them?'

'I don't know if it's principals, Dave. Maybe London go-betweens, or hired muscle. But you can work from there.'

'Names?'

'Not names. Area. Bachelor was afraid of people coming down from a certain London area.'

'Christ, Si, area? This isn't – '

'A particular South London area.'

'Some particular South London areas are so full of villains we'd be questing till the Last Trump.'

Simeon sat down now and smiled with fondness. 'That's what I mean about books, Dave. Reading. What Erica got bowled over by. Last Trump. This from a hardback?'

'So which district?'

'Hang on, Dave. We've got a deal, then?'

'Half a deal. I'd have to see whether what you tell me takes us forward. I've got people pressuring me – Bullfinch himself. There must be results, Simeon.'

'I heard Bullfinch wanted it all closed down.'

'You hear rubbish.'

'Shit, Dave.' He stood up and paced again, full of rage and

honest dignity. 'Deal with a cop and watch their offer pulled back faster than it's offered.'

'Have I ever played dirty with you, Simeon?'

'Have you ever played clean?'

'You're free, running girls.'

'I'm free because you couldn't make a case stick.'

'We could have enhanced the evidence, Si. A routine skill for Glyndwr.'

'I'm running girls because you people like it organised, not random. *Am* I running girls, anyway? They're here.'

'They work – are working at this moment.'

'For how long? They're not giving their all, Dave. Grudging. Nothing worse than a half-cock floozy, especially Erica, with her gravity to start with, anyway.'

'Which London area then, Si, or shall I make a suggestion?'

Simeon was on the other side of the room, standing in front of Brade's picture of Mevagissy or somewhere else quaint, but turned quickly, alight with new anger. 'What? You going to bloody con me, say you knew all along where Sweet Bachelor meant? You're going to say I'm offering nothing? No *quid* for your *quo*? So you can keep infringing on my girls.'

Brade went to his old pine desk and brought over a memo pad and two pencils. He tore off a couple of sheets and gave one to Simeon. 'You write it on yours and I'll do it on mine. If they're not the same, the girls are out today.'

They each wrote, folded the sheets and exchanged them. 'What does yours say, Sim? Mine – that's to say yours – is New Cross. They stay, for now.'

'Bastard,' Simeon said, reading Brade's, silently.

'But useful to have it confirmed, kid. I don't consider this at all a wasted effort. And I'm going to talk things over with Louise and Erica.'

'Talk them over when you've all got clothes on and no fuck-pulse.'

16

Fear took a hard hold on Julian Corbett. All his worries – Drinkwater, Hamer, Don Samson, Yeo, Brade – still fermented. Paul Yeo wanted a meeting and they went to that Pontcanna café again.

'Not to harass you, but any sign of the weapon you're getting for me, Jule?'

'Very much in hand.'

'I'm unprotected. This bloody South London Procedure. Myself, I don't understand cultures and communities. I'm alone.'

'So evil, so unwarranted, Paul, the way they respond.'

Corbett wondered for a second if he should tell him now that Don Samson longed to deal and stay peaceful. Half a second. Corbett could not do it. There was Drinkwater and Lance Hamer to think about. And there was a job to line up. Corbett might be scared but he still had to act like a fixer.

'Since those plans, I've shifted our bedroom, Jule. Carol wonders what the hell it's all about. I can't tell her. A woman doesn't expect this sort of life. I don't know how long she'll take it.' Yeo tightened up his face, so Corbett saw what he considered the German hardness and beakiness. 'Jule, I've got to tell you: I've decided – I'm not doing this bloody job for your friends, either of these bloody jobs. Not the bank driving and certainly not the job on Samson.'

Corbett, in his positive way, pounced on the 'certainly'. Did it mean Yeo might do the bank, even if he would not kill Don for them?

'This would be Paul Yeo in roles all wrong for him, Jule. Am I a number three or four or ten in a team, just a Wheels? Those days are over. And I'm no hit-man, either.'

Yeo spent half his time sorting out who or what he was, talking about himself third person. It was a pain. It was a peril.

'Jule, if I've learned one thing, it's play to my strengths. They don't include Drinkwater's and Hamer's mad schemes. Tell your friends it's not on.'

He kept his voice low, but anyone could sense he was talking dynamite and an old couple stared across the café over their mugs of hot chocolate. 'You keep calling them my friends, Paul. They're not. No special understanding – simply business contacts.'

'But don't tell them yet. Get me the armament first.'

'They can be a troublesome pair, Paul.'

'I'll deal with that when it happens. First, Samson. I have to be ready.'

'Grief, rage, the culture – they don't stop to think, Paul. Not only Don and Billy. There's the lad, Amiable.'

'I'll *make* them stop and think. But that's if it ever happens, Jule. Half the time I suspect those two louts, Hamer and bloody Drinkwater, did the plans themselves, anyway. Or were helped. No connection with Don Samson.'

'With help? From where? How could they work that, Paul?'

'I don't know. How the hell is Don Samson supposed to have done it?'

Corbett reckoned he stayed fully deadpan. He had had a lot of practice. 'I got Drinkwater and Lance Hamer a rented cottage outside Cardiff. I'll have to tell them what you say, Paul.'

'It's tricky for you. I'm sorry.'

Yes, tricky. Drinkwater and Hamer were sure to think Corbett had passed on Samson's peace offer to him, and that Paul had decided to buy the quiet life: no need to knock Don out of the firing line because cash could do it. Lance sounded gentle and Drinkwater liked a giggle, but no question they could slip fast into standard savagery once things upset them. 'I can't predict how they'll react, Paul, if you back out.'

'Not back out.' Yeo still controlled his voice, but this was close to a snarl. The old couple stared again. 'Paul Yeo was never in. What's known in business as not taking up an option. Do you see Don at all?'

'Not in the present circumstances. I don't think that would be right.'

'So, get me this pistol, yes? Tomorrow? Why not today?'

'I'll certainly pull out all the stops, Paul.'

Yeo stood up. 'I have to get to the *Splott*. We're sailing in half an hour.'

He liked tycooning now and then, lording it from his owner's cabin, the bullshitting sod.

Corbett went for a booster drink at the Starboard Light. A week ago, he might have returned to the manse and looked for help and consolation from Henrietta. Lately, he had come to feel she was drifting from him. Usually, he could discuss every problem with her, covering all details, and she would switch on that great brain and guide him, buttress him, restore him. Now, though, he was aware of new distance between them, and kept his terrors secret. He was a middleman caught where middlemen always were caught, smack in the middle.

Floyd must have noticed the cooling and after she left for work this morning had said: 'She sniffing around someone else, Jule?'

'Hardly.'

'Appetite can get to Hen in strong form. Before you, she practised variety, when she could get it with those looks, and I was never certain marriage could hold her. Someone new on the pitch?'

'To my knowledge, no.'

'She said two of your friends met her from work while you were in London. Probably a pair, but she thought one could be AC-DC. Did he make an impression?'

Drinkwater? Henrietta was so bright, but could easily be pushed off balance by attention from someone loud and glib and strange. That you could say of most women, though.

'She's a wonderful girl and spells of fierce restlessness are part of that wonder, Jule,' Floyd had said.

'I know she's wonderful.'

17

Brade said: 'What interests me, Maximilian, is whether Olive ever spoke of abuse when a child – that's to say, of course, more of a child than when you first started banging her. You must have had many a long, intimate conversation, and I know you had her confidence. One could read that in everything she said.'

Maximilian, propped on his racy, metal-hung, beige sofa,

gazed at Brade, no part of his face and no movement of his body showing what he thought. Max was at home now but still looked bedraggled, though noble in profile occasionally. Luckily, most of his businesses had kept turning over while he was away, and he seemed to have recruited at least one new earning girl. Brade had heard of no money problems, and Maximilian's status held in dockland, although he had been mauled by a woman in church.

Brade said: 'This is the kind of childhood sexual trauma that can push girls on to the streets later. They lose all sense of emotional content in the act, or have never developed one. Easy for them to see it as commercial.'

'Respect, respect – this is my watchword, my only what you might call "technique" with women, regardless of their social station or chosen career. You've got her father in the frame, then? He was opening her up early and wouldn't let her go?'

'We wonder. And to a lesser degree, the mother.'

'Mother? Her?' Maximilian cried. He moved abruptly in shock on the sofa and winced at the pain he gave his leg. 'She attacked and foul-mouthed me so stupidly because she thought *I'd* corrupted Olive, surely.'

'Maybe.'

'Kill your own daughter?'

'Families are wondrous organisms. This would be to reclaim her. It does happen.'

'Reclaim her in a box?'

'It does happen. It gives permanence. Glyndwr has checked on availability and they're both floating free on the night.'

'Daily I weep for that girl, Dave.'

'I know. We had hospital bulletins.'

'But then there's Sweet Bachelor.'

'I've never taken it as certain they were killed by the same person, Max. The weapons were different.'

'Alarming, Dave. Two killers possibly living on this patch.'

'I can't persuade Bullfinch to leave protection on you any longer,' Brade replied.

Max was in a heavy dark blue twill dressing-gown, vermilion pyjamas and rest-home, brown slippers. The leg was out of plaster, but he still needed sticks, and his repaired ear seemed entirely secure though not completely ear-like all over. He had a big, very magnificent third-floor flat in one of the renovated old warehouses on the marina, with a fine view of where Bachelor was pulled bleeding from the mock dock. Max's furnishings were mainly tubular, which Brade had an idea might be *passé*, and there were rugs on polished boards, like those Room of my Own features they did in the *Observer*.

'My problem, Max, is that Bullfinch would prefer no progress.'

Maximilian wagged his head. 'Being sweetened to keep things peaceful-looking?'

'We can line up a dead London lad for both these killings, and that would suit him. Two cases closed at once, plus no trials to pollute the Bay air and maybe queer his commission. I need something to shake him, Max.'

'Abuse?'

'To strengthen motive.'

Maximilian nodded slowly. 'I'm going to have to try to recall whether she ever mentioned anything like that, and report back.'

'Good.'

'You really believe it? One of the parents? Both?' Maximilian asked. 'But I heard you thought some big, metropolitan side to it.'

'I don't know, Max. London? Ivor Lestocque – who's still missing, with Miriam – why? Jule, even? Yourself, Max, regardless of what the hospital says? But I've got to keep the inquiry alive, somehow – stop Bullfinch shutting it down. He can't do that if I say it might be Daddy or Mummy.'

Brade heard someone stirring elsewhere in the flat. It was late afternoon and Max's new helper might be getting spruced for clients finishing at the office. She sounded delightfully light on her feet. Some tarts plodded, as though resentful. In a while, she came in, quite tall, dressed in red leather and with a crimson bandanna around her reddish hair. Max liked a trace of brightness. She was what Glyndwr would probably call a *jolie laide* – lips, eyes, nose, all slightly too big, but giving a very amiable, lively look. Her body was slim-to-thin and her legs very long, a little bony, yet not at all off-putting, as far as Brade was concerned, anyway, or her customers, clearly. He stood and gave one of his neat bows.

'This is Dave, Petronella.' Max smiled at her hearteningly. 'Petronella, Dave.'

Brade went over and shook her hand. She smelled as good as Louise's place, nothing cheap, and was about Olive's age or a little less. Brade saw she wondered if Maximilian had brought him in for trade and did not know whether to flourish her attractions. 'Just an old mate of Max, Petronella,' he said.

'I thought I'd take a stroll now, Max. Will you be all right, love? Your orange squash?'

'Things renew themselves you see, Dave,' Maximilian said.

In the night, Brade was sitting at home, having a chat with Louise and Erica after they came in from work, when his doorbell went. 'Christ, Dave, you ought to have one of those voice boxes,' Louise said. 'Not even a spy-hole?'

'It's usually pretty cloistered here.'

'You'll open?' Erica asked.

'I have to be available.'

The girls had not brought house coats with them when they moved in, only basics, and usually took their top gear off and sat around in something of Brade's. Louise had on an old police cape, from when he was uniformed, and Erica wore an even older Cardiff High School black and white rugby shirt down to her knees, faded now and streaked with resistant grime. Cardiff High had been quite a snooty place and he doubted whether his old headmaster would have approved a black tart in the colours. But things had improved.

When he opened the door, he saw Fiona, Sweet Bachelor's pre-Miriam wife, wearing the three-quarter length green-brown wool coat she had on that day at Bethel. 'This *is* a treat,' he cried. 'Where's your friend, Harvey?'

'That turd,' she replied. 'Vamoosed.'

'Do you know Louise and Erica, a couple of chums of mine? What will it be, a drink or tea? A drink, obviously.'

'I'll see to that,' Louise said, standing. The cape looked great, her pale skin made to seem even paler and finer by the navyness of the heavy cloth. Brade's number on each side of the collar band glinted silver against her cheeks, like ear-rings.

'I didn't want to phone or go to the nick, Dave. Or come here in daylight.'

'It's a trek for you,' Brade replied.

Louise handed her a sound whisky and topped up her own, Erica's and Brade's.

'This would be about money then?' Louise said. 'What Bachelor cut up for.'

Fiona did not answer. She loosened the coat and shook out her short, fair hair. There was something fine about her, but probably not money, or Harvey and his pipe would still have been on parade.

Louise might have been thinking the same. 'The buzz is, zilch in Bachelor's estate,' she said. 'Or something like £37? I had this from my solicitor, a regular.'

'I heard that, too,' Erica added. 'It's a bugger, Fiona. You're in the will for a quarter, yes, and what's a quarter of fuck-all? It's finalised?'

'Yes, £37 the full estate, Dave. Obviously, it means he had it in cash, stored around his places,' Fiona cried loudly. 'It never saw probate. Miriam's cornered the lot. It could be anything – right up to three or four hundred grand.'

'Outrageous,' Brade said.

'I heard that figure, too,' Erica said. 'Four, not three. From a very reliable source, a lovely payer.'

'So you can see why I'm here, Dave.' Fiona was still giving it volume.

Brade said: 'We have to think of the neighbours. Cynthia next door gets up early to feed her cats.'

Erica said: 'Dave might be able to help. He's got a heart.'

'It would figure, not to use banks, and so on,' Louise said. 'Some trouble, and people like Dave can start poking into your statements.'

Fiona said: 'All the property mortgaged up to the roof, but there would have been cash stacks, no question. Deposit boxes?'

'My solicitor can't always get it up but he's a dear lad and I hear quite sharp in court,' Louise replied. 'If you're contesting I could mention your name.'

'Nothing official,' Fiona said. 'It could be awkward. If it's handled like that and the money's found there'd be queries on where Bachelor got it. Like you say, Louise. It might disappear again, to the authorities. I wondered if Dave could do some pressurising. We always look to Dave.'

'Of course,' Erica replied for him.

'I know you don't ever take cuts, Dave, but obviously there would be an honorarium,' Fiona said.

'Information?'

'You do deals, I hear.'

'Policing *is* deals,' Erica replied. 'He had Simeon here trying to move us out and making offers.'

'I'm getting fond of Llandaff Green and matins, plus the sense of religious history,' Louise said. 'Might stay.'

'You know something about Bachelor's business?' Brade asked. 'London connections, say? Why Ivor was missing, *is* missing?'

Louise refilled the glasses.

'Ivor went abroad somewhere, scared he could get framed, I suppose. Or scared someone from Bachelor's outfit might ask why he was left unprotected. Miriam's joined him, I hear. Do what you can for me, Dave, will you?'

'He'll definitely look at it,' Louise replied for him.

'Jesus, though, to have cohabited with something like Sweet Bachelor and then get nothing,' Erica remarked. 'That's filthy. Of course Dave will help.'

'I don't know the major connections themselves,' Fiona said, 'but there were people those connections used – used here . . . well, to clear the way, deal with difficulties, do messages and so on. This is a family.'

Brade was going to ask whether the name might be Samson, but then decided it would be cruel – the kind of ploy you could and should pull on Simeon de Courville, but not on a woman in mourning for at least a hundred or so grand in notes.

'Samson,' she whispered.

'I don't think I got that,' Louise replied, leaning forward in the cape to hear better.

'I think I did,' Brade said.

'South London. New Cross,' Fiona added.

'This could be invaluable,' Brade told her.

'I find it all incredibly exciting,' Erica said.

'Turning you on, is it?' Fiona asked. 'I won't hang about. Do what you can, Dave.'

When Fiona had gone, Erica, out of the rugby shirt, and looking very different from anyone Brade saw in his school-days out of a rugby shirt, asked: 'You knew all that, did you? Why so kindly? You hoping to get something going with her in due course?'

18

Lance Hamer said: 'Look, I'm sorry for coming to your home with work matters, Paul, but this is an emergency, a real one. And we're not known, so still no tail, I'm sure of it.'

Where the hell was the weapon Corbett promised? He tried to work out from Hamer's voice if he knew Yeo was refusing, refusing twice. With Jule, you were never sure what he had said or half said or said twisted or not said at all. Hamer seemed anxious, not angry. Where was Drinkwater?

'Now you're here you're here, Lance.' They were in the drawing-room at Highcross. When Hamer's voice first came on the gates intercom, Yeo had thought for a second, Don Samson. Stupid. If Don came stalking would he announce himself, for God's sake? Yeo had felt so relieved he pressed open-up. In any case, only a mixture of low fences and hedges guarded the grounds, and anyone could get in. Your true county families always had a wall, at least around the house. Next on his list.

They stood near the window, gazing down over fields towards the Bristol Channel. Bay advertisements preferred to throw the word 'Atlantic' about. It had more oomph and grandeur and infinitely greater sewage dilution than the Channel. But it was the Channel that gave Yeo sand. Carol was in the garden, sweeping leaves, and looked up for a moment and waved. Yeo waved back. It was happy, peaceful. It was being in touch with the soil, being part of a landscape. 'My girlfriend,' Yeo said. 'She volunteered. One of the gardeners got gout.' There were no gardeners, but why tell Hamer?

'To be frank, Paul, I'm bloody terrified about Otis Drinkwater. He's grand in so many ways, but he can't handle this bank job, Paul. All at once, I see it. And now Julian Corbett gets out of touch. How are we supposed to operate?'

'What do you mean, out of touch?'

'Difficult to reach. Paul, is Jule fragile, like Otis?'

'How do you mean, fragile?'

'Changeable. Big talk, then shit scared. I've watched it happen to Otis.'

'Jule's got problems.'

Hamer sharpened. 'The woman? That's part of all this. She's taken a shine to Otis. Women do. Maybe they've got something going. She's turned into a pain, and Otis is too feeble and nice to tell her, get lost.' One of the retrievers wandered towards Carol. 'You've got everything here, Paul.'

'We're settling in.'

'It's his way – Otis. Always has been. A period of consistency, but then every so often this lurch into chaos. There's fear, there's a turn to girls. Break-up. This is a known psychological state. You get it in kids mostly. Paul, obviously he's not really interested in women.' Bitterness and disgust crackled in his voice.

'No, I – ?'

'He gets so he needs to hurt me, for no reason, only malice and power, and he knows taking a woman will do it, any woman.'

'I'm sorry.'

Hamer grew passionate. 'Paul, you – you could return him to reason so easily and put his morale back to rights. Then we have a lovely, sure-fire project here. I can forgive Otis. Haven't I in the past a score of times? No back-biting to spoil our work plans, honestly. I can understand what she sees in Otis. Well, obviously. But it's not right.'

Yeo felt sorry for him. 'What did you mean, Lance, she's being a pain?'

'Hanging about.'

'Christ, you told Henrietta how to get in touch? Some security!'

'Otis gave her the cottage address. I said no, but he has this genuine, kindly streak – a credit, in a way.'

'You're saying the bank thing could be off because of all this?'

Or should it be both jobs off? Jule had not spoken. If Henrietta had drifted that way he might want nothing to do with them. Perhaps there would be no need for Yeo to bow out, no need to offend them or to look fragile, *changeable*. He felt bucked, yet suddenly disappointed as well. His problems were as ever. He still needed the boost. He still had to build his identity, and it cost.

Hamer shrugged. 'Is Jule opting out? If so, we're one short, and another's cracking up and posing girl-struck. What Otis needs now is brisk leadership, Paul. Don't get me wrong, I'm not putting myself down and perhaps I could handle it with someone else. But Otis wouldn't take that from me.'

They sat down. Yeo had begun to like the sound of things. An element in him still yearned to be called upon like de Gaulle, as long as he could keep control, take the lead. With Hamer in this state it looked easy to keep control, like reassuring a child. 'Malt whisky and rum are all I keep, Lance,' he said.

'Whisky would be rich, Paul.'

Yeo poured a couple of malts. 'What you're asking is, me take over?'

'Well . . .?'

'I'm not sure.' You made the ground right first. 'Straight commerce could be as much as I can handle, Lance, if things keep moving as lately.'

'Two or three points, really, Paul. Most important, I think he'd wear leadership from you. You're quality.'

'I try.'

'All right, I hear around you're a bit of a hotchpotch – name changed far back, ancestors from all over. Does it matter? I still read capacity. Second, I think you could get to Jule and bring him back in. Even talk to Henrietta. Convince her Otis is not for her. Oh, please, Paul. People respect your views. Get her and Jule back together. Such a tragic, unnecessary split.'

'Henrietta's a fine girl in many ways.' They were both sitting on one of the big leather chesterfields now, Hamer half turned towards Yeo, as if intent on catching everything he said and hinted at, Yeo looking ahead, towards the window, relaxed but thoughtful. Anyone glancing in would sense immediately where the power was. Yeo liked that.

'Otis is warm and seems young, plus all the laughs,' Hamer replied. 'Girls think life's going to be total merry-making and kid themselves they can end his AC-DC phase, turn him for ever hetero. Women love that challenge – believe they're reclaiming – the presumptuous, sexist bandits.'

Yeo sighed. 'At this stage, I don't even know what the job is or where, for God's sake.'

'That's Otis, too. I've told him – if he wants to work with quality people he's mad to sit on secrets. This is *some* whisky.'

'Fourteen years old.' He had bought it when they moved to Highcross, for ambience. No Valpolicella house, this.

'Incredible. I mean, I don't mean incredible like I don't believe it. Just incredible how good it is.'

Yeo smiled. Hamer was tripping over his friendliness. The house and so on hit him with awe. 'What kind of money, Lance? I assume respectable, or you wouldn't be bothering me. But exactly? And the target?'

'This goes into hundreds of grand, Paul.'

Yeo stopped himself from laughing outright – the deferential, hushed voice at the amount. In a way it was touching, yes, and made Hamer radiate a youthfulness as good as Drinkwater's, never mind the pink and white bald acres and phlegm-heavy lungs. Yeo waited.

'Of course, figures like that you're used to,' Hamer said. 'Businessman and previous gainful outings.'

Yeo applied modesty. That was part of man management, too. 'I don't think hundreds of grand grow on trees, if that's what you mean.' But he still spoke towards the other side of the room, still kept it unexcited.

'Thanks, Paul. We expect six hundred grand. Just over half a Big One.'

'And split among four? Wages or a bank? Well, you said bank. It's got to be a bank. I'd know of that much moving about.'

Hamer laughed. 'You would, Paul. You've got this area sewn up. You and your family might have been outsiders once. You've changed all that. It's a bank tip. But over the Severn Bridge.'

'What level?'

'Level?'

'Does it come from a cleaning lady or the chairman?'

'Otis has done banks before, genuine takings.'

'We've got to pay off a tipster? Making five?'

'Not a full share, Paul.'

'A fee?'

'Fifty grand.'

'No sliding scale?'

'Fifty regardless, even if it goes to over a Big One, and that's possible.'

'A million's a lot of freight. So, I ask again, is this tip from a good level? One step up from a clerk – if he'll take that sort of fee?'

'Higher. Otis is brilliant. He can find someone like this and still keep the costs tight. He did business training, knows all the workable ratios.'

'But he didn't know not to fuck a partner's woman until wind-down. Lesson One at Harvard Business School. Has Drinkwater heard of tact? Is Jule likely to work with him after this, for God's sake?'

'Except you speak a word. You alone can talk to their souls, Paul. You're local. All that German stuff – rubbish. You're in touch with them. All right, so you tyred Tommy Samson in the street. People know that could not be helped. Most people.'

'Not Don.'

'You can deal with anything, Paul.' Hamer was laying it on. But the problems he listed intrigued Yeo. They could be dealt with, and on his conditions.

Yeo sat well back, very relaxed. 'Here's the first of my terms: I'm not taking out Don Samson for you.'

'Oh.' The contentment bolted. His breath went altogether for a while. It was clear Jule had not contacted them. 'This is a turn-around.' He held out his glass for more whisky. It could not be ruder, but Yeo splashed some in. A host was a host.

He said: 'Why do you have to see off Don, anyway?'

Hamer put a hand over his nose and eyes for a second. 'This will knock Otis hard, and he's already crumbling.'

'I'll tell you, for your own ears, I was going to pull out altogether – no Don and no bank, either. Look at me. Look at this place. Look at my straight business operation and its potential. No police trouble. Do I risk that?'

'There'd be nothing to link Don Samson's death with here or you.'

'Maybe. Jule's casual. And you don't know Brade or his number two, Glyndwr Jenkins. Black. That boy's got something to prove. He and his family want integration through success, something I understand. Anyway, there's no link with Samson, because I'm not doing it. But, if you like, I *will* handle the bank, and try to get Jule back in.' Yeo sat back again, happy with a good compromise, the essence of business.

Hamer's voice was full of plea. 'We never regarded you as an exterminator, Paul, but we thought self-protection, because Don's going to come for you, otherwise. That would just happen to solve our problem at the same time.'

'He might *not* come.'

'Paul, be reasonable. You mashed his beloved son for a galloped exit, no police anywhere in sight. The Procedure. Don's – '

Yeo stood and spoke as he walked to the window to watch Carol. He was talking over his shoulder. 'Yes, police *were* there, or almost, I swear it. I swear it.' His voice nearly failed, and for a second he felt dominance of this meeting running away. He paused, and then took care to speak at proper volume. He faced Hamer. 'Look, this is take it or leave it, Lance. I'll run the bank matter, do the leadership, for forty per cent of the gross – that's before the fifty grand comes out. Forty per cent of the full total. I'm signing without knowing the detail, pig in a poke, and there's not many in my bracket would do that. If you want it, I'm here. That's as far as I go. You need Don dead, you see to it.'

'Which would be doing you a very nice favour, wouldn't it?' Suddenly he sounded evil.

'You say.'

'I'll have to talk to Otis.'

'Of course you will. Talk about the craziness of tying himself to Henrietta and hurting Jule. Does he understand her father's a famous minister? They're still prized in this part of the world. Learn local culture.'

19

Brade had a sad little meeting in the flat with Erica and Louise. It was lunchtime after what sounded like very good business the night before, so both girls had been looking game and cheerful. Each wore one of his suit jackets over little. It would excite him a bit to put them on himself after this. Anything helped.

'I have to go to London for a day or two,' he said. 'Think you'll be all right? I'll tell Glyndwr to keep an eye, but it's no fortress. There's Simeon and so on. I'll get back fast. It's a worry.'

'Christ, we'll miss you, Dave,' Louise replied. Hers was a grey, Jaeger suit jacket, and she had the collar turned up like some girl in a French film, nicely framing her face and red-brown hair. 'Look, I don't want Glyndwr thinking free availability just because we're in your place and I conferred it once when low.'

'Why London?' Erica asked.

'Bullfinch wants to shut down the cases, blame the killings on a dead man.' Eventually, Brade had been forced to tell him about Tommy Samson and Bullfinch immediately decided Samson did the murders. Brilliantly tidy.

'Yes, so why London?' Erica said. 'What do we do for conversation?'

'We've got a lot of pointers to a dead New Cross kid for Olive and maybe Bachelor – what Fiona said the other night, and others. So handy. But true? I must keep the inquiries open. I've convinced Bullfinch we can't wrap it until I've checked if the lad has alibis. Had.'

'Hoping so?' Erica asked.

'Hoping so.'

'You wanting to get who instead?' Louise said.

'Me wanting to get who did it – did them. One of the team? Max? Ivor? Yes, Ivor. People behind any of these in London? Parents? Harvey? In any case, me wanting to get someone or more than one we can put questions to – someone who's not ashes.'

'You're targeting Alec Rice?' Erica said. 'My God, though, families.'

'Jealous? You had something with Olive, Dave?' Louise asked. 'Why so committed? Would you behave the same for me?'

'Stop it,' he yelled, hearing inside his head a sudden singing roar of what could be blood pressure or a bursting clot. 'It's not going to happen to you. I'll give you Glyn's home number. The least sign of crisis ring him. I mean, if the Merc's seen this end of town, anything.'

'Simeon won't try brutalities, Dave,' Erica said. 'A cop lair, alongside a grey cathedral, the bourgeoisie all about. People like Simeon don't act off their ground, where they're in control.'

'No, not in fucking control,' Brade replied, shouting again.

'No?' Erica said, glancing towards the party wall and Cynthia's place.

'That's *my* ground, *my* place. If I pull this settee over to near the door you'll be able to shove it into position before you go to bed.'

'Settee's naff, Dave. Say sofa,' Louise told him.

'It's not too heavy,' Brade said.

'Tat, like everything here,' Louise replied. 'So what good if it's not heavy?'

'A couple of minutes' delay while you phone.'

'If you're so worried, why not let it die?' Louise said. 'Do it Bullfinch's way.'

Erica said: 'Bcause he can't. Dave's got that lovely hero thing.'

He loved south-east London, run-down and various like the work patch at home, exploited people fervently scheming to milk the system. Just more of them. Deptford Town Hall had a small statue of Nelson and his ship high outside, and you could not get more heroic than that. If Horatio wanted to sleep at peace in his hammock he would have to blind-eye on plenty visible from there. The young, local CID expert on the Samsons was a fattish-faced sergeant, Arnold Aphik. Brade saw at once that Aphik's soft leather, plain black shoes must have cost even more than his own Charles Laity boots. They came up fast in London. Brade did not mind kowtowing to top town flash, as long as he knew he would be back home and king again soon. 'I was in the Big Box with Tommy,' Aphik said.

'Yes?'

'Same class, Shillay Comprehensive School, aka the Big Box. He went his way. A family like that, what else? One day they'll get the message. I'm still around in this nine hundred quid suit and pensionable. Where's Tommy? You've heard about the Elvis turn he did? Great. He'd get even ancient teachers singing and doing pelvic lech thrusts.'

He had the voice of these feverish streets, not genial but authentic. Brade could hear him shouting for Millwall. Aphik walked him around, obviously proud to show off the peeling realm with its pavement sphinxes of at least Rottweiler shit. They passed the dark-walled Venue club and Aphik nodded towards a group of bay-fronted old villas. 'Chaucer Court, where I was brought up. Touch of the literaries and the royals. We call it Crack City now.' He branched off and led Brade into a big, scruffy, noisy, multi-flatted Victorian house. They climbed to the third landing and he knocked a door. A woman in her twenties opened it and when she saw Aphik turned and went slowly and silently back into the apartment, leaving them to follow. A dark-haired girl of about two waddled out from an inner room and took her hand, also staying silent.

'Here's Dave, a friend of mine from Wales, Fran,' Aphik chortled. 'About Tommy.'

'Go on.'

'He wants to do his best by him. It's like a mission. This one's Tommy's, Dave,' Aphik said, nodding towards the child.

The room was not bad, probably sprucer than his own before Louise and Erica purged it, though not as neat as their places. Two windows looked towards the middle of London, high-rises poking up through smears of body mist far off. All the furniture seemed superior to Brade's, and it could be real velour on one of the cerise armchairs. 'I wondered if you knew whether Tommy did any work in Cardiff last summer,' Brade said.

'What work?'

'I don't mean banks. Proper work – seeing people, fixing things up. Trouble-shooting and so on?'

'He did travel a lot.'

'Of course.'

'What's that mean, of course?'

'Dave's trying to help you, Fran.'

'So why's he with you?'

'Or help Tommy – help the memory of Tommy. Fairness is operating. They're like that in Wales.'

'In *South* Wales,' Brade said.

'I don't need help with the memory of Tommy,' she replied.

Brade said: Well, look, I've got to ask this, Fran. Did he have a girl down my way – might have taken her to Blackpool before the raid?'

'He's going to tell me?'

'Did he wander?'

138

'He's going to tell me? This a whore or something? What's she saying about him?'

'Did he make trips to Cardiff, Fran? This was a girl called Olive.'

'Was?'

'Or ever speak of someone called Bachelor Percy, a heavy, but with charm?'

Aphik said: 'Can we sit down?' He pulled a bag of Turkish delight squares from his pocket and the child released her mother's hand and went unsmiling towards his chair for them, probably a regular drill. Fran folded down into the cerise chair. She was dark-haired with a longish face and good, jutting features – nose, chin, eyebrows – plus heavy lips, rather like Richard Gere, but enough not. She sounded beaten yet looked strong. Brade was used to reading hatred in people's eyes and found it here. Tommy would have picked someone from the culture, so you had to expect hatred. It looked as though Aphik and maybe others had given her a lot of interrogation since Tommy's death, but the hate probably went back before that.

'I'm interested in the nights of June 30 and July 2 last year,' Brade said.

'What happened?'

'Was Tommy away?'

'God, am I going to remember dates?'

'If he was away for a long time you might.'

'No, he wasn't.'

'Short absences?'

'He travelled. He made money.'

'You don't keep a diary?' Brade asked.

The contempt left her eyes briefly and was replaced by laughter. 'Prick,' she replied, 'in your pretty boots. Am I a writer?'

The little girl liked this lightening of mood and smiled, too, her teeth full of pale chunks of sweets. But Brade began to feel oppressed by the loathing and contempt from her mother and stood, preparing to leave.

'You told me you'd let me know one day how it all went at Blackpool,' she said to Aphik.

'Fran, you don't want to hear that. Let it lie, now,' he replied. 'A minute ago you said you needed no help with memories.'

139

'Just big-mouthing, were you?' Brade said.

She looked away from him into the empty fireplace. A paraffin heater burned on one-third power in the room, nowhere near beating the cold. Brade and Aphik had kept their raincoats on. Fran was in what looked like a couple of sweaters and the bottom of a track suit. The child also had on a kind of track suit, bulked out by woollens underneath. Some money must have come to her from Blackpool, though. Lads were generally good like that. What had she done with it?

Aphik pulled folded papers from his breast pocket. 'If you really want, Fran. And if Dave's got the time.'

'Sod Dave. What's he trying to do – offload all unsolveds in his domain on Tommy? The old ploy. Find a dead, dispose of the outstandings and put the hunt tally up.'

'You never heard the name Olive?' Brade replied.

'Didn't know there were still people around called Olive. What we waiting for?'

'I'm thinking about Sarah,' Aphik said.

'She's a baby. She doesn't understand. Perhaps she ought to know, anyway.'

'She ought to know how they can slip to hell, yes,' Aphik said.

'One of them. The other three are fine and rich, the gutless wonders.'

'Oh, Christ, why don't you leave it alone, Fran.' Brade sat down again.

Aphik got the sheets in order. 'This comes from the local police. To start with, we have stuff from outside the bank – witnesses who first spotted something when Tommy and the other two pulled on balaclavas, plus the driver with wide-frame glasses under the wool – but we don't think he did, eventually.'

'What?' Brade said.

'Drive. Blackpool police also found a woman lately who had a good look at one of them as he ran up to the assembly point, mid-thirties from his physique, thin. He was masked, but she says eyes like some blond actor who played Nazis, and agreed when they showed her a pic of Anton Diffring. One day it might help.' He flipped over the top sheet. 'Then, bank people describing Tommy's part inside, threatening the security van boys with a pistol. This we know now was a Modelo A-90, fifteen rounds.

140

Cockney accent saying, "Get flat and give it or you're dead" – saying it very level, no shouting.'

She nodded and smiled: 'Corny. Yes, that would be Tom.' Once again the child noticed and, taking heart, smiled herself. Brade saw suddenly why Fran wanted to hear this. She longed to be told the winning parts. These would not continue in this story, and she knew it, but never mind. Tommy was on top then, the culture doing its bright, rough best. What did it matter he'd been bedding another girl, as long as he'd had this moment of eminence? He had been an emperor then, and emperors took women as they wished. None of this was much use to Brade, but it gripped him. An education. Tommy had been another sort of hero? 'Yes, exactly Tommy,' she murmured.

'Tommy,' the child chortled.

'Your brave dad,' Fran said.

'Dad,' the child stated.

'Tommy takes the last two cash bags as the raid ends,' Aphik said. 'He's in red and white trainers, jeans and a purple wind-cheater, plus balaclava, none of it identified as his by you, of course, Fran, but what does it matter?' He looked squarely at her. 'Because we had the body, didn't we?'

'I identified that.'

'You were good.'

'I had to see him, that's all.'

Aphik said: 'Yes, he was a fine lad.'

'Fuck off.'

Aphik smiled now. The little girl did not respond, though. 'We come outside,' Aphik said, returning to the papers. 'They're backing towards the Senator. Someone shouts, "Let's get there," sounding panicky, probably not Cockney, probably not Tommy.'

'Not Tommy.'

'Even an educated voice. Not Tommy,' Aphik said.

This lad talked like someone who had been around since the beginning of time, seen it all and made notes. Yet he would be only twenty-five, Tommy Samson's year, and you could still imagine what he looked like in a school group picture. He had fair hair and a round, fat face full of a sort of friendliness, a police sort, so not everyone would believe it. Soon he would grow a sharp moustache to look older at promotion boards.

'A bank security guard, Norman Hector Peters, has followed them and comes out from the bank while they're still retreating to the car,' Aphik said. 'Two of them keep going, but Tommy very deliberately puts down his sacks and carefully fires a couple of shots at Norman Hector Peters.'

She nodded again. 'I like it.'

'He misses.'

'Was he trying to hit? It could be a warning only. Anyway, he tried. He fought back.'

'Shot at a helpless man,' Aphik said.

'At the law.'

'Tommy gets up and bends to recover the bags. It's awkward. He can use only one hand because of the pistol. As he's doing this, Norman Hector Peters makes a dash at him down the steps. He's quite a lad,' Aphik said, 'law or not.'

'He's death, but, yes, he's quite a lad.'

'I wouldn't say *he* was death. That's the driver,' Aphik replied.

'Peters started it.'

Aphik paused. 'Who finished it, Fran? Why not let us get him for you?'

She yawned, perhaps real, perhaps to show she had heard the questions from him and the rest time and again. Fair teeth. 'Do you think he'd be alive if I knew – if any of the Samsons knew?'

Brade muttered: 'Don't say that. It's evil.'

She seemed about to laugh again, then said to Aphik: 'So go on.'

'It gets rough, Fran.'

'Nothing's as rough as waiting for him to claw his way from the coma pit and knowing he won't.'

'Three witnesses say there was some sort of confusion at the car. The driver had been sitting balaclavaed behind the wheel and he brought the Senator up near the bank, then opened both nearside doors. Know anyone with glasses, Fran?'

'Wide frames? Warren Beatty?'

'Bonnie and Clyde return.' Aphik had a chuckle, a dead chuckle, like some pensioner over his day-centre dinner. 'My governor said Warren Beatty, too.'

'Liar. You bleeding liar,' she screamed, 'I don't joke like police.'

The child lowered her head and foraged in the empty sweet bag, as if embarrassed and frightened by the outburst.

'Just before they come out of the bank the driver struggles over and sits in the passenger seat, instead. He's still there when the other two arrive and witnesses saw frantic arguing. One man's into the back with his sacks, sort of lying out, half helpless on the rear seat, everything gone, his strength, his control. What's said between the man outside and the driver we don't know, nobody close enough – you can believe that – there's a lot of armament about. The driver won't shift. Witnesses think he'd frozen. Some say police two-tones could be heard by now. It's tense. The man in the back is howling and audible, "Write him off. Fucking drive. Drive." We assume he's shouting at the man outside, but it's not clear whether he's telling him to write the driver off and take over himself or to write Tommy off, who's still trying to get to the car. This is panic, but these people are pros by the look, so even now no names used. Tommy's about fifty yards ahead of the car. We don't think the Senator was where they planned, because a cleaning vehicle had the spot. Eventually, the man outside dumps his sacks on the driver's lap, slams the passenger door shut and runs around the bonnet to get behind the wheel. We think the Anton Diffring. The Senator moves forward a little way, its nearside rear door open. Apparently, the substitute driver's trying to make it easy for Tommy – going to meet him. I'm paraphrasing.'

'Bollocks,' Fran said. 'The driver's getting clear.'

'One, two, three witnesses told police he waited.'

'He thought about his skin and loot.'

'They're closer to pedestrians now, and witnesses say the man in the back was still screaming – some message like: "Go, go, go, you bastard. Christ, where's a real Wheels?" That's their word for a driver.'

'Really,' Fran said.

'Nothing useful on accent, except it sounded like the educated one. He's frantic. Know the type, Dave, Fran? Peters has reached Tommy. He could have turned and blown Peters away with the pistol – '

'I said he didn't want to hurt anyone.'

143

'Peters bangs down with his truncheon from behind on Tommy's wrist and he loses the gun. Peters grapples with him. He's a big lad, and fit, as well as gutsy.'

'All right, all right. I've heard it before. Law and order recruits the best – him and you.'

'So they fight and wrestle on the pavement. Tommy has dropped the money sacks as well, to get his hands free. One tripper witness, a woman, is very cool, picks up the automatic and points it, also two-handed – they learn from TV – points it at Tommy and Tommy seems to see it and throws himself to one side and stumbles out into the road. Peters says he tried to hold him, actually thought he was escaping. But Tommy is off balance, tottering, and the Senator is right up to them by now, one door still open, welcoming, and hits him with the front near side, not a big blow but enough to finish off the stumble, so he's down and the car goes over him with front and rear nearside wheels.'

'But it was just dawdling, waiting for him to get in,' Brade said. 'He couldn't stop?'

Fran looked at him as if he had said what she wanted to say, and what all the Samsons wanted to say, and had said half-hourly since, but she didn't switch off the hate.

'Peters tells us his impression was – he's concentrating on the fight and could be wrong – but his impression was that a couple of seconds earlier the driver had upped the speed, maybe to twenty. Other witnesses say the same. And once he'd hit him he really put his foot down.'

'Writing Tommy off,' Fran said. It was clipped, definite, QED.

'Perhaps he'd decided there was no chance,' Aphik replied. 'The damage was done. Make the best of things – save three.'

'Three plus most of the take,' she said.

'Of course. What else? They couldn't stop and give mouth to mouth. They belt away, rear door still open when last seen. Police arrive a minute or two later. Tommy's bags of cash stayed on the pavement, one with a fifty note sticking from the top and waving in the little breeze like what our arty woman observer from a flower shop describes here as ... as "a small hand through a grating".'

Suddenly she turned to Brade. 'Do you buy it?'

'What?'

'That it was Tommy's own fault. Arnie's line.'

'I've never said that,' Aphik replied. 'I don't give a shit whose fault. Tommy was there. That make it his fault? I'd say so.'

'So, do you buy it?' she asked Brade again.

'Tommy hung about.'

'He tried to stop the pursuit,' she said. 'He was thinking of the whole job, the whole team. His way.'

She needed to believe this. Why not? After all, Brade was here to do the lad a kind of service. 'Maybe they could have stopped. Yes.'

She nodded and almost smiled. 'I think Tommy comes out of it big.'

'He comes out of it dead,' Aphik told her.

'But decent,' Fran said.

She must know Aphik would not accept that and she glanced at Brade again. 'He'd have killed an unarmed man,' he said. You did not piss on law and order for just a smile. You did not go into an alliance against one of your own. She smiled, anyway, and stoked up the hate in her eyes, as if he had confirmed for her that all police at all times were police and nothing more. He switched off from her eyes again.

Brade left with Aphik and they walked back to the car. Old tar letters scrawled on a wall in Cold Blow Lane read, 'The Den is a Yuppie-Free Zone.' Aphik said: 'I suppose no help to you?'

'I liked her.'

'Oh, sure. She was mine for a year, before Tommy came on the scene with the bloody guitar. I thought permanent.'

'Great eyes.'

'I saw you feeding there and elsewhere. So, you'll hit Tommy with your murders, too?'

'I got nothing that said he couldn't have been in Cardiff, and nothing that said he was.'

'He's capable of it, naturally – guns, knives, Tommy wouldn't hold back. Didn't hold back at Blackpool. He'd handle a contract.'

'Is this Aphik, CID, talking, or Arnie Aphik, needing to prove he did right to ditch local culture, or Arnold Aphik, beaten lover?'

'Fair questions. Look, we'd rather you don't see Don Samson at present. He wouldn't know anything about Cardiff, anyway.'

145

'Sure of that?'

'We're not sure of anything, but we don't want you calling on him. You're brighter than you look and sound, Dave, but this is a delicate one. Our thinking is, he'll have to move very soon against the three in the car, under The Procedure.'

'He'll lead to them?'

'That's it. Why I laid it on that at least two and maybe the original driver all helped do for Tommy. Don denies knowledge of the crew, like Fran, but I ask you. We'll get the three then, and maybe Don and some of his people for attempted this or that – or better, if we time it so we're too late. It would be a nice capture. He has to think he's being left alone now. Then he'll get it under way, Dave.'

'It's been an eye-opener.'

'She fancied you.'

'Not that I could see.'

'Never actually spat in your face. But I heard you prefer pictures.'

'Safer.'

It was late evening when Brade arrived back in Cardiff and he did not go home but walked to his office in Bute Street. The girls would be out working now and he urgently wanted to check they were all right. If orders said forget Olive, he worried all the more about Louise and Erica. You could not preside over a patch where girls were getting savaged all the time. He went to Erica's beat. He could not see her, or Simeon, supervising from the Merc and collecting. Turning back, he made his way down Bute Street towards the docks. Normally, it would have settled him nicely to be back on the patch, grandly unwelcome to many and feared, seeing folk he knew or half knew, and who knew him but gave no sign: Aphik had his spot, Brade had his, and no reason why the London one should be superior.

Tonight, though, his anxieties kept at him and mounted when he could not find Louise around her favourite areas near the Exchange, either. Maximilian's Petronella he did see in James Street, negotiating with what appeared to be three well-dressed foreigners, two white, one black, full of gloss and merriment, perhaps diplomats with day business at the Welsh Office or Welsh Development Agency. Petronella seemed a good kid, and would know Maximilian had some money to make up, even

146

though things ticked over while he was sick. She gave Brade a small, friendly wave, and he thought he heard her say, 'A hundred?', which would most likely be for all, though they'd be on good expenses and any girl would sense how high she could go. If they agreed immediately, Petronella might gently add, 'Each.'

In Mount Stuart Square one light seemed to be burning in Bethel Chapel, although the manse was dark. He tried the door but found it locked. Someone moved inside, apparently having heard the latch lifted. In a moment, Floyd, short of a dog-collar and breath, opened up. 'Why, Dave,' he said. 'I thought it might be some member seeking help or consolation.' They went in and Brade saw Louise near the blood text putting her clothes straight and tidying a pew.

Floyd said: 'Henrietta's back.'

'Was she away?' Brade replied.

'Some strain between her and Julian. Possibly she's been slagging it. Always something of a furnace down there. The way she's made. A nice reconciliation. It might last. I wanted to get out of the manse – let them have the run of it tonight.'

'Constructive,' Brade said.

'Jule was badly hit. He's been keeping very much to himself. Louise and I were discussing reform of the House of Lords.'

'It still makes me uneasy to stand here, just where Olive was,' Louise said.

'Is Erica all right?' Brade asked.

'Of course she's all right. You think we can't survive without you?' Louise replied.

'Dave, I hear you might be shutting down on Olive and Sweet Bachelor. The Bay. Big money. It brings its pressures. We're small fry, even you.'

'You thought it was Erica at the door, did you?' he replied.

'Over Bethel's doorway are inscribed the words, "All Are Welcome", Dave,' Floyd said.

20

Paul Yeo was phoned at Highcross by Lance Hamer, keen to fix a meeting about what he called 'the new command structure'. Yeo would not let him into the Farm again, this time with Drinkwater, nor did he want to see them anywhere around the docks. And it was time to change from the Pontcanna café. Yeo suggested a small car-park alongside the Red House in Ferry Road: at low tide fine views over mud to Rat Island. You could see the progress of Cardiff's barrage from here. It had already generated all kinds of other construction and made a lot of sand business for Yeo. If the meeting turned sticky he would remind himself and those two he could do without them. He needed something like this to fortify him: Jule Corbett still had not come up with the armament, and Yeo felt exposed.

He considered not going. But, Christ, he had to believe he could manage them. What use trying to build yourself a good identity if a couple of wandering nobodies could wreck it? He was not a rabbit scared in a hole, but Paul Yeo in twenty acres with sea views, and a shipowner, thanks very much: jumped up from kraut nowhere, yes, but jumped up high. Did German have words for *nouveau riche*? All the same, Carol saw he was edgy and asked why, but he told her the *Splott* had trouble. He checked his tyre lever was under the driving seat.

This was a spot where the Bay transformation in general had already begun to show, not just the barrage. Ferry Road used to be only car breakers, tips, small-time engineering shops and junk yards. A few remained but now there was also Windsor Quay under construction, a smart new housing development at the edge of the mud, with an outlook to the docks or Penarth Head and the Holm islands. A new elevated link road led to the docks tunnels. Smell the future.

Hamer and Drinkwater arrived in a sodding VW and came and joined Yeo in his Rover, Hamer in the front. It was just after 4 p.m., and the light had begun to go. Drinkwater said: 'Paul, I had the message: you'll do the bank, but not Don Samson?'

'Exactly.' It came out as he wanted, short, hard, undebatable, and he reached down on the door side and fondled the tyre lever.

'I put your points to Otis absolutely straight, Paul,' Hamer said.

'Not a word Lance likes. We have to accept your terms, Paul. As simple as that.'

Letting go of the lever, Yeo half turned and could still get a reasonable sight of Drinkwater's glossy skin, really not bad for around fifty. 'You'll forget about the Don Samson side of things?' Yeo said.

Drinkwater went into a biggish, very comfortable, moist laugh. 'No chance. Look, it's not forgettable, Paul. But Lance will handle things. We can't neglect that sort of chance. Don has hurt us, you know – gone out of his way to.' He kept his voice light, possibly to show they would certainly not brew everlasting venom about this, as long as they could kill Samson Thursday week.

'No problems finishing Don,' Hamer said. 'We just thought you'd be glad of the opening.'

'We need you absolutely for the bank, so we take your conditions, Paul. The Blackpool flair. We want a pro.'

'Thanks, Otis.'

'Are we going to try to lean on someone like Paul Yeo – your lineage?' Hamer asked, shaking his nice round baldness to show the absurdity. 'We're on foreign soil, too, and you hold our hands.'

Yeo had arrived early and parked near the pub, gazing back towards Rat Island's foreshore and the nice old Hamadryad hospital. He always bought British cars, of course. The view was not your standard picturesque, but on the mud flats, oyster catchers, gulls and a sheldrake brown-nosed away, and more gulls glided and harangued above. Naturalists fretted about what would happen to bird life when the barrage was completed. He fretted himself. Not just this habitat but some of the place's history would disappear under a lagoon, and he valued history, almost as much as the future. What was anyone without a history?

Now Hamer leaned closer, confidentially, breathing that noisy way he had, like wind through a corn field, his large, brown eyes making a plea. He seemed to think about putting a hand on

Yeo's leg and decided, no. 'But, in turn, we'd like you to agree to a small change in how we do the bank, Paul.' He hesitated and then rushed the words. 'It's Corbett.'

'This is a pain, regrettable, but necessary,' Drinkwater said.

'Otis and I both see him as the sole but desperate weakness in our outing, Paul. We decided this quite independently, no influencing each other. Look, we three can handle it, or possibly Otis will find someone else, even so late.'

'Jule's been bloody hard to contact lately. Perhaps you know, Paul. Does that give confidence? He's hiding from colleagues, lying low with father-in-law, apparently. What's he doing, seeking sanctuary?' It was a kind of joke, an old kind and Drinkwater generally made a production of jokes, but did not laugh this time. The grey moustache looked greyer because of worry and the shadows, like Field Marshal Haig's in Great War books.

'What we hear about Blackpool, he didn't show up too well in the car,' Drinkwater went on. 'We risk that again?'

'Nobody was completely great,' Yeo said.

Low water, and no shipping moved. Tomorrow, the *Splott* would be bustling out visible from here towards Flat Holm again, as dredgers had been for sixty or seventy years. Now and then Yeo liked a trip. He had no need to go. There was a good crew and a good captain. But Yeo enjoyed plodding out in her and enjoyed even more plodding back at night towards the Cardiff lights, a hold full of sellable sand or gravel aboard, the men grouped forward, ready to be off and away as soon as she docked. To them, the ship was a pay packet. He understood. For Yeo, it was this and status. That old thug Bachelor Percy had recognised how important the boat was to Yeo and offered in his crude way to 'protect' it for him. Yeo told him he did his own protection. Percy had not liked this. Pity. No, Yeo was not a scared rabbit in a hole. People discovered that.

'Basically, with Jule it comes down to the woman, I think,' Drinkwater said. 'She's made him even more jumpy.' He sank back a degree further into the half-darkness, bowed his head and held up one hand to acknowledge error. 'All right, Lance. I see you looking. Yes, I blame myself for what happened with Henrietta. I could have held back, pushed her off.'

'Ha!' Hamer snapped and struck the glove compartment with his fist in triumph. 'Well, at last, we have an admission.'

'In fact, I *should* have held back. A whim. She's not something to bowl anyone over, is she?'

'Jule's very fond of her,' Yeo replied. 'More, really – dependent.'

'I did misread things,' Drinkwater said. 'Oh, yes, a brain.'

'What you did was cut loose,' Hamer told him. 'Juvenile, importunate and disgusting. It's not the first time. Any opportunity. Gender, looks – immaterial. Otis, it can be heartbreaking.'

'Anyway, there's resentment in Jule Corbett, no question,' Drinkwater replied. 'Understandable. Yes, but it means I can't trust him to behave right.'

'Oh, that's really lovely, coming from you,' Hamer said, with a hell of gasp. 'How do you think it sounds to Paul?'

'We can't run a job with bad feeling between two of the people,' Drinkwater replied. 'I've done damage. I'm sorry. We mustn't let it get worse, fatal.'

'Of course, you'll ask how we set about dropping him?' Hamer said. 'He's not going to volunteer, is he? Jule knows the pickings available in this job.'

'But just leave that to us. To me. I brought it on, so I'll deal with Jule.'

'"Deal with Jule"?' Yeo said.

'Only talking to him,' Drinkwater said at once.

'I won't have Corbett hurt.'

'That's not going to be necessary,' Drinkwater said.

'If he's hurt or worse we've no chance at all,' Yeo replied. 'Brade and his people will be everywhere. Jule's father-in-law is a docks cornerstone, greatly loved, and people look after him. Girls give it to him free.'

Hamer controlled his voice and stared ahead through the windscreen out into the dark: 'Otis will tell Jule, or authorise me to, that as long as he quits with good grace – and I stress that, with good grace and no sabotaging or leaking – if he agrees to that, Otis will leave the girl alone. Obviously, he'll be leaving the girl alone, anyway, won't you Otis?' He paused then yelled: 'Fucking won't you, Otis?'

'Of course. I sent her back, didn't I?'

'But Jule's not to know that Otis has already sworn off, is he? He'll be scared of losing her again.'

'And she'd come if I called, Paul. There was what she termed

151

"rapport", which, apparently, she's short of with Jule and previously. I'm not bragging. Just how it is.'

'Irresistible, isn't he, Paul, the cock-happy, old grease spot?' Hamer turned and glared at him. Hamer's life must be repeated agony. 'So rapport's what they call it now.'

'I foresee no problems,' Drinkwater replied.

'Three really can handle it?' Yeo asked.

'Three good ones are better than three good ones plus a panic king,' Hamer said. 'In any case, you're two on your own, Paul.'

'I concentrate hard on being just one, as a matter of fact.'

When they had gone, Yeo sat for a little while in the dark. Suddenly, he was sickened by his responses to those two. Jesus, he had felt a rush of obnoxious pleasure when Drinkwater praised him, called him a professional because he had escaped from Blackpool with the funds and brought Jule and Flanders out intact. But one missing. He had annihilated a kid there. Drinkwater called this flair?

In pain, Yeo decided he would motor up to Blackpool next day to the raid site. If he was in the same spot again, he could do a playback of the whole thing, convince himself it had been inevitable, console himself. The buildings and roads, the smell of the town, would remind him in detail. Of course, he had run it through his mind repeatedly, but that was here, at a distance, in Highcross, or out on the *Splott*, and maybe he had cleaned up his recollections to suit. No maybe. He had. He knew himself well.

In the morning, he asked Carol whether she wanted to come and explained his agony – pleaded with her to come. She could not see any point, felt it would be morbid and dangerous. Probably. 'Self-indulgent,' she added. Probably that, too. He went, just the same.

Obviously, he would not make a show. At least one woman had taken a good, close gaze at him masked-up just before the raid – though perhaps a holiday-maker and far from Blackpool now. He must be careful. Of course, Hamer and Drinkwater would say it hardly mattered whether Tommy could have been saved. What counted was what Don Samson thought – 'perceived', in the jargon. If Samson believed Tommy had been sacrificed the culture dictated what came next, and soon.

Yeo parked far away and walked to near the bank. The town

152

was in winter hibernation, most of its tacky, cheerful souvenir stores, chip shops, noiserama pin-ball places and pizza dens closed. Blackpool looked almost sedate. Yeo preferred its summer buzz and the season's friendly, pervasive reek of junk food, ciggies and ale. He would have preferred the summer crowds, too, so he could merge. Fragments of mist or low cloud hung around the top of the daft tower and the sea sounded ratty.

Seeing the bank again, Yeo recalled why they had thought it would be a doddle. The building had a wide front, easy, shallow steps, big doors, a choice of side-street exits. Even with the snag of that bloody cleansing truck, Flanders had been able to park fairly close. Yeo walked quickly past, then turned and did it again, had to, despite all his resolutions. He could identify the spot where he hit Tommy and went over him: no bloodstains now, but it was in his head for ever, the different stages in the feel of it, the way the vehicle bucked then came down. And he saw again the mirror view: Tommy's body in that purple shirt still moving a bit and a bag with money fluttering cheerfully at the unzipped top, like children's hands through a car sun-roof – how he had thought of it then, even panic-dazed.

When they left the Senator, Flanders behind the wheel had seemed right enough, recovered from the nerviness. Of course, Yeo had heard of drivers who cracked and ditched their people to make a dash and save themselves. Never of one seizing up the way Flanders did, though. Would a good leader have spotted sooner how bad he was? Without that shock of finding him in the wrong seat, perhaps things would have stayed rational, and Tommy might have had a chance. Had Tommy cared all that much about a chance, though? There had been moments here on the day when Tommy Samson seemed indifferent to safety and to life, his own life. That strange impression came back to Yeo as he strode these streets.

But he returned to self-examination, in that style of his. Had he come apart just as badly as Flanders or Jule? Had that shock over Flanders plus Corbett's screaming and state taken Yeo's guts? Taken his judgement? Over and over since, he had told himself he was in command of his brain and body then, had stayed in command, would have stopped for Tommy if it had been even half possible. Until yesterday and today he had been able to convince himself that his mind had operated well enough here to make such a judgement – was able to measure half-chances or less. And it had been less, a lot less, hadn't it?

Tommy, with that security ape on him, and some woman waving Tommy's automatic, stumbled into the road, just ahead of the car. Yeo was doing below twenty, he could swear to this, but was still too close to avoid him. If Tommy hadn't been already staggering the little bump might not have knocked him down, but he spun and went straight on to hands and knees at the front wheel. There had been no chance at all, nothing near half. As Yeo walked past the spot now, he was seeing Tommy Samson stagger like a drunk, still gripping a sack of cash and looking at Yeo with his dark eyes as he tumbled, possibly even a little smile because he had managed to keep the money, and certainly expecting Yeo to stop. But Corbett was yelling about the guard, telling Yeo to keep going. It would have been useless banging the brakes, wouldn't it? They would still have gone over Tommy. But wouldn't someone with real leadership have ignored Corbett?

Because of the impact, Yeo had lost his grip on the steering wheel for a moment and his foot came up off the pedal, slowing the car right down, almost stalling. Corbett had howled at him to correct and even Flanders might have come out of zombiedom and shouted. And, correcting, Yeo banged the accelerator. That was how it had been.

You could argue that Jule or Yeo himself should have shot the guard after Tommy lost his gun. They were both tooled up. So was Flanders, though not in a marksman state. But Tommy and the guard were wrestling and clawing at each other, and to put a bullet into the right one would have been so tricky.

They said Graham Flanders was in Jersey, girling, blueing his gains, no thrift, no guilt. How they were, some of them. Corbett had wanted to stop Flanders' share or slash it, but Yeo said he took as agreed. He was part of the outfit – a dud part, but things could go wrong for anyone.

Yeo walked up to where they had made their side-street turn, the rear door still swinging. After a couple more miles, Corbett had recovered enough to tug it shut. By then they were nearly at the change car, anyway. Needing to organise the switch then, Yeo had pushed Tommy Samson out of his head. Now, though, walking for the fourth and last time past where the car had hit and ploughed, Yeo could feel some of the horror of the day at the boy's mistakes, and above all Tommy's failure to see he had a duty to the rest of them. He thought the fight was one to one, like jousting, and still couldn't win it. Tommy had been exactly the type you wanted no partnership with in business, rough business or straight business – a boy clever enough to see possibilities, but too doom-laden and suicidal to turn them into sweet reward. Stop to help him and that guard would have been into the car, too. Finish. Not just no takings, no liberty again this century. That would really turn you into Nowhere Man, for half the rest of your earning life a jail number. Surely Don Samson had heard what a high-gloss shambles his kid made of it. He must know there could be no blame, except on Tommy, and no cause for vengeance. Perhaps Don Samson knew why his son seemed so indifferent to staying alive. Those alleged attack plans of Highcross were a fraud to scare and pressurise, probably done by that positive thinker, Jule.

Turning his back on the bank and stepping out towards his car, Yeo felt mostly sadness now, little rage, except with himself for getting involved with Tommy Samson in the first place. You could not keep up anger or blame against the dead, especially an Elvis clone. Even if he had lived he might have been for ever wrong in the head. Yeo found he still did not know whether he had failed Tommy Samson, and whether Tommy Samson had deserved to be failed. It had been a useless trip.

Great to see the chimneys of Highcross on the evening skyline again. The thrill made him recall Laurence Olivier bringing home his new bride, Joan Fontaine, in that original *Rebecca* on TV, and her suddenly glimpsing the grand house, Manderley. As a word, it had punch to it, quality, timelessness, 'Manderley'. The name Highcross Farm seemed a bit feeble, not really sexy. People might imagine only a place with cows shitting in their unplanned way. These were genuine, big old stone chimneys, part of the history of the place, and some of them still in use when he lit log fires, which Carol adored. Those chimneys were part of the picture and had to be kept, although they cost an arm and a leg to maintain. Again, obligations that came with privilege. If he had to, he would fight for this place, against Samson, or anyone else.

21

In the Toledo, Jule Corbett saw everyone knew Henrietta had done a run somewhere, and then returned. Nothing was spelled out, but he could sense the giggles, plus some sympathy – and wonderment that he took her back. He felt angered, by the sympathy as much as anything. They saw him as a victim, pitied him, thought he forgave to keep his billet, bought him burgundy and soda and told him to drink up and forget. Some of the tarts were especially kind. Really, few thought much of Henrietta. People did not see how deep and emotional she was, nor how much he needed her. Or if they did see this second thing, were amazed by it. Although he hated Otis Drinkwater for what had happened and had him very much in mind, he could never hate Henrietta.

He decided to ask her to take a couple of days' leave from the bank and come to London with him, when he went back to report to Don Samson. For all sorts of tactical reasons, she would not be able to go to the actual meeting, but they could be together on the train and for the afternoon and evening in London after the lunch with Don, doing galleries, perhaps a theatre or *Guardian*-commended film. This was the kind of outing Corbett had always enjoyed, and he knew she had, too. Henrietta would see he still loved her. It could be a tricky session with Don, and he would feel more able to cope if she were not far away. In any case, did he want her left alone in Cardiff again, for God's sake?

Les Sendanta and a few of his International Corporate Enterprises people were in the Toledo, loud and exultant, Les telling the world about some important visit Dave Brade made to Chatsworth. Although History Man was certainly not part of ICE, a solitary, he stumped about the bar doing a savage imitation of Maximilian on sticks and holding his damaged ear in place, just to give Les a grin, like a court jester for the king. Control in the realm was slipping from Brade. He and Jenkins had not been in the club at night for weeks since the verdicts. They could not throw their weight about any longer. The Toledo was off limits now. Of course, Sendanta and the other little monarchs would themselves be shoved under by Bay developments pretty soon. Did they know and were they making the most of their time? Sendanta's noise was the *Titanic* orchestra.

On the way back to the manse at about 1.30 a.m. Corbett suddenly felt he was being followed, perhaps by two. It scared him right through, but he managed to keep his pace steady, and did not turn his head to look. He wished he had done more about getting armament, not just for Yeo but for himself. What would he see if he did glance back? Maybe Drinkwater and Hamer, or a couple of Don Samson's people or family, or ICE boys because he had not done the full curtsey to Les, or a pair of Brade's boys following the Tommy trail. If you worked in the middle you had enemies all sides. The street was deserted except for Corbett and the shadows. In any case, around here at 1.30 a.m. you did not expect help from Joe Public: Joe rushed by on the other side. The footsteps behind kept with him for a few hundred yards, then the sound stopped. For a second he was relieved, but soon had the notion that they had turned into Mount Stuart Square and would head him off before the manse. That's supposing there were only the two. Was he being driven towards a reception? All the same, he speeded up and had his key out early. Sweat-aided, it slid sweetly into the lock although his hand was jumping about. He let himself in and closed the door. In the hall Floyd kept a bardic chair won years ago for Welsh language poetry at some Eisteddfod, and Corbett collapsed into it now, under a big photograph of Patterson peek-a-boo boxing Johansson for the title. God, what a sick show of nerves. Another.

Someone tapped on the door, not with the metal knocker but knuckles, possibly even fingernails, very quietly. 'Jule.'

The voice could be Hamer's. There was no open quarrel yet with him or Drinkwater, but those two might not always wait, and why act like this so late? Corbett got up quietly and pushed the two bolts home. The top one made a small sound.

'Jule, what you doing? Here's a friend. In disgrace but a true friend.'

Not Hamer. This was a voice he heard every agonising time he rescreened Blackpool in his brain, from the early part only. 'Graham?' he whispered. 'Graham Flanders?'

'Of course.'

'On your own?'

'Well, no, Jule. Me and a colleague, a fine colleague.'

Corbett pulled back the bolts and unlocked the door. Flanders' big spectacles glinted under the street light. A short, thin, younger man in a brown bomber jacket and jeans stood just behind. 'Come in. I thought you were in Jersey.' Corbett closed the door. 'This is not a good situation, Graham.'

'Jersey's great but expensive,' Flanders said.

Corbett took them to the kitchen and closed the door. 'Look, you had your full share, Gray.'

'You bloody well objected.'

'Yes, but – '

'I don't hold it against you, Jule.'

'It's the past. No good coming here for cash, though.'

'No, not cash, Jule. This is Mark. He was lying low in Jersey, too. Both caught by the cost of living you could say. Too much money in that economy – belonging to others. And too many spending girls.'

Floyd, in the kind of dark silk dressing-gown you saw in old British movies, opened the kitchen door. 'I heard voices.'

'New friends from the club,' Corbett said. He did introductions. 'We came back for coffee and a little business talk.'

'Perhaps I'll join you,' Floyd replied. 'One gets minimal sleep. I've a daughter to worry about, you know,' he told Flanders and Mark. 'Incorrigibly eager. Jule will tell you. We have to bring her within bounds, you see, while not impairing her naturalness.'

'This is a problem, sir,' Flanders replied.

'You're not local.'

'A visitor,' Corbett said. He made coffee and they sat around the big, clean, pine table.

'Jule knows all sorts,' Floyd said.

'That fits me,' Flanders replied.

'Tolerant, even uxorious, to my daughter, but essentially a villain, though I'm not clear how,' Floyd said. 'Probably lost. You two lads the same?'

'None of us is perfect,' Flanders replied.

'What Protestantism's all about – a recognition of sinfulness then salvation through Grace.'

158

'The Atonement's always been a puzzle to me,' Mark said.

'The actual balance-sheet connection between Christ's death and our redemption?' Floyd asked. 'True, Mark, *il y a des lacunes*.'

They had some discussion on this until about 3.30, when Floyd thought he might be able to sleep and left them. 'Try to keep it quiet, Jule, or Henrietta hearing males will come wagging her needs.'

When he had gone, Flanders said: 'It's work we're after, Jule. OK, this seems crazy to you, post Blackpool.'

'I put a line through your name. So did Yeo.'

'Not me, Jule, obviously,' Flanders replied, head lowered for a moment, and his voice almost down to a shamed whisper. 'Mark. He's got pedigree.'

'But not in the police form book,' Mark said.

'Would I bring someone with known previous to Jule and Paul Yeo?'

'This was driving, also front-lining at one bank, one building society, two cash vans,' Mark said. 'I can give chapter and verse. Nobody hurt in any of them, and decent rewards. Enough for eighteen months in Jersey.'

The accent was somewhere north of Manchester. He would be about twenty-seven, dark, with one of those useful, long, straight-nosed faces that looked honourable, even considerate.

'We're having a grand time over there in CI, then the money goes and Mark says he'll have to look for another job, Jule. At which point, I have an idea, namely Jule Corbett with his finger in all those fat pies. Our arrangement, me and Mark, is, I put him in touch, we split any takings, sixty-forty, me forty that is, being only the link. Well, doing your sort of work, Jule. Am I going to put myself forward in any principal capacity after that tragedy, especially to people who were there?' He waited for Corbett to say something tender. He could wait. Behind the pleasant goggles, Flanders still looked like a fucking disaster. 'I read in the papers Tommy snuffed it at last,' Flanders said. 'Don and that Billy – they Proceduring? Can they name all in the Senator? How? Tommy never came round enough to spill, did he? You can see what I'd like is a quick one for Mark, then retreat to my Jersey niche. Perhaps you'll meet her one day.'

Flanders wore what seemed a good, grey wool suit, and a blue shirt and silvery tie. He appeared pretty sound now, not too

159

much overweight and still powerful in the shoulders and neck. Yes, he talked too much but had a lot of words to make up for after the Blackpool paralysis. He sported thick blond hair, which he used to keep in a bit of a pigtail, though that had been lopped. Before Blackpool, Corbett had always liked him as much as was needed. Flanders asked the right questions and stuck at it. Nobody could have forecast blackout.

'Well, yes, as a matter of fact, I'm toying with ideas for what could be a juicy job, Gray.'

Flanders grinned and gave a brief, muted whistle.

'A tricky one. Needing to act pretty fast,' Corbett said.

'Even better,' Flanders said.

'And we're short of some people.'

'How many?' Mark asked.

'If you come, one.'

'I've got a contact – someone solid I rang work-hunting. He's looking, too.'

'Paul Yeo in on this?' Flanders asked. 'I heard he was in the frame for a killing here – some heavy who threatened him.'

'Yeo's clean,' Corbett said.

'Yeo's great, Mark. I told you.'

Flanders stared down at the table for a moment, thinking. 'Won't Don Samson have something terminal lined up for him?'

'Why we need speed.'

Flanders asked again: 'Don and his goons know who was in the car?'

'He knows who was driving when Tommy got hit. He knows I was there.'

'And?'

'That's all.'

'Not who *should* have been driving?'

'No.'

'Wouldn't Tommy have told him that – discussing things with dear daddy before it happened?'

'Leave it, Gray,' Mark said. 'Jule's told you.'

'Yes, all right, but listen, Jule – does Don know how you wanted to stop Yeo smashing Tommy, really tried? And me. If he's got my name. We definitely expected Yeo to drive round him, or even stop, didn't we?'

'Of course.'

'Not just accelerate regardless. I thought a hell of a lot of Tommy Samson myself,' Flanders said. 'Witty.'

'One of the best.'

Flanders nodded for a time. 'So this job?'

'The point is, we need to get in before some others, Gray. Ahead of a couple of louts.' Dawn started putting a little more light into the kitchen. Corbett saw the questions in Flanders' eyes. Mark waited, his fine face steady. 'These two might be troublesome. Called Hamer and Drinkwater. London.'

'Never heard of them.' Flanders had another laugh. 'But we beat them to it, yes? You know the details of it? Slip in on their project early? Disappear.'

'If we can. I'm supposed to be with them. But they want me out, I know it.'

'A hijack. Sure we can.' Flanders sounded ready to go and do it now, whatever it was, because he knew he didn't have to. One of life's best spectators.

'These two piss about, Gray. I can't stand it. They've got something against Don Samson, so try to push Paul into blowing him away before the job – making it part of the operation, all sewn up together. Mad. Something go wrong with the Samson side of it and the whole lot comes adrift. It's basic you never let one job depend on another. Injuries, police ripples, God knows what.'

'I love how you understand method,' Flanders replied. 'Paul to act a hit-man? Don't make me laugh.'

'But they tell him he's got to move first or Don will do him. On paper it's the perfect squeeze.'

'Loony. So we don't wait? And bring Yeo in with us, instead?' Flanders said.

'Right. There's always good money in this target. It can be done any day.'

'Why hang about?' Flanders chortled. 'They don't deserve to collect.'

Corbett said: 'Gray, I've got my loyalties, yes, and it's *their* job, really. Over the bridge in Bristol. But if they're going to mess it all up, edge me out, I – '

'Crazy.'

'And there's another thing, a hellish thing. I don't want any talk about this, you understand – but, well . . .'

'What, Jule? Not pillaging your wife?' Mark asked. 'Did I pick up hints from Floyd?'

'It could be.'

'That's horrible,' Flanders said.

'You're good to that woman.'

'It's my way. And I can't operate without her, Gray, Mark. Guys who'd do that, banging a partner's partner before a big job, do I owe them any sodding thing at all?'

'I remember Henrietta as a very lovely, sheltered kid,' Flanders remarked.

'Terrific IQ, but she can be led, I don't deny, and she has this itch, as her father said. Plus they're career gays. I don't object, but what's being passed around?'

'You've got no obligations, Jule,' Flanders said.

'How I feel. It's a blessing you turned up, Graham, Mark.'

Flanders smiled. 'Just a blessing we got urgent broke. Floyd a whore hater?'

'Not a bit.'

'Some are – ministers,' Flanders replied. 'I wondered about this dead girl, Floyd obviously keen on boxing, violence. The pictures in the hall. Cleansing the world?'

Corbett showed them out before full daylight. Mark paused alongside the bardic chair in the hall. 'Floyd's into *cynghanedd*, those Welsh verse forms, yes? I'll be in touch with a great lad. Leave it to me.'

'I'd still do it, if you asked, Jule,' Flanders whispered. 'Make the fourth.' His head was on one side, his arms hanging limp, like a child pleading for a circus trip.

'I'm relying on you, Mark,' Corbett replied.

Henrietta and he went up to London by the early train first class. As ever the carriage was full of Welsh Office civil servants carrying their little bits of paper in executive briefcases between the place in Cathays Park, Cardiff, and the one in Whitehall, with lumps of dining-car kipper on their chins. Perhaps some of the bits of paper were about the Bay. Would there be money left for the state's contribution when this gang had claimed exes?

'I never think of myself long term with anyone but you, Jule,' she told him.

'Darling, I know it.'

'Always I was sure to return.'

162

'Thank God.' She looked orderly and mild today in a full-length tweed coat.

'Novelty, Jule – I have this appalling thirst for the exotic.'

'Drinkwater's that?'

'I know, I know, I get it from Daddy.' Under the *Guardian* he put his hand up her skirt and found her. 'Purr, purr,' she said.

Around Didcot, he went to the bar for a half-bottle of champagne and some orange juice so they could celebrate with Buck's Fizz. When he returned, she was openly, and noisily, weeping. Across the gangway three functionaries in perfect, drab suits gazed at her, appalled.

He put drinks and glasses on the table and sat down, placing his hand on her arm. 'What is it, love?' he whispered, hoping she would get the message and answer like that.

But she spoke in a normal voice, normal except ravaged by raucous sobs. 'Oh, Jule, I still want him, that's all. Have to be with him. A fever.'

Jesus, he could have done without this. For a second he froze, then pulled his hand away. He tried to arrange his body in the seat to obscure her and muffle the words. 'Drinkwater?'

'Jule, I can't help it. This weeping – shamed rage with myself, that's all. What does Otis care? And how can I be so cruel to you?' She turned to stare out of the window and hide her face from the audience.

Replacing his hand on the arm of her coat, Corbett gently stroked her through it. 'I can't bear to see you in agony.'

'Otis prefers that bloody bald Hamer,' she said over her shoulder. 'I mean did you ever see a slobbier neck.'

'How Drinkwater is, darling.'

'So I weep, weep.' In a while, she turned back to him. Now she did lower the volume. 'Jule, I'm going to have to find him.'

'But – '

'He doesn't want me? Don't say it. Don't.' She spoke in a scorching whisper. 'He thinks me unlovely?'

'As I say, how he's made, Henrietta, that's all. Can he appreciate a beautiful woman? I need you, and you need me. Go to him when?'

'Oh, I don't know. Very soon.'

These words came out like from some antique ham actress. Corbett poured orange juice into the glasses, then sent the

163

champagne cork flying and added the wine. He handed hers to Henrietta.

'I know I owe you a lot, Jule. How can I be such a cow? It can't all be Daddy's fault.'

'Here's to us, then,' he said. 'We'll have a great day.'

'Here's to us.' She let him wipe her face with his free hand, then poked her tongue out at the three opposite.

He had to ring Samson's house from a pay phone at Paddington to find the name of today's meeting place – typical big-headed security. Henrietta took a taxi to Knightsbridge and the shops. She seemed recovered now, lifted a bit by the drinks, but Corbett did not like letting her go. Henrietta was not someone you let go or did not let go, though. She did as she wanted. What Floyd called her naturalness.

Samson had picked a really top-class restaurant in Garrick Street, genuinely French, with tasteful arched windows. It was a fine street, containing one of the smartest clubs in London, where people had to wait up to ten years for membership, or for ever if you were Don. Inside the restaurant, there were red-brick walls and good pictures of birds and food. Samson had on a great navy blue pin-stripe suit, really Cabinet class, and was looking as polished as anyone with his kind of face and morality could.

'We'll do meat and something red this time, Jule? Morgon?'

'I'm in contact with a couple of lads from London in the way of business, Don,' Jule said during the beautiful hors-d'oeuvre. 'I think you know them. They know you. Dangerous people.'

'A lot of them are. It's the filthy air.'

'A boy called Drinkwater?' Corbett asked.

'Otis? Fifty-odd-year-old boy? Can't stop laughing? Coupled with Lance Hamer?'

'Often. Don, it hurts to say this, but they hate you. Especially Drinkwater. He's coming for you. He's kitted out.'

'Drinkwater? He doesn't usually handle their heavy work, Jule. Not Hamer? When?'

'Any time. Tomorrow. Couple of days? At the latest, a couple of days. Definitely Drinkwater.'

'Up here?'

'Right.'

Samson nodded and continued eating. 'They're trying to get themselves in down there – your area. Or get someone else in,

164

someone bigger. Same kind of work as me. I'm competition. They'd have orders to take me out, from someone in the City, maybe. Probably.'

The waiters brought Corbett a steak and lamb cutlets for Samson. It looked great. Don poured the red. 'Let me know what you think, Jule,' he said. Corbett made like an expert and gave a short, definite nod, no creepy shit about roundness or smoky, blackcurranty texture. 'Good, Jule, forgive: how do you know this?' Samson's old rat eyes shone with rat caginess. 'You kitted Otis yourself? I mean, this is great insights, but – '

'No, would I arm someone to come after a business friend – I hope I can call you that, Don?'

'I don't know what else . . .'

'But I have to talk to them a lot. Well, we were mooting a project together. This could be extra to their main activities, I suppose. All right, we're even partners to a degree, but some things I can't take. I mean, we have these great lunches, you and I. We've got mutuality, and linked by the death of Tommy. Don, I could give you an address for Drinkwater in my area. Nice and isolated on a hill.'

'I could do a pre-emptive?'

'Must. You don't like stirring off your ground, but you'll have surprise. Safer than waiting for him.'

Samson fiddled away at the great food again. No wonder he stayed bony. 'Sounds sane, Jule. Just Drinkwater? Look, sorry to keep on, but you're sure Drinkwater? Not Hamer? I knew they had intentions, but I thought probably at some swimming do.'

'Sooner. Urgent. And definitely Drinkwater the danger man. Hamer as well, if you like, but Otis is the one actually coming. He's Mr Macho in the pair, yes?'

'Now and then he'll take a girl.'

'Oh?'

'So what's in this for you, Jule? Why do you want Drinkwater taken out? You fancy Lance Hamer? That porky neck send you? I thought you were through and through hetero.'

At the next table, a skinny, youngish man in a green shirt and khaki jacket seemed to be trying to talk the lad with him to take a post at 'one hundred and twenty K, plus BMW, plus assisted mortgage, plus an entertainment account here'. Some venue.

Corbett said: 'In it for me? Don, nothing, I swear. I told you, just I can't stand by and see you targeted. You need to know your real enemy, that's all. It's not Paul Yeo. Look, I know The Procedure – '

'Fuck The Procedure. Out of date.'

'You're pragmatic, Don.'

'That what I am?'

'Yeo's not the enemy, and definitely not other people in that Senator when Tommy – well, when Tommy fell.'

'Fell. I like that. A soldier. Noble. In battle. What – you need Paul for something, do you? Yeo in another project, Jule? He's all right, and I'm still thinking about that deal we spoke of, skip the vendetta. We're grown up.'

'Well, he might bite. He's thinking about it, too.'

'You've spoken to him?'

'Of course. Immediately. This project would help him find the readies for the deal, Don.'

'What am I going to do, anyway, wipe out half the universe? I'm Himmler?' He summoned more Morgon. 'The women around me say I'm not strong enough to be myself, to resist the culture, Jule. We'll see.' The bridge of his nose shone with purple defiance. 'Anyway, safety's something else. A first concern. So, Otis Drinkwater. I'd better have this hillside address then, Jule. I'm ready. This is a service. I'm not going to forget.' He pulled out a very slim and classy, red, leather-bound notebook and gold-plated propelling pencil.

'Thanks, Don. The least I could do. By a kinky castle.'

'You're playing fair, are you? Well, thanks again. Listen, Jule, I'm not prejudiced about gays, never. More ways than one to satisfaction. But they do get some foul ideas in their chummy heads, yes?' Again Samson went before the sweet, leaving a stack of fifties nude on the table for Corbett to do the bill. 'The rest for your costs, Jule. And we must talk fees soon.' Corbett had some Roquefort and a couple of vintage ports, unhurried. He felt clever and a bit masterful.

Perhaps it radiated and Henrietta seemed committed to him again when they met in the Hayward Gallery for brilliant Impressionists, though she had bought a yellow, summer-weight trouser suit which would be all wrong with her legs, but which she might think would get to Drinkwater's main taste. The summer was a good way off, though. She stated that she was in love with Monet and bought a print of a red sun in fog over yardarms. In bed at their Gloucester Road hotel she said: 'Give me frenzy, Jule, would you?'

'What you dreamed of while you were away, you wicked wanderer?' She liked condemnation, as long as it recognised power in her.

'Intolerably, Jule.'

'True, Henrietta?'

'So true.'

You did your best to try to believe stuff like this. They fought a little, in that spasmodic, half-serious way she liked, and then he closed with her, her arms and legs lovingly locked across his back again and her mouth against his ear whispering his name over and over and always getting it right. He wanted to look after her, to be stalwart for her, not just now, in bed, but in every part of her life. If only she knew how much she needed him, as her father often said. And then, when it came to Corbett's own needs, she brought that unique, stunning amplitude to his life which he could not do without. Yes, hard to understand, but that's how things were and had been for years. It meant he could not bear doubts about her and with any luck would not have to much longer.

When they tired, Henrietta got out of bed and tried the trouser suit on. 'Perhaps my legs are heavy for this style?'

'It's you,' he replied.

22

Sweet Bachelor's widow Miriam let them in and they followed her upstairs. Lights burned everywhere. 'Palatial,' Jenkins said.

'Thank God we had your personal number, Dave,' Miriam said. 'I called you at once. She's dead, no question.'

'I thought you were abroad, Miriam.'

'Back yesterday.'

'And Ivor?' Brade said.

'He came back, too,' she replied.

The house had four bedrooms, three big reception, three

bathrooms, and a granny flat, but for no granny: Ivor Lestocque, Percy's bodyguard, used to live there. About five years before Percy died, he and Fiona had moved home from dockland to this fine, new-built, mega-executive place in one of Cardiff's most lustrous suburbs, Lisvane. When they divorced he married Miriam and brought her here. His Baptist background had made Percy regard it as bad form to live with a woman prior to marriage.

Wearing blue boxer shorts, Lestocque was sitting on the bed in the main bedroom. 'Dave, Miriam had no option.'

'But why, why was she here?' Miriam whispered.

Brade crouched over the body for a moment, then straightened. 'Not many would recognise her as Fiona. So little of the face intact. What the hell did you hit her with, the poor duck?'

Lestocque said: 'This was one shot only. This is permitted minimum force against an intruder – after 2 a.m., for Christ's sake.'

Glyndwr Jenkins was getting a closer look at the damage, where Fiona had folded down against the open bedroom door. Glyn had that raging curiosity of the very bright, and it meant nothing much could put him off. Her face must have rubbed the door as she dropped and it was smeared with thick blood and some particles. In bending, Glyn had got some of this on his hair, where it shone on the blackness like a flare path. The Scene of Crime people would not be pleased. 'Well, it has to be a .44 or .45,' he said.

Lestocque stood and stepped to the body, pulling down her skirt which had gone high above the knees when she fell. Behind him on the other side of the huge duvet was a revolver, not one Brade recognised. Moving closer, he read the marking: 'Röhm, model 57, calibre .45.'

'That's a strengthened job,' Jenkins said.

'Fiona still had keys to this place,' Miriam told them.

'She must have had a tip you were back, and thought you'd have the remains of Bachelor's loot in your luggage. She came looking for her true legacy, driven wild by envy,' Brade replied.

'Dull cow.' Miriam was beautifully dressed, for any time let alone the middle of the night. You wondered where the money came from. No, you didn't, you knew where the money came from, but you wondered how she had cornered it all.

'Where did you get the gun, then, Miriam?' Brade asked.

'One of Bachelor's, obviously. It was in the drawer, I heard movement – downstairs, I thought and . . . well, you can see.' She sobbed.

'In bed together?' Jenkins asked Lestocque.

'This is a steady, decent relationship,' Miriam replied.

'She needed looking after when Bachelor went,' Lestocque said.

'*He* needed looking after the night he was hit,' Jenkins replied.

'I've explained all that,' Lestocque cried. 'This is cohabitation.'

'You're in bed and hear something, Miriam?' Brade said. 'What next?'

'I get out and find the gun. I'm standing by the bed when the door's pushed wide. It was already part open,' she replied.

'The gun's not on safety?' Jenkins asked.

'I don't know anything about that. I just pointed and fired.'

'You don't know guns?' Jenkins asked.

'Would I, for Christ's sake?' Miriam said.

'Very neat shooting,' Jenkins replied.

'Where's Ivor when this is going on?' Brade asked.

'Still asleep. It was so quick.'

'Asleep? The gifted bodyguard,' Brade said.

'I thought she was pointing something,' Miriam said.

'Or perhaps just pointing,' Jenkins said. 'At Ivor in your bed? Accusatory?'

'What's it to Fiona? To anyone?' Miriam replied.

'*I'm* interested,' Brade said.

'How do you get on with the neighbours?' Jenkins asked.

'Who did the art, Ivor?' Brade asked. 'Very beautiful.' On his chest and back Lestocque had wide, multi-coloured tattoos. Several seemed based on the Bible, including Daniel in the lions' den and the crossing of the Red Sea. Brade did not mind the Scriptures pictorially. It was texts that angered and dismayed him. Brade took off his jacket and shirt to show Miriam and Lestocque his own chest tattoos – pairs of naked women, but in artistic poses, not vulgar – pre-Raphaelite ladies, the tattooist had said. The names written beneath were Delphine, Marguerite, Romola and Venetia. Lestocque came over and studied them admiringly and Brade could sort out on him across the shoulder what seemed to be the feeding of the five thousand. Maybe tattoos looked richer on a black background, but Brade could not do much about that.

In a while he re-dressed: 'Did you see something pointing, Ivor? This person at the door?'

'I was asleep until the gun went off,' Lestocque said. 'Miriam told me.'

'Who did you think it might be, Miriam?' Jenkins asked.

'It could be so many,' Lestocque replied. 'Bachelor had widespread interests.'

'Bachelor's dead six months,' Jenkins said.

'People see Miriam as part of his operation. One reason I'm here.'

'Asleep,' Jenkins said.

'Well, why I was here originally, living in the flat.'

'They wouldn't be coming after *you*, Ivor, would they?' Jenkins asked.

'Which people especially, Ivor?' Brade asked.

'In the dark I couldn't even tell it was a woman,' Miriam replied. 'Her hair under that bobble hat.'

Jenkins was searching Fiona, before the Scene of Crime people came and messed things up. 'She's got a couple of black plastic bags in her coat pocket.'

'To take the bundles of fifties she'd come for,' Miriam replied.

'Was she getting warm?' Brade asked. 'Where are they?'

'I'd love to know,' Miriam replied.

Brade said: 'This would be a woman who felt let down, cheated. She'd believe herself isolated. Her legal whiz-kid, Harvey, quit, seeing no instant money or prospects. This was do-it-yourself debt collecting.'

'There's no debt to Fiona,' Miriam replied.

'But she was not someone we were expecting, Dave,' Lestocque said.

'Who?' Jenkins replied.

'What?'

'Who *were* you expecting?'

'I've told you – I can't put a name, but far-flung and lethal.'

Brade said: 'You'll have to try to put a name, names. Otherwise, I'm not sure how this will go for Miriam in court. Glyn and

170

I would like to help, believe me, but we need something solid to make your story work, Ivor.'

'You creep, Dave,' Miriam replied.

'Murder, manslaughter, accident or justifiable killing?' Brade said. 'That's what we'll have to sort out. Or Glyn will. He's the smart bugger of the two.'

'You're the smart bugger, Dave, and not just out of two,' Miriam replied.

'Why I zoom up the ladder.'

'You're *too* smart for them,' she said.

'Stop buttering him, Miriam, he loves it,' Jenkins remarked. 'And believes it. He shoves the clever, hard stuff on to me so he can stay everyone's pal. This yearning to be all-round loved. Rather pathetic? So damn bourgeois whitey.'

Brade said: 'Some neighbour might have heard the shot and phoned. We'll have a brigade here soon.'

The property was no distance from where Sir Julian Hodge himself, millionaire and more, once had a spread. The built-in wardrobes would take all the *Ben Hur* costumes and still warehouse a ton of untaxed gains. Fiona might have been heading for them, not the suitcases. She knew the amenities.

'Timing's so important in all this,' Jenkins said, still crouched by the body.

'It happened only forty minutes ago,' Miriam replied. 'Get some clothes on, Ivor, will you? It looks casual.' She had obviously made a real effort herself: a blouse, waistcoat and simple skirt, hair smoothed down and fixed behind – altogether much classier, much more Lisvane, than that day in the Toledo.

'I don't think Glyndwr means the timing of death,' Brade said.

'What else?'

'This is delicate, love, but, faced tonight with this relationship, we're bound to wonder when you and Ivor first took to each other, aren't we?' Jenkins said.

'What the hell's that got to do with it?' Miriam was standing in front of a pale, real wood dressing-table and in the big mirror Brade could see her hair worked into a tight, nicely shaped bun. He always liked the schoolmistress touch.

'Bachelor's dead. We don't know how,' Brade replied.

For a second there was silence except the rustle and rattle of money, keys and cosmetics as Jenkins went quickly through Fiona's handbag. 'Oh, Christ, meaning I did him to get Miriam?' Lestocque cried.

'Miriam and a lot more, though Miriam on her own is considerable,' Brade replied.

'This is filthy, Dave, even by police standards,' she said.

'How people outside might view it,' Jenkins replied, over his shoulder. 'Surely, there are two possibilities. Either, Ivor leaves him unprotected by arrangement with someone major that night. Or he sees Bachelor off himself, as a permanent way to Miriam – or because someone big somewhere finds Bachelor a hindrance to his Bay plans and has the standard notion that he'll suborn the minder to remove him.'

'Suborn – that's buy, Ivor,' Brade said.

Jenkins waved an arm to indicate Miriam, the bed, the room, the house and then the wardrobes. 'Yes, motives aplenty.'

'I told you, this only began after Bachelor died,' she said. 'We comforted each other, both desolated.'

'But Ivor did the fleeing abroad first,' Brade said.

'It was arranged that I'd follow.'

'Nice,' Jenkins said.

'You think I'd do that to someone as great as Percy – that I'd risk it?' Lestocque asked.

Jenkins said: 'Think: there's such a smell of money around you, Miriam, it turns poor old Fiona burglar. I've got to say this, it could do the same to Ivor.'

Brade said: 'We reach the next stage. Say Fiona had rumbled all this and came here to bargain. She'll give silence about how Sweet Bachelor died in exchange for her share, as she regards it. But, Miriam, nobly protecting lover boy, you dish up something different. You and Mr Röhm impose silence.'

Lestocque had pulled on a sweat shirt and pair of jeans. He stood in front of one of the wardrobes, handsomely aquiline, tall, lithe and shattered, and Brade tried to decide whether it was possessively, protectively of what might be in there. 'Jesus, what are they trying to prove, Miriam?' Lestocque asked.

'That they're on top,' she said. 'What else do they ever try to prove? They're screwing you for names – for everything about everything you know.'

Brade sat on the bed, alongside the revolver. 'Listen, Miriam, you'll forgive me, but Bachelor is not a priority. I want to know who did Olive Rice. Anything that points me, I'm interested in.'

'You were doing something there, too?' she replied. 'I thought six months ago you were into your magazine and jerking-off phase.'

'But Percy deserves attention, too, obviously,' Brade added. 'And it's still possible the two are linked, despite different weapons. That would be a basic precaution.'

'Some tart has precedence in your book?' Miriam snarled.

'*This* tart, not some,' Brade gently replied.

Lestocque said: 'I heard you thought her father might have cut loose. Even her mother. How am I involved?'

'I could – could – push for justifiable killing or accident here, Miriam,' Brade replied.

'If I talk you mean?' Lestocque said. 'What am I supposed to tell you? I don't know a thing about Olive Rice.'

'Something like this, was it?' Brade replied. 'The little empires starting to fight each other in dockland, all scared they're going under. So, the scrap around the Toledo. Bachelor or you or another of Bachelor's helpers sees to Olive, to knock Maximilian some more, because he can't be got at personally as he's in hospital and guarded.'

'God, he'd already been sufficiently got at, hadn't he – a broken leg and the rest,' Miriam replied.

Brade said: 'Olive's to force the message home. Then maybe someone for Maximilian retaliates and does Sweet Bachelor.'

'Maximilian hasn't got people like that,' Lestocque said. 'Not real troops. Carl Minter gives him some pushing aid, now and then, obviously. And there's Hubert. At a pinch he can do protection – enforcement – but they're not top-class claws, Dave.'

'For fuck's sake, don't dig your own grave, Ivor,' Jenkins replied.

'How's that?'

'If you moved out of the way on the night, people like Hubert, even Carl, could handle it, surely,' Brade said. 'Bachelor was grey and getting on, maybe worn down a bit by Miriam's requirements, which you can testify to now.' He sighed. 'Or, I fear, we're pushed back to looking at you, personally, as Bach-

173

elor's killer, Ivor. That's what Glyndwr means.' Brade ran his hand over his hair as signal to Glyndwr. 'You're festooned with Fiona.'

Jenkins produced a comb and cleaned himself, then went to one of the bathrooms to swill it.

'Or then again, might some London connection have done Bachelor?' Brade asked.

'We'd have trips to London sometimes, yes,' Lestocque replied.

Jenkins, returning, said: 'Why don't we go and sit in the drawing-room. I just had a look. Tasteful. The bathroom's tasteful, too, but the drawing-room is supremely tasteful.'

They sat facing one another on two long, white leather sofas, Brade and Lestocque together and Miriam and Glyndwr. He was right about the room. It had a huge, blue Chinese carpet and what looked to Brade like genuine paintings of some kind on the walls, not up to Ivor's tattoo lions for zing but ungarish. Genuine books stood on white alcove shelving, including thumbed paperbacks. A miniature flag had been framed under glass and hung over the fireplace, possibly of the country where Percy or his family originated, though he had always been uncommunicative about that. Brade thought it might be Norway or one of those spots.

Lestocque said: 'We'd go to London and Bachelor would have to ring someone from a pay phone for the meeting place, usually a good restaurant with a French or Hungarian name.'

'Ring who?' Brade asked.

'I never heard.'

'But, Miriam, I expect he told you who he was going to see?' Brade asked.

'You're joking. Wives come and go. They might turn vindictive, talk. Look at Fiona.'

'We did. But you were minding him, Ivor, so you went to the rendezvous?' Jenkins asked.

'I delivered him and picked him up. I never joined them. The other party's insistence, according to Bachelor. When I returned for him the other party had always left early. He didn't eat too much, I gather.'

'So what else did you gather?' Brade asked.

'This was a sort of middle-grade heavy, acting for someone

174

much bigger up there, someone maybe more or less respectable, or a syndicate, but needing a way in to our dockland development.'

'A partnership with Bachelor?' Jenkins asked.

'You make that sound hilarious,' Miriam said. 'Percy had standing.'

'Along those lines. Bachelor didn't swallow it all, not just like that,' Lestocque told them. 'He was doing it step by step, that's how I saw it. Feeling things out. My impression – he thought they'd partner him as starters, to get in, then squash him. Well, Dave, you knew Bachelor. He believed nobody, especially nobody from London.'

'So, had we reached the time when they told you to get rid of him?' Jenkins asked.

'You black sod,' Miriam replied.

'Which part of London was this anorexic gourmet from?' Brade asked.

'I'm not told.'

'Who put Bachelor in touch with the London end?' Jenkins asked.

'Don't know that either,' Lestocque said.

'You'll tell us the restaurants? Maybe we can work back. The table would have been booked under a cover name, I suppose, and payment in cash.'

'Never the same one. So next to no use, Dave?' Lestocque asked.

'Don't sell the fucking pass,' Miriam said.

'I'm going to ring in now and report Fiona dead and possibly an accident,' Brade replied. 'Nobody's 999ed, clearly. This must be the kind of neighbourhood where they hear gunfire and suppose a clay pigeon party.'

'Thanks, Dave,' Lestocque said.

'How do we know?' Miriam asked.

'What?' Brade said.

'You'll say accident?'

'You can listen.'

'I mean how do we know you'll keep saying it when we're not around?' Miriam said.

'That's a point,' Brade replied.

'Don't aggravate, love,' Lestocque told Miriam.

175

She shrugged and put a small smile on her run-of-the-mill, short-nosed, very prosperous face. 'I suppose I do trust Dave, really.'

Jenkins, staring up at a corner of the brilliant white ceiling, said: 'Well, look at that now, the blood coming through like in *Tess*.'

23

They drove through the early part of the night to sort out Drinkwater. That was Billy's phrase, 'to sort out', and Don Samson did not like it – so crude and final. You had to be crude and final, though, now and again. With him in the Opel, Don took Billy and Jason, his sister's boy. Samson aimed to arrive at about 12.30 a.m. and find Drinkwater helpless in bed. Samson wanted to be back at New Cross for a late breakfast. This was important, sometimes called among younger lads, 'Alibi Muesli'. There might be another morning visit by Detective Sergeant Arnold Aphik and/or associates. Aphik hovered, that way they had.

The Opel belonged to Jason Young's girlfriend. Samson had left his Audi outside the house, another sign he was spending the night at home. As a small joke, Samson had one day started calling Jason Amiable. Jokes that small usually died in the incubator, but the name had stuck. Billy drove. He had a nice cheerful way with him and knew guns inside out. They were both fine, Billy and Amiable, at taking orders.

Corbett? Could you believe him? Could you believe any middleman? They had so many what you might call loyalties – if you were a fool – plus above all, of course, their own interests. Well, this was believing him, wasn't it, three people going a hundred and fifty miles in the dark to some country shack in fucking Wales and carrying half an armoury? What Corbett said fitted a fraction with what Samson had thought himself – Drinkwater and Hamer might be hunting him. Those two wanted a settled and long-term spot in Bay land, maybe for themselves, maybe for a master. The world was at it. Don Samson could be in the way. Possibly Bachelor had got in the way, too.

If Drinkwater was hunting, Drinkwater had better be stopped and stopped now. Samson had thought they'd try at the water polo event, and Hamer, not the other one. He still half thought so. But if you believed some of Corbett's message you had to believe it all. So, get to Otis fast. If you could help it, never let the opposition pick place and time. And, although Samson hated this sort of work off his patch, there was something to say for distance and a lot to say for a cottage with no neighbours.

Obviously, Samson would have to do Drinkwater himself. You could not ask your son or your sister's boy to handle that, even if Billy did love weaponry. These two he needed with him only in case of trouble from Lance Hamer, or elsewhere. As a matter of fact, all this evil with Drinkwater probably started even before the business angle. It could be something Samson said once about Hamer. He had mentioned the size of Hamer's eyes and his wheeze breathing and inquired if he had angina and might fall dead soon, leaving poor Drinkwater widowered. You could see this as a caring remark. But Drinkwater grew quite sour. Perhaps Otis honestly could not bear the thought of life without Hamer. That relationship might have real love and depth, despite the way Drinkwater varied.

'If they're in the same room, the same bed?' Billy asked. 'Hamer's going to see us, which means possible evidence later.'

'Well, that would be a problem,' Samson replied. 'I don't need Hamer dead, so Corbett says, but, yes, Lance could be a talker.' They had covered it three times before, with the same answers. He did not know anything about executing people, for God's sake. Was he the IRA? Two or three times in his life he had carried a gun on tricky jobs, but never needed to fire, nor ever been in activity when anyone needed to fire. Leave that to New York. This was very different, anyway – blasting someone in bed. Blasting two in bed seemed far more than twice as bad. This trip was supposed to be defensive, not the pheasant season.

Lying out on the back seat, Amiable giggled in his sleep, sat up for a moment, eyes open, then slumped back down. He had a wide, trusting sort of face like his mother's when a young girl. Often, it made Samson miserable to look at him and get carried back to those days. His sister, Joy, had almost married out of all this, an authentic biscuit company manager from Croydon. But then it suddenly finished for reasons he never heard, so eventually she ended up with Basil Young, and with Amiable. Life did not let many leap the wall, especially women.

By the time they found Tongwynlais village it was just after midnight. Corbett had drawn a map for him. The little, run-down cottage Jule said Hamer and Drinkwater rented was on the side of a hill. They woke Amiable. 'You stay at the front door. Come up if we call,' Samson said. 'Fast and ready.' There were no houses anywhere near and the only breaks in the dark came from Cardiff's distant glow and from floodlights on a weird, fairy-tale sort of castle with pointed towers stuck on the side of another hill, opposite. Christ, what a place. No wonder they wanted independence down here, they were so different. 'Billy, I do the first shooting. Maybe the only shooting. I hope so. This could be a total phoney. This could be Corbett messing me about for some private reason, or just getting it wrong. I'm not into knocking off a Taff old-age pensioner. We identify, right?'

'Of course,' Billy said.

They left the car, without closing any doors, for silence. Samson went ahead. For a couple of seconds they stood in the overgrown front garden, listening. Samson brought a Davis P-32 from his pocket and Billy and Amiable did the same with a couple of Service Six revolvers. The sight of it all nearly turned Samson's stomach. A spurt of wind rattled some branches and hoping that would mask the sound he broke a pane in the door with the gun butt, put his hand through and turned the catch. The door seemed to open into the main downstairs room and he could make out a bare, polished wood staircase in the corner. That meant noise if you rushed.

He moved forward and began to climb, putting his feet down carefully. Behind, Billy did the same. For a big lad he could be really delicate. Billy was truly gifted, had been since a small kid. Well, they had both been out of the ordinary, Tom and Billy, and he always suspected Norah had thought more of Tommy, though she would never say so, obviously. A mother did not show preferences, but Tommy could do the guitar and had the looks – dark, thin, a bit drawn, as if needing a good feed, which would bring out sympathy in a woman.

Samson turned once on the third or fourth stair and gave Billy a very brief smile, hardly a smile at all and, in any case, maybe in the darkness Billy could not see it. Never mind. The boy would sense it was a message, a good message, father to son, father to the one son who was left and who really mattered. Playing the guitar was great, but not everything. That glance said he and Billy looked after each other and went into dangers together – lousy quaint cottage, crazy castle, hill-and-jungle Wales, it didn't matter where. They were blood and that made them strong. Amiable was sort of blood, too, and quite a decent kind, although so dozy, yet in some ways an outsider, just an extra hand, tonight as ever. But Billy was a partner. They had an outfit, Donald Samson and Son. It would go on. This couple of rough-house schemers, Drinkwater and Hamer, could never break up that solid, traditional team. It just would not be allowed.

All the same, he still dreaded finding them in bed together, sleeping like a couple, maybe one with an arm around the other. He did not care that they were two blokes. He would have been just as grieved if they were a man and a girl. It was the thought of killing someone in a bed alongside somebody else: they were together, warm and close, and then suddenly one of them is bleeding and smashed and nothing any longer, and the pillow and duvet's a wet mess, and one of them is waking up to hear the other coughing and croaking his way into the past. For Samson, a domestic situation had a lot of aura, and the bedroom part really weighed. It made people so wide open to anything rough – sleep, brains switched off, relaxed, no clothes, contentment. Bursting in with armament had to be foul. It was like police, for God's sake.

So, on the little landing, he had another moment's pause and listened – tried to pick up the sound of breathing through the door of what must be a bedroom, and to sort out whether it was one or two. Billy had a point. If it was two and they left one – if they left Hamer – the police might have him soon and even down here in a place like Wales they knew about giving pressure and Hamer would talk. Christ, he thought, just get on with it. Kill one, kill two. What's magic or holy about a bed? Do it and disappear. Save yourself.

He put his left hand on the door knob, lifting the gun in the

179

other, and heard Billy right behind whisper from so far down in himself that it hardly rated as a sound at all, 'Right, Dad.' There was no need. Samson knew the boy was all right and ready, but he felt glad of the words, pleased especially over 'dad', like a child answering his father about something ordinary and harmless. This outing would do so much for the family.

As he began slowly turning the knob all the quietness suddenly ended, and a door just to the right of Samson and Billy was violently pulled fully open from inside and Samson recognised Drinkwater standing there, no mistake, even without lights, in a calf-length blue-and-gold-striped nightshirt and tan boots which he must have just pulled on. Two-handed, he held a big pistol, maybe a Magnum, pointed at Billy because Billy stood closest, and so close a drunk or baby could do it.

'Not another of my boys,' Samson screamed. 'Do me, me.'

When Drinkwater's pistol went off it went off three times, even four, and right afterwards there came another of those sounds from far down in Billy, not a good, comradely whisper this time, but the kind of sound that Samson had imagined coming from Drinkwater in the bed, the sort of noise that said goodbye without saying anything even similar to goodbye as far as the actual words went, only a weak rumble like phlegm starting on the way up from the chest, but never going to make it and slipping back: that gasping, crackling gurgle, not resembling the happy gurgle of a fed baby, but a stricken gurgle, someone choking, someone giving everything up. Billy went down with a great clatter, falling on his Service Six. Weeping, Samson bent to him at once and, as he did, Drinkwater fired twice again.

Afterwards, Samson knew the bullets had gone over his head because of that. At the time, he was just aware that the door he had been trying opened behind him and then someone crashed down on him, maybe shot instead of him, so there were three of them in a heap on the landing, Billy, then Samson and, on top, Hamer. Samson did not realise at once it was Hamer, but he found out pretty soon, the fat neck, the baldness skidding against Samson's cheek. Blood from Hamer flooded down, soaking through Samson's jacket to his shoulder and arm, and swilling over Billy's face beneath him, filling his eye sockets and making everything look ten times worse, though it could not be.

180

He heard Drinkwater yelling Hamer's name in agony, 'Lance, Lance, Lance. Jesus, I've hit you. Please.' The 'Please' – as if Hamer was only fooling about and would get up all right again in a second because Drinkwater had not meant it, and return to happy times with him. Hamer had nothing on except a medallion on a chain around his porky neck, which hung against Samson's face warm from the bed and Hamer's body, like some sort of intimacy, one Samson did not want. Frantically, he struggled to get his weight off Billy and out from under Hamer, who was more weight still on Billy. Then he heard Amiable shouting as he came running up the stairs, too late, also as ever, but not to be blamed.

'Don't anybody move,' he was yelling. All that time in front of old films on TV when the betting shop was shut had given the bugger a way with crisis words. As Samson pulled himself upright, Drinkwater's door was pushed shut and a moment afterwards came the sound of a window in the room going up hard. Amiable started firing then – anywhere, really, but it turned out that one bullet did hit the door, went through and finished in a chest of drawers. A car started outside and Samson heard it turn and speed away.

'What's with Billy?' Amiable said. He peered down in the dark. 'His eyes bleeding? How it looks.' He glanced at Hamer. 'And this one. He the lad we wanted? I hope so.' Amiable took the chain and medallion and put them in his pocket.

The door where Drinkwater had appeared opened again and Samson saw a woman also in night gear there. Amiable jerked around and might have fired, but Samson pulled his arm down. 'A girl, a girl,' he yelled. 'Drinkwater was sleeping with a girl.'

'They heard us break in?' Amiable replied.

'This is terrible,' she said. 'Otis has gone down the drainpipe, no proper clothes, urgently to fetch a doctor for Lance. It will be all right. Poor Lance. Poor, poor Otis.'

24

The day of the bank outing, Corbett and Floyd had breakfast together in the manse kitchen. Henrietta's new absence unsettled Corbett. After the return from London she had seemed to try for contentment with him. And then exit again. But Corbett did not feel too bad – able to eat and talk. Floyd liked making breakfasts and would sing while at the stove, hymns occasionally, but more often songs that seemed to come from wartime, to do with separation and yearning: there was one called 'Room 504', and another about wanting to sleep so he could dream, and to dream so he could be with the one he loved. His voice was as deep as a mine, rich in mournfulness, like a whole generation regretting loss. This morning he was doing black pudding, bacon, fried bread and tomatoes, wearing now his scarlet dressing-gown, which had *Champ* in golden letters across the shoulders.

He pushed a heavily loaded plate in front of Corbett and gave himself more still. Henrietta said his cooking was rubbish, but he could manage a frying pan all right. The tea was in the real china cups. 'If she comes back while you're away on your trip, Jule? Do I allow her in again?'

'Well, of course, Floyd. Welcome her. Be Christian. This is almost part of your church.'

'One day she'll go for keeps, Jule.'

'If I thought she didn't need me, I believe I could bear that.'

'But the humiliation. Someone other than yourself holding her, giving her anecdotes, snuggling up.' He seemed to growl.

'I don't see it like that. If she found she needed someone else, that's how it would have to be.'

But who said Drinkwater would be available for much longer, or any longer at all, even if she did need him? *Go, go, go, Don Samson.* Corbett saw Floyd shake his head in wonder, maybe admiration.

Henrietta might be in danger if she was at that Tongwynlais cottage, and where else would she be? There could be confusion and wild shooting, especially if Samson and his team arrived at night, which was probable. Henrietta was the kind of girl who might even think she had a duty to protect her man. But it was too late to do anything about that now. He had stressed and stressed again to Samson that Drinkwater was the only target.

'There's obviously a rotten side to you, Jule, yet sometimes I feel you're a saint. The selflessness,' Floyd remarked.

'Baptists don't have saints.'

'How long will it take, this business matter?'

'Half a day? I'll come straight back.'

'Yes, please. I don't think I can guarantee my own patience with her any longer. A terrible thing for a minister to say about his daughter. It isn't even as if she was irresistibly driven by being beautiful or young now.'

'She's Henrietta.' Corbett washed up, only reasonable after Floyd had handled all the cooking. 'If she does arrive, don't do an interrogation, a raking over, will you, Floyd? Tell her everything is going to be brilliantly different, in all sorts of ways. Comforting is what she will need.'

'Yes?'

Corbett went upstairs for the Beretta, ready under his pillow, then walked to a junction about half a mile away and waited. He had no idea what kind of stolen car to expect, but it would be something powerful. Mark and the other new lad would be in it already, and then the three would go for Yeo. Graham Flanders waited at home somewhere, no hazard this time, dreaming of forty per cent of a quarter.

25

About an hour after Carol saw Paul Yeo off from Highcross to wherever he was going she took a last look around the house and gardens. She hated the place – had come to hate it. This final tour was a sort of sweet triumph over the house and grounds, a happy, unlingering goodbye. Every part of it she loathed, inside and out: the period fireplaces and the period woodwork and cornices, the period staircase, the period wardrobes and clothes presses, the period windows, and even the views – patio, paddocks, the fields and then the grey-brown Channel. Stuff the lot and all they stood for.

Her cheerio letter to Paul was on the mantelpiece over one of the downstairs period fireplaces. Her car, with a couple of full suitcases in the boot, stood at the front door, pointed towards escape. On the remote control, not period, she had already opened the gates ready for exit. The suitcases contained only her own stuff, and not all of that. She wanted nothing that belonged to the house or to Paul. If things went all right, he would return from what he called his business trip this afternoon and find Highcross wholly as he liked it and wanted it, except that she would not be here.

The letter would hurt him, no question. Hurt but not devastate. After a time, the house and the grounds and the fields and the outlook to the sea would work their steady solace on his dodgy, unsatisfiable soul. It was why he had bought the spread. It spoke to him and for him. It spoke in place of his history and his family, those embarrassments he wished to deny. It was why she had to leave. Her letter ended: *You don't really need me. Your life's about you, you, you, the new you you're scheming to concoct. Your lust to build a true Paul Yeo means nobody else is anything, including me. You are the* Splott, *you are Highcross, you are flight from the name and roots of the Köllers, you are money in the bank. I'm not in love with any of those. Something's gone missing, Paul, and I can't cope with the loss. I'm interested in your unstoppable hunt for yourself, of course I am. But me, I have a self, too. This is another matter that's got lost. Ta-ta, then, Carol.* Period.

A bit high-flown, possibly, but she did not rewrite. She had some money, personally saved. Her plan was to drive anywhere. The imprecision thrilled her. As she started the car, though, she realised her departure was not entirely self-financed: Paul had bought the Escort. Christ, but it was difficult to get full freedom, full independence, full gesture rights straight off. Perhaps one day she would be able to send him payment for the car. *Please find enclosed one retrospective liberty cheque.*

What she had to have immediately, though, was distance between herself and this blanketing idyll and the life Paul had boxed himself and her into. The Escort was the simplest means to that, a piece of privilege she was using to ditch privilege. Few women had such means, and so they stayed stuck or they ran and then were forced back. As she heard it, this had happened to that wild wife of Jule Corbett. Henrietta was a woman who looked for a kind of freedom, too. But it was a poor kind. She seemed to scoot from one man to another, and, in the end, had to return to where she started.

Carol pushed the accelerator down as she reached the motorway. Jesus, would she be forced back one day, too? She would miss Paul, of course, and was missing him already. His fierce obsessions stifled her, yet there was also something good and brave and even lovable about them, something that made her feel proud, as well as sorry for him. But they also forced him into stupid risk-taking, stupid criminality, stupid greed. That project he went out on early today would almost certainly be something crooked and she hoped he would come back from it all right. She would keep the radio on for news. He wanted to rob his way to status, the age-old, almost touching story, and the sort of ruthless short cuts to power and position that over the centuries put half Britain's upper class where it was now, including royalty. Paul, the man from nowhere, looked at those families, read their histories, and said, right, me too.

What turned her off, and finally forced her to pack and vamoose, was that his quest for status left her none. And so, as *Private Eye* would say, farewell landed lad, bank raider and shipowner. To Carol these rated equal. They all excluded her and trampled her, or would if she let them. Hunt solo then, Paul. Look after yourself. Yes, look after yourself, only.

26

At his office, Brade had a telephone call from Aphik.

'Dave. Just needed to hear your lilting tones again. Maybe some small movement this end. I have a name and from your realm. Do you know a Julian Corbett?'

'That rings a bell, Arnie.'

'Lives in a manse.'

'I can put a face to him now.'

'The computer says nothing.'

'Entrepreneur and so on. Clean. Where did you meet him?'

'L'Estaminet.'

'You want me to do the hick bit and ask what that is?'

'You know?'

'The WC2 restaurant that replaced the Inigo Jones?'

'We didn't actually meet this Corbett there, Dave, but off and on we watch Samson in case he starts The Procedure and leads to our other Blackpool people.'

'Corbett ate with Don Samson there?'

'A pleasing repast, with two bottles of Morgon, and Julian stayed on for the cheese. Don never hangs around.'

'He's usually called Jule.'

'You *do* know him, then?'

'A man about dockland.'

'I stayed behind him after the luncheon, not knowing who the hell he was at this stage. He rendezvoused with a woman at the Hayward Gallery. Not too pretty. Sexy, though. Dark? Heavyish? Mid-thirties, like him.'

'His wife.'

'Have I been disrespectful?'

'She can take it.'

'As I said. She got all loud and groupie about Monet and bought a print. That misty port thing.'

'Le Havre.'

'Sometimes I think you're a dark horse, Dave.'

'Unbridled.'

'She paid by Access.'

'Identification.'

'It took us a little while to find she was married and the name of her husband. They have a joint bank account, though he's got a private one, too.'

'He would.'

'So, Jule and Samson – what's the link, Dave? Don knows Arnie Aphik too well for me to do close surveillance myself, but I had two lads at a table near them talking like young business thrusters and gutsing our expenses allowance for the next three months. They said Don and Corbett plainly knew each other already.'

'What else did they hear?'

'A definite trade discussion. Possibly an address given. Don leaves what looked to my boys like fifteen or twenty fifties on the table for Jule to settle. That's going it a bit for two, even at L'Estaminet. This could be a very promising connection, yes, Dave?'

'You want me to have a word with Jule?'

'Oblique, Dave.'

'Really?'

'Sorry.'

'Jule could have bumped into Tommy down here, of course. It might be a condolences visit to the dad. How's Fran?'

'Safely in the past.'

'I'm sorry, Arnie.'

'What we wonder is if this was to do with The Procedure. Corbett up there to give him guidance – the address or whatever? Locating vengeance targets for him? Could it have been people from your realm in the Blackpool car, Dave? There's the Tommy end, after all.'

'He's made no clear, stalking moves?'

Aphik gave this some silence. Then he said: 'Dave, we've been guilty of what might be a grave slip. We were watching the house, as we do now and then, but his Audi's outside and this lulls. The oldest trick. You'd never have bought it, Dave.'

'I've bought worse, often.'

'We only tumble to it when Don's wife's – second wife, called Eloise no less, a cracker – well, we only tumble when Eloise's current boyfriend turns up at the house around 1 a.m. That's not likely if Don or the armament boy, Billy, are present. She's been on the phone, hasn't she, to say the place is safe? That means for most of the night, at least. Don and the boy have gone out over the back, probably, and maybe picked up another car. But whithering, Dave? Arnie Aphik has no answer. This is *mea* very personally *culpa*. I was in our car. Still haven't slept. The boyfriend leaves about 4 a.m. We go, too, and search for Don at known haunts. Nothing. When I call on him at the earliest decent visiting hour, just after 9.30, he comes down looking brilliantly tousled in a dressing-gown, smelling of soap, and rubbing the sleepy dust out of his peepers, dear old thing. But something pretty serious has happened, Dave. I can see they're both deep in turmoil, and especially Don.'

'He's found alien hair on the pillow and reproached Eloise?'

187

'A real, terrible sadness.'

'You sound quite moved, Arnie, for the Met.'

'They're only local folk who went wrong, Dave – who went wrong because it was a tradition to go wrong.'

'Ah, fucking philosophy. I'll speak to Jule, so roundabout he won't know I've said a word.'

Raging Bullfinch was due in dockland later that morning to show a party of high-rank police from overseas around the Bay project and discuss problems such development brought for law and order. Some of the talk would be done in Brade's Bute Street office, and he and Jenkins tidied it now and brought in a few decent chairs. On the walls he had four photographs of Olive Rice from different angles and front and back in the muck of that abandoned office block. Police pictures naturally concentrated on wounds, though the face was clear enough in two of them, and almost matchable to the cheery, untrusting but hopeful face Brade used to see around the tart beats and clubs. There was no operational need for the pictures, and he had nothing similar on Bachelor Percy, though a set existed, of course. The Olive collection was to make sure he did not forget with time that someone had to be got for this and that it ought to be the right one. If he could get the right one for Bachelor, too, that would be grand, but, as he had told Miriam, Bachelor lagged far back.

Glyndwr asked whether the photographs should come down temporarily in case Bullfinch and his friends misinterpreted Brade's motives.

'Misinterpret how?'

'Unhealthy obsessiveness, Dave.'

'That's not misinterpretation.'

'I mean, with Bullfinch wanting to wrap it. These are going to hit the visitors, make the case look . . .'

'Alive?'

'As it were.'

'Fuck him and them,' Brade said. Jenkins was a priceless lad. He could have let Brade rile the brass without interfering, so making him easier to pass on the ladder. Glyndwr was certainly in love with his career, but occasionally seemed to fret more about Brade's prospects than his own. Yes, occasionally.

'London points us now towards Jule,' Brade told Jenkins, as they moved ancient papers into a locker.

'I suppose we've both thought of that. In the Toledo on the night, and up to his ears in complexities. Bullfinch will hate the idea – reflections on Floyd, Pope of the patch, whatever the rumours about him and Louise. Aren't you supposed to have got rid of these, Dave?'

The magazines that Brade's neighbours had sent to Bullfinch were beneath some pamphlets outlining what to do if you found a bomb or an animal with rabies. 'Burning went against the grain,' Brade said. He found room for them in his safe.

'I don't see Jule Corbett as a killer – either or both,' Jenkins said. 'I've been wondering about Harvey – trying to terrorise Bachelor into coughing up to Fiona, and it goes wrong?'

'Harvey terrorising Sweet Bachelor?'

'Harvey could have a rough side.'

'Jule's educated and sensitive,' Brade replied. 'Pressure can hit them hard, push them to violent aberration.'

'For God's sake, Dave, I'm educated and sensitive. Jule's only from some bloody ex-poly.'

'OK, Balliol.'

'You going to talk to him?'

'Talk to him or have a quiet look at him.'

'How can you have a quiet look at him? He'll spot you straight off.'

'Eminence does have problems.'

'This is Dave Brade,' Bullfinch told his group. 'He's very much at the sharp end of our dockland operations, and a fervent disciple of the Bay project. And here's Glyndwr Jenkins, unparalleled on data, very Welsh, but not to a fault.'

They were from France, Denmark and Italy, the Italian a woman. Someone from Publicity at the Bay office tagged along, and someone from the Welsh Office. Jenkins knew him from Oxford, or the Pricerite checkout queue.

'Shall we process, then?' Bullfinch remarked.

The tall, grave, balding Dane studied Brade's Olive pictures. 'She looks very winning.'

'Exactly what she was,' Brade said.

'Dave's very much in touch with people at all levels on this patch,' Bullfinch said. 'Crucial.'

'Hardly an assault by someone experienced,' the Dane replied. 'The unnecessary wounds. The frenzy.'

'Dave sees them all as unnecessary,' Jenkins said.

'Touché.'

'I love this build of girl,' the Italian remarked.

'Which features?' Jenkins asked.

'Narrowish shoulders yet sweet tits. Magnificently slim legs, but the arse not negligible.'

'Thank you, ma'am,' Brade replied. 'I'll find the sod who did it.' He wondered whether he could offer her the magazines.

They went in three cars, Brade with Bullfinch, his driver and the Dane. Bullfinch's radio reported a successful bank raid in Bristol and alerted South Wales police in case this was the escape route. The party looked at the marina development, the Bachelor death site, the new hotels and offices, the Olive death site, the media studios in the Square, the Toledo, the new link road, the street battle locations.

'In Copenhagen we are inclined to let them destroy one another,' the Dane remarked.

'We should have,' Brade replied.

'Or they destroy you.'

'Touché.'

'Supply them arms if necessary. You've got a problem with juries not believing you?' the Dane asked. 'I don't mean you, personally, Dave, but police in general.'

'Him personally,' Jenkins remarked.

'So it is better if things can be kept out of court. Let these elements hit as you say shit from one another. Supply only traffic police to direct vehicles around the bodies and get the ambulance through, but obviously not too soon. Everyone is then happy. Criminals feel fully realised, when allowed to sort out their own little antagonisms. It is within their culture, you see.'

Bullfinch wanted them to see the Allsop prize-winning piece of impermanent architecture, lying like a white zeppelin alongside the handsome, old red-brick port authority headquarters. 'Here we house our Bay exhibition for visitors such as your good selves,' Bullfinch announced. 'Inside, one may walk to what is virtually a great lens at the front and look out over the estuarial bay which has given the Bay its name. And ponder the future. The construction will be removed in due course, symbolising, I like to think, continual, progressive change: the kind of change we are witnessing at last in dockland, and are part of.'

Bullfinch waited outside with Brade, while the party entered. 'Miriam, Dave,' Bullfinch said. 'We should be able to keep the case fairly low key, I think. Accident, yes. Miriam will get minor trouble for possession of a gun, but it's virtually something planted on her by Bachelor.'

'I thought Lestocque probably killed Fiona, sir, and Miriam was covering for him. A sweet relationship. I cried accident, but just to see how things would develop.'

'What things?'

Brade said: 'I mean, with Ivor's record she'd have known we wouldn't buy the accident story. So, she stepped in. Even possession of a firearm would be grave for Lestocque.'

'Cover up? I can't see that,' Bullfinch replied.

'A career bodyguard yet he sleeps through an intrusion.'

'Oh, he might have been on something – pissed or high.'

'Quality of the shooting, sir.'

'Very close. Who'd miss at that range?'

'Many.'

Bullfinch saw the visitors begin to reappear and hissed: 'Drop it, Brade. Leave things the way they are. You're manufacturing complexities and needless trouble – quite needless. Is your race prejudice showing, do you think – *white woman couldn't do it, black man could, white woman takes rap for black man*.' Turning to the Italian, he cried: 'Isn't it panoramic, though? You saw the Norwegian church for seamen? And isn't this artefact deliciously ephemeral?'

They went back to Brade's room. The Bay and Welsh Office people were excluded and Bullfinch gave a documented run-down of problems produced by bringing 'extensive and expensive' middle-class, marina-type housing into a traditionally underprivileged area, and of the outbreaks of 'raw panic and *sauve qui peut*' among established criminal firms as bigger interests began to intrude. He invited questions.

'We have some crimes, such as the killing of this girl,' the Frenchman said. 'This can happen when a client discovers the girl has been with a gay. This produces great fear, great rage.'

'It *is* worrying,' Brade replied.

'This would suggest someone fairly young. Older men are

191

troubled less, angered less. The incubation is so long it means an old man might die of something else, anyway, by then.'

'How old are you, Dave?' Jenkins asked.

Bullfinch said: 'We have a very strong possible in the frame for both these killings. Dave and Glyndwr worked admirably on the cases: exemplary patience and thoroughness.'

'Thank you, sir,' Brade replied.

'I see intimations of promotion in this work for each of them,' Bullfinch said.

'I wonder, did either, both, of you two, Dave, Glyndwr, fuck this girl from time to time?' the Italian inquired. 'Or more regularly? Did you, that is, know her quite closely? Would you judge her the kind to open her mouth, by which I mean, of course, open her mouth as to other clients, or as to sensitive matters she might have been told, thus making her a target?'

'This was a very young girl,' Bullfinch replied.

'Oh, I can see that,' the Italian said. 'Oh, yes, indeed.'

The Dane said: 'We had a recent doubler. This was a man killed for jealousy and money, and a tart because she happened to see something. Tarts get into some very out-of-the-way places, murderous places. But, located as we are close to what was once called Tiger Bay, am I, indeed, teaching my grandmother to suck eggs?'

'*Eggs* I don't think my grandmother ever sucked,' the Italian replied. 'She was a tart herself, and cast off by the family. Then along comes a film called *Cabiria*, before my time, but it's on TV, and apparently whoring took a real step up.'

'I always thought of Cabiria when I saw Olive,' Brade said.

'Oh, your girl is considerably riper,' the Italian replied. 'Could the father keep his hands off her, do you know? Or the mother?'

'You hot climate people!' Bullfinch declared.

'Yet I would also like to ask about the parents,' the Dane remarked.

27

In the afternoon, Corbett closed the curtains and lay on the bed alone, now and then trembling throughout his body and sweating as he relived the morning raid, and now and then laughing in convulsions – fist in his mouth at these times to stop the mad noise, because of Floyd downstairs. When Corbett had left him he was in the kitchen skinning a hare donated by some church member, and crooning another miserable song, about letters tied with blue among his souvenirs and finding a broken heart there, also. One thing you could be sure of: no other manse in the world had so much cash in it. Lay not up for yourself treasure on earth? Lay it down in suitcases under your bed.

At about five o'clock, Floyd knocked on the door and came in with a cup of tea. He had washed well after the hare and smelled of carbolic. Just the same, a thin line of blood streaked his forehead, which looked off key with the dog-collar and tuft-cut grey hair. Corbett sat up and rubbed his eyes as if he had been asleep.

'Don't rush, Jule, but Dave Brade and Glyndwr are down below. I told them you were resting and they're content to wait. I've given them tea and we talked of Liston. Do you realise that when he beat Floyd nobody knew whether Liston was forty-five or thirty?'

'You said resting?'

'Well, yes, after a business trip. They understood. Dave said you get about. I remarked this was putting it mildly. They think Hen's at work, so that's all right. Is there armament in this room?' He moved his head around like a scenting dog. 'That whiff of a handgun – oil, metal, savagery.'

'Well, I hope not. Whose would it be?' Corbett drank. 'I'll look for Henrietta tonight, when it's dark. We don't want display.'

'The suitcase you came back with after these negotiations, Jule?'

Corbett got out of bed and began to tidy himself. 'Papers, samples. They're part of the business we're trying to float.'

He gazed at Corbett with those noble, graveside eyes, despairing of mankind. 'So, I won't ask what business or where the cases are now. I'll get further lies. Do you want me to come with you, looking for her? This could be dangerous? Well, obviously, the people you hob-nob with.'

'It's not necessary, Floyd. I feel confident.'

'Yea. That could be your end. You ought to do a runner – suitcase, armament, the whole thing. Go now. Forget her.'

'I can't.'

'Honestly? When I look at Henrietta in full light these days I think she's so forgettable. On the other hand, I see some Sunday School girls, one especially – Michelle-Sue: such skin and happy leg movements. Impossible to associate Henrietta now with that dinky age. Find something fresher? Run and come back later.'

'Desertion.'

'She's the deserter.'

'Only a spasm, a gesture.'

Floyd came downstairs with him. 'You're looking brilliantly reinvigorated, Jule,' Jenkins said.

'Just a general chinwag again,' Brade remarked. 'Certainly not worth waking somebody for after a trying business trip. Where was this one, Jule? Floyd says not the capital.'

'Only a half-day,' Floyd said.

'But exhausting all the same,' Brade said. 'It's not the distance or venue but the intensity of these things, I imagine.'

'Yes, intense,' Corbett replied.

'People have a gem in you, Jule,' Jenkins said, 'the total blank-wall discretion.'

'The essence of his work,' Floyd replied. 'Where two or three are gathered together, there is Jule in the midst, dreaming of his cut, keeping their secrets.'

They were sitting in the lovely, big, light lounge again. Brade said: 'I still get nowhere with local inquiries. We want to do something on London connections. I wondered if you could help us, Jule.'

'Naturally, in total confidence,' Jenkins remarked.

'My work is always that, as you mentioned, Glyndwr,' Corbett replied. 'If I give you names, you or your Met friends would go and harass. Where am I then, Dave? Would I ever see further work? Do you imagine for a moment they wouldn't know who'd pointed the finger?'

'What interests us primarily is any London connection with the man I mentioned before called Tommy Something,' Brade replied.

Floyd had a guffaw this time. 'Is Jule supposed to spend business gatherings in smart London suites canvassing those present in case they know someone called Tommy?'

'Why don't you fuck off, Floyd?' Jenkins replied.

'Not in the manse, Glyn,' Brade said.

Floyd maintained his smile. 'Don't fret, Dave. I like it. What I hate above all is the mealy-mouthed. Our Lord spoke simply, directly, provocatively.'

'Yes, well, why don't you fuck off, Floyd,' Brade said. 'Go play with your Patterson dolls.'

Corbett gave his voice a reasonable, mild tone. 'I believe I've said before, Dave, that the people I'm negotiating with in London are conventional, and in many instances, eminent business folk – unlikely to be in touch with the kind of man who, as I understand it from you, comes here to knife a whore and execute Sweet Bachelor.'

'But some of these eminent folk might use heavier material to clear a path,' Brade replied.

'I don't understand what that means, "clear a path". These are people, companies, thinking of investing considerable monies here. Money "clears the path". That's what business at their level is about, Dave. If there should be any other mediation necessary, that is my function, surely. I'd be failing, I'd be superfluous, if additional aid were needed. The kind of business people I deal with do not pay for the same service twice.'

'So why don't you and Glyndwr fuck off now, Dave,' Floyd remarked.

At about 11 p.m. Corbett drove out to Tongwynlais and parked some way from the cottage he had found for Drinkwater and Hamer. He kept an eye on the mirror, wondering about a tail after that afternoon visit. You could never tell what Brade knew – what any detective worth his pay knew. But Brade would realise he could not hope to shadow Corbett, and nor could Jenkins. Before leaving, he had tried to telephone Don Samson from a public box to ask if he had been to the cottage but reached only an answering service and rang off. In his pocket he carried the Beretta Floyd claimed to have scented in the bedroom. Floyd was gifted and yearned to be famed among preachers for street savvy.

Corbett started to climb on foot the rough little path up the hillside. He took it slowly, keeping out of the moonlight. If Drinkwater and Hamer were here, intact, it could be stressful. The raid must have made the news by now and, after all, it was *their* bank. They must jump to the right conclusions. There might be a lot of rage, all coming Corbett's way.

He could make out the cottage. There seemed to be no lights. All the same, he stayed put for a while in the shadow of a hedge, watching, and brought the Beretta from his pocket. He might have surprise here. He must bring Henrietta back. When he told her about a meaty future and a good catch today she would come with him, surely. Jesus, she could really prefer life with these people?

Floodlit and moonlit, that crazy ornamental fortress, Castell Coch by Burges, gleamed on the neighbouring hillside, above the cottage. Corbett began to edge forward, the Beretta in his hand, down against his leg. As he came nearer to the cottage, he stopped again. He thought he heard moaning from somewhere inside. It was irregular and urgent, the sort of sound Henrietta sometimes made when she was getting into her stride. Angry and sick he went closer, through the little front garden, and in a moment could pinpoint the noise. It came from behind an upstairs curtained window at the side of the cottage. That made him worse for a second. Now, though, he thought it might be a man's voice, not Henrietta's, and a man in pain, rather than ecstasy. He worked his way quietly around the building, seeking an uncovered window. He had no luck. The noise continued.

The front door was not part of the original building but a modern, mock-solid thing, with a big, mock-brass knocker. Corbett was about to give it some genuine shoulder when he looked down and saw in the moonlight a heavy stain across the step, something like that smear on Floyd's forehead, but drier and wider – about the width of a body, as though someone bleeding badly had been dragged out from the cottage a while ago. If it had been day he reckoned he could have followed the marks on the garden path.

He put a bit of body pressure to the door and felt it yield a little. Lifting the Beretta to the ready, he moved back a few inches and then shoved hard forward. The door burst open at once. He stayed outside. It gave direct into a living-room and he peered through the darkness, the Beretta held two-handed. As soon as he had bearings he entered. It would be stupid to stand framed in the doorway, silver-spotlighted by the moon. The place seemed well furnished. He felt carpet under his feet and crouched low behind a big, soft leather armchair. In a second, he could make out stairs leading down into this room, again a modern style job, varnished boards on metal supports. He propped his body against the chair and sighted the Beretta on the top stair. Someone could be on the ground floor too, he realised that, and kept alert. His back was to a wall and the chair gave him good cover on one side. The Beretta was a first-class stopper and he made sure he did handgun practice at least every few months. At this range, he could not fail. He waited, feeling pretty good – triumphant, rich. Would that bugger Floyd go sniffing under the bed?

Corbett heard movement at the head of the stairs, careful, subtle, quiet movement, though not quiet enough. An urge to shout a warning, a threat, took hold for a second, but shouting told your position. He fought to keep his breathing silent.

Then, in a big whisper, Henrietta suddenly said: 'Who is it? Otis, darling, you're back?' She was whispering, and still out of sight. 'But why break in? You have a key.' He kept quiet.

'Please,' she said. There was a pause. Then she spoke again, as if to herself: 'Oh, no, no, please, not you others.'

Some of the moonlight found its way through a landing window and he saw a shadow move briefly across the top stairs. 'You've returned, you people?' she said. 'Why? Surely enough terrible damage?'

'Henrietta,' he whispered back.

She went silent for a few seconds. 'Jule?'

'Drinkwater not here? Who's with you, then?'

197

'Jule?' He tried to work out whether she sounded pleased or disappointed. God, he was sighting a pistol on the sound of her voice, yet still cared only about how she rated him.

'You're all right?' he said.

'Are you alone? Not with those people?'

'Come down the stairs, Henrietta. You – are *you* alone?'

She did not answer, and did not appear.

'I've come to fetch you, Henrietta. Yes, alone.'

'Well, I knew you wouldn't be with those people, really.'

'Which people?'

'Terrible, terrible, here, Jule. There's someone terribly injured.' Now she sounded as if she were about to weep.

'But you – you're all right?' he said. 'Please, come down. Let me see you.'

'Lance Hamer,' she replied. 'Dying.'

He stood and, the gun still out in front, walked to the foot of the stairs. He spoke at normal voice. 'You've nothing to do with these people. You must come with me now, Henrietta. Things are good – I mean things with me. I'm coming upstairs.'

But he waited, as if needing permission. He still could not see her. Henrietta's voice came from the landing at the side of the stairs. 'Jule, you didn't really send those terrible people, did you?'

'Which people?' he asked again.

'London people? Terrible. Otis said you'd sent them. Oh, I couldn't believe.'

'Which London people?'

'You know some London people, don't you? Look, I think of that Samson you used to go to see.'

'Samson was here?' He gave it full surprise.

'Otis said so. Three. People from his family.'

'I'm going to come up, Henrietta.' He climbed fast. As he did, he heard another burst of moaning from one of the bedrooms. When he reached the top of the stairs, he found Henrietta sitting on the floor of the little landing, her back against the wall and legs stretched out. She had on an old green track suit that he had seen Floyd exercising in once or twice. She was staring towards the room where the noise had come from and did not turn her head when Corbett arrived by her side.

'This is a dangerous place for you,' she said.

'It's where you are.'

'Otis will come back. He's gone for a doctor.'

'Gone how long?'

'It can't be just *any* doctor, Jule. A doctor who is discreet. All sorts of things happened here.'

'Gone how long?'

'Since the early hours.'

'And you really expect to see him again?'

Now she did look up at Corbett. 'Oh, yes. He'll return. He worries about Lance. Only about Lance.'

Corbett walked a few steps across the landing and looked into the bedroom where the sounds had come from. He saw a four-poster bed, with what seemed in the half-dark to be expensive, silk hangings in mauve. There was something royal about it, except that Hamer lay there, uncovered, hunched up on his side, and wearing underclothes. His head was bent forward, his chin on his chest, and Corbett could make out little of his face. He groaned again as Corbett watched. It was as if Hamer had folded himself around some appalling pain, perhaps in the stomach, though Corbett saw no injury, nor blood marks on the bedding.

'Otis said to stay with him, Jule.'

'If you came away, we could phone somewhere anonymously. Get him help at once.'

'Otis didn't want anything like that.'

'Sod Otis. It might take him a day or more to find that sort of doctor.'

She shrugged and almost gave a smile. Corbett went closer to the bed. Hamer's eyes were closed and he might be sleeping, or in a coma. Once, though, he reached out with a hand, clutching at the air, his fingers working fiercely.

'He'll be dead if someone doesn't see him soon, Henrietta. Perhaps he'll die in any case.' He had no real hate for Hamer, not Hamer. He must not die of neglect. Corbett knew he had brought these injuries on him.

'Someone has to be here,' Henrietta said.

Corbett went back to her. She had not moved and was staring at her feet. 'I'm part to blame, Jule. These people, the London people, they never expected to find a woman here. I heard one of them yell, "A girl, a girl," and the confusion seemed worse because of me. And so, this.'

'Don't be stupid. Not your fault. They were here to kill.'

'Oh, yes, they were here to kill. How do you know that, Jule? But they went into panic. It was Otis they wanted. Some long-time grievance? And these people lost someone of their own, too. They dragged him, took him away in a car.'

'I saw the marks.'

'Otis heard them arrive and had time to get something on, reach a gun and fire – fire and fire and fire, Jule. It could have been Otis who hit Lance, you see. Can you understand what that would do to Otis? Lance was part of him. Is.' She glanced up, then back down. 'Why did you do that, Jule? Send them here?'

He sat on the landing alongside her, the Beretta in his lap, and put a hand over hers on the carpet. She made no response.

'Why? You know why,' he said.

She shrugged again. 'You ought to get clear.'

'He's not coming back.'

'I almost wish you were right. It would mean he'd forgotten Lance.'

'Oh, Henrietta, I do love you,' he said, releasing her hand. 'You need me so much.'

She followed her own thoughts. 'Even if Otis never comes back, I can't really leave Lance here dying, can I?'

He considered that. 'No, of course you can't. You're a lovely Christian person, Henrietta.'

'Don't use that word about me, even in joke. The word "lovely".'

28

'Obviously I wouldn't normally intrude on a thing like this, Don, a family thing, a happy thing, but there's some really bad news, I'm afraid,' Aphik, the boy detective, said. 'You had to be told at once. This is family, too.' He had one of those all-direction short haircuts to show he knew about modes as well as twenty-four-hour snooping.

Samson was at the Sports Centre, watching Eloise play her

water polo match. They had decided they must come, despite everything. To stay away would signal they knew something was wrong. Samson had a Smith and Wesson in a waist holster under his jacket. Amiable and another lad were somewhere handy, in case of trouble, but Samson had seen no sign of anything, and there probably could not be anything, now. For occasional moments he had been almost able to forget Billy and that Welsh cottage and enjoy the game. Eloise would have cried off because of what had happened, but now she was here she played full out. Of course, she was not Billy's mother. He was unsure whether what she felt was grief or disgust with the whole life she had let herself in for with him. He wondered how long he could hold her.

At water polo, she was as tough and dirty as any of them, and faster than most, a beautiful, tearaway crawl. She had scored once, a real bullet of a throw, and looked up at him in the balcony and waved, grinning under her tight little numbered hat, eyes shining as blue as the pool. He had felt proud then, but still uncertain of her. The spectator area was not full and Aphik had slipped into the next seat. 'So what news, for God's sake?' Samson said, playing the part. 'Family? Don't I get any peace?'

'It's Billy, Don,' Aphik replied. This evening, he was in a double-breasted navy blazer that must have cost four or five hundred, the informality of it maybe to suit the sporty venue. This lad definitely had a future, sod him.

The yelling from supporters boomed, the way it did in swimming baths. 'I didn't hear,' Samson told him.

'Billy.'

'Billy? Yes?' It hurt Samson even to speak his name to this trifle and especially when speaking his name brought back those pictures – Billy folded and silent on the floor in the back of that borrowed car – Billy stiff and pushed gently into the river during a swift detour from the Severn Bridge on their way home – the traces of Billy in the car really worked on later by Samson and Amiable, and scrubbed out more or less completely from the carpet and seating. No complaints from Amiable's girlfriend, and they brimmed the tank for her as a general thank-you. He had not weighted Billy. They all wanted him recovered before the fish got to work.

'He's been found, Don.'

'Billy? I didn't know he was missing. He went on a trip somewhere, that's all.'

'In the sea, as a matter of fact.' Aphik glanced down at the water.

Eloise pushed someone under and pinched the ball for a sprint at goal.

'You're saying he's drowned? Where?' Samson said.

'Can we go outside? It doesn't seem the best place here.'

Aphik led the way. Samson stood. As he followed, he saw Eloise glance up again and he gave a good smile, but she had seen Aphik and would know it was trouble.

The detective waited in the corridor near the Sports Centre notice-board. A door opened for a moment and Samson heard people grunting and hard-breathing with lifting bars. 'Washed up in South Wales, Don. Fully dressed. Wallet, the lot, in his pockets. No robbery. No attempt to hide who he is.'

'God. How did he get in the sea?'

'Not drowned. He'd been shot. We think twice. Could be three.'

'Oh, Jesus.'

'Why I came at once, you see,' Aphik said.

'Thanks.'

'It's not good, Don. A couple of children found him.'

'Oh, poor kids.'

They went into a canteen full of people with Adidas bags, and men in trainers walking that cocky, wing three-quarter style. Samson bought tea and they sat down at a table. 'Have you been in touch with his mother?' he asked.

'Norah? No, she doesn't know. I thought you'd want to tell her, Don.'

'Right.'

'Look, it's terrible: Tommy, now this. I feel for you. I didn't know Billy so well, but even so.'

'Thanks.'

'Don, maybe this is not the time, but we think we might be tracing one of the people from the Blackpool Senator. This is someone who's been spending hot money from another bank outing. Spending a lot – Jersey. The lad's name is Graham Flanders, according to Jersey police. He has wide-frame spec-

202

tacles, like the ones spotted at Blackpool. We think the failed Wheels.'

'Yes?'

'It's no comfort now, I realise that.' He leaned across the table and a for a moment Samson thought the detective was going to grip his arm in love and sympathy. But Aphik drew back and simply nodded sadly.

Samson said: 'And I'm here enjoying myself, watching swimming. I feel a kind of guilt. You understand?'

'You couldn't know, Don. When did you see Billy last?' Groups of men and girls in track suits at two tables nearby started a battle throwing plastic cups at each other, dregs flying all ways. Some of it trailed across Aphik's blazer and there was a big laughing all round. He stood up and went and took the meatiest-looking man by the throat and had him suddenly lying on his back across a table, scattering more cups and badminton rackets. Aphik held him there for a while preaching a few points, then reached to another table, took a brown sauce bottle and squirted several heaps on to the man's face and track suit.

'This place is going downhill, Don,' he said, returning. 'Symptomatic of the break-up of law and order, would you say? But then, you eat in Wheeler's and the Gay Hussar and L'Estaminet – you wouldn't be used to it.'

Amiable looked into the canteen to check all was well. Samson told him with his eyes to disappear.

'Who?' Samson asked. 'Who the hell would want to kill our Billy?'

'We're in the dark, Don. At this stage. You tooled up on some account?' Aphik nodded down towards the Smith and Wesson under Samson's jacket. 'What goes on?'

'South Wales?'

'Near Newport. The kids were fishing.'

'What's he doing down there?'

'We think he might have been put into the Severn. The experts are looking at tide and currents for us. Very strong and swift.' Aphik leaned across the table again. 'Did he mention a trip?'

'Billy? He got around. He didn't always say where. Where did it happen, the shooting?'

'We don't know. He might have been carried in a vehicle from anywhere. There could be some mess.' He frowned. 'Excuse me,

Don. No need to say that. Once in the head, once, possibly twice in the chest. Not very close. Someone blazing off, in a panic? Unprofessional. We hear of no shoot-outs, yet. So, a remote spot?'

'Well, I don't want his mother told any of the details, nor Eloise.'

'I shouldn't think we'd need to hold the body for long. God, you're strong. You take tough news bloody well. It *is* news, is it? We'll keep clear of the funeral again. It's only decent. This is full tragedy. Even a cop can see that.'

29

Brade went out to see Olive's father again, but Rice was at a caravan auction in West Wales, or so they said. Tomorrow would do. When Brade returned to Bute Street, Jenkins announced: 'You've got an invitation from Miriam, Dave. Rang twice. She'd like to see you at Lisvane, alone. Maybe she fancies you, now Ivor's not around. I hear he's taken off again. Restless fellow. He's probably afraid you're going to do him for Fiona. More? Anyway, it sounds good. No witnesses wanted.'

'It sounds like treachery.'

'What I mean – good. She's after a deal?'

'What deal?'

'Maybe that she'll tell all about Ivor as long as you keep her name out of the papers if there's a trial – shield her from the select neighbours.'

'Her name's already been in the papers – discovery of the body in her house, for God's sake. Nobody could keep things quiet from now on, there were charges.'

'People don't realise how powerless we are. They think courts can be fixed. Some can.'

'Not this.'

Jenkins said: 'Well don't tell her till she's coughed. You're so stupidly decent, honky decent.'

'And she'll say Ivor did the other two as well?'

'Many pointers.'

In front of his Olive pin-ups, Brade snarled: 'I want Rice. A couple of those foreign cops went straight to him, or her. They thought it standard fatherly business.'

'Europe's seedy.'

'Bullfinch said something like that. This profession's seedy.'

'But, then again, we also want Corbett.'

'Could be. Second choice. Why does he deny knowledge of Tommy's surname? I deliberately held that back. Why doesn't he say he knows the father?'

Jenkins said: 'Business ethics, as he pleaded very movingly, I thought. Your trouble, Dave, is you can't see Bullfinch might get something right. I sympathise, but the bugger *could* by accident. Possibly it *was* Tommy Samson after all. Myself, I still like the look of Harvey.'

Brade began to yell. 'That's only for bloody Bachelor. I'm looking for who did Olive.'

'Bit at a time, Dave.'

'There's no time left.'

Brade drove out to Lisvane. Would Olive Rice's doctor cough if he thought there had been childhood abuse? Probably not. They loved all the corny power and kudos that came with consulting room privacy.

In her brilliant lounge, Miriam said: 'I want to give some clarification, Dave.'

Brade sat down and readmired the carpet.

'I'm not ashamed of how I live my life now,' she said. Miriam was standing against red velvet curtains, drawn back and towering behind her like an angry pillar.

'What clarification?' Brade asked.

She said: 'First, I want you to promise to go easy on Ivor. I know you think he killed Fiona.'

So, she had not called him here to betray Lestocque. The opposite. 'I've said Accident, so far,' Brade replied. He did not tell her Bullfinch seemed to want Accident, too, for his own purposes. Keep some pressure on. 'All right, Miriam, love, how do we deal? Is there a drink?'

She brought him gin and dry vermouth and mixed herself one. 'The thing between Ivor and me, it's entirely post-Bachelor.'

'Of course. You told us.'

'Never mind "of course", you snide bastard. This is true. It's to the point.' She was back to her denim today, but still looked pretty fair. 'Before me, Ivor went to girls – tarts.'

'Some do, Miriam. It's sad, but where would a whole division of Bachelor's empire have been without?'

'Ivor would never go to Percy's girls.' She came and sat opposite him. 'He didn't believe in exploitation – pulling rank on a girl and not paying.'

'Delicacy.'

'Olive Rice. He went there. I believe you thought highly of her, too, Dave.'

'A lovely kid.'

'With a great – '

'Heart. Oh, yes, indomitable. Well, not finally.'

Miriam put on an expounding tone. 'Olive was into some kind of serious thing with a regular visitor from London, a missionary called Tommy Samson. He did business with Percy, so Ivor knew him.'

'We heard of this lad.'

'I should hope so. I can tell you, Dave, Bachelor feared Tommy and those who were behind Tommy. Things were not going right.'

'Being squeezed?'

'Olive mentioned this relationship to Ivor.'

'That's like her. She was very open,' Brade replied.

'He said Olive seemed really proud of it. She told him this special lad could be very jealous, was growing possessive, and asked Ivor to be careful when he left her place – not be seen. I don't know about this next bit, but Ivor thought she was telling him Tommy Samson might be especially vindictive with her, even violent – I mean, you know, violent . . . murderous – if he knew she went with a black? This could be just Ivor's sensitivity. Why I asked you to come without Glyndwr.'

'Glyn's not touchy.'

'Nice. This night, as Ivor's leaving her, he thinks he spots Tommy in the street, and also thinks Tommy saw him, though Tommy doesn't let on. So Ivor keeps going, in the opposite direction, hoping he was wrong. He believes Tommy went immediately into Olive's place.'

Brade began to concentrate hard and did not touch his glass

when she replaced the martini. He needed to feel what she was telling him at its worst, not blurred by booze. 'You mean Tommy Samson killed her out of jealousy?' he whispered. Oh, God, did Raging Bullfinch, that Traffic refugee, have this right? Oh, God, was it possible, tolerable, to go to him and concede that? Oh, God, was the easy way out sometimes the correct one? It *was* all down to a dead Londoner? Or was Miriam loading it on the outsider with this neat concoction, to help dear Ivor, the paramour?

'After that night, Olive dropped out of sight. Girls do, as you know, Dave, but Ivor began to worry. Eventually, he went looking for her.' She took a breath or two. 'He found her, where your lot found her a bit later. Of course, Ivor panics, because he's been with her, and it's known to other girls. He does a bunk. While he's gone, you find Olive, and Bachelor, who's unprotected, gets killed.' She opened her palms, as if to show she had handed him everything, all the answers. Perhaps she had. He did not want them.

'What kind of differences between Percy and this lad?'

'Look, Dave, Bachelor didn't unburden his soul to me, or anyone, but it was something like this – Samson and maybe Samson's family in London work for some genuine big wheel, maybe a builder, maybe a developer, who's coming into the Bay and requires a degree of protection. Bachelor was going to handle this. It's second nature. He has the resources, he thinks. Then queries start. The big wheel is interested in really hi-tech protection – against arson and organised pillage. He's already suffered both apparently in other Bay-type schemes where competition was grim. His insurance cover is at the bone because of claims. So, he demands the protection is foolproof. The Samsons doubted whether Sweet Bachelor was up to it. They came to regard him as small-time and amateur.'

'It will happen to all of them.'

'Bachelor wouldn't wear it, Dave. Couldn't. He tried to fight back. I think, and Ivor thinks, that Tommy took him out, probably on orders. As I understand it, that lad could be a charmer and then flip suddenly into violence.'

'Yes, that might have killed him, as a matter of fact.'

'So it adds up?'

'It sort of adds up. I mean, do we know Ivor hadn't been bought by some outfit? And then there's the sexual side, plus a money side – wanting Bachelor out of the way because of you.'

'I've told you, the thing between Ivor and me didn't start until after his death.'

'Yes, you have, Miriam.'

She mulled that for a while. 'Can you make it favourable for Ivor?'

It was touching in a way, her concern for him. Love for him? 'Why didn't Ivor tell me this himself?' Brade asked. He did drink now. 'Don't answer. People like Ivor never talk to police, though they might ask their women to.'

'He's afraid to admit he was with Olive so near her death. He knows what your sort would make of that. You'd have him cuffed in a flash.'

Brade stood: 'No, we would have discussed things with him. We'll still have to discuss things with him. He's in touch?'

'What do I say to him, Dave?'

Brade said: 'Say you told me and that I admire his taste in tarts.'

'He knows.'

'In women generally.'

'You don't have to say that, Dave.'

'Miriam, you won't ask your next-doors in for tea, will you, until you've got rid of the ceiling stain?'

30

In the mauve-draped bed, Hamer became conscious briefly, seemed to rally. Still hunched on his side and groaning now and then, he awoke with a shout of several unintelligible words which roused Corbett, where he was sleeping in a chair. Hamer gazed across the room at him, almost with friendliness. They had a bedside lamp on, but covered with a towel to keep the light low. 'Some tangle, this, Jule,' he said. 'I'm going to snuff it on one of those keep-a-welcome hillsides? All your doing? You send Don Samson, and take the bank for yourselves, yes? We should have foreseen that. I must be getting sleepy.' He closed his eyes again. 'Well, yes, I am.'

'What are you talking about, Lance?' Corbett replied, appalled by this evil clarity.

'Is Otis here?' he replied.

'He's coming,' Henrietta answered. She had been dozing in a chair, too, but was standing close to Hamer now, leaning over him in the bed. She began to weep. 'Arriving very, very soon, Lance.'

'No,' Hamer replied. 'Not at all.' He managed to shake the big jowls like a peeved judge.

'Oh, yes, yes,' Henrietta told him.

'He's gone. Only sensible.'

'Never,' she replied.

'Well, if he comes it will be because of you,' Hamer told her. 'Somehow you've managed it.' He paused and tried to gather more strength to explain. He gave up, though.

'No, Lance. He'll come for *you*. You must believe it.'

'You're good people. Really, she's a great girl, Jule.'

Hamer closed his eyes. 'Otis always had an exit plan in case of something like this. He's not coming, not for me, not for you, Henrietta. He laughs a lot, but he's a thinker, too. About his skin.' He groaned. 'Sorry,' he muttered, without opening his eyes.

'He told me he feels linked to you for ever, Lance,' she said. It was not clear if he could still hear and she bent lower and spoke the words again. In the small glow from the lamp Corbett saw some of her tears fall on Hamer's bald head, and slide down across face and neck, like skidding lard in Floyd's frying pan. 'Yes, linked to you for ever, Lance. I'm only here to make sure you're fine when he arrives with the friendly doctor. That's the whole story.'

They went over the cottage clearing up after he died. They had had to bring in food while they waited, best part of two nights and a day. 'No, you're both right. He won't show,' Henrietta said. 'God, we're into Friday. He's scared. Let's go, Jule.' She covered the body and drew the mauve drapes. Now Hamer could not be seen, the bed looked more than ever like a royal bier.

They went back to the manse and in their bedroom Corbett

209

unlocked the cases and checked the money. It was 2 a.m. and they slept until Floyd woke them with cooked breakfasts on trays. He said Grace then sat down at the bedside while they ate. 'I heard you come in. Somehow I sensed this was a new new beginning. I thought it possibly wiser not to greet you then.'

'Terrible hours we keep, Floyd, but I eventually located Henrietta and last night we decided all we wanted was to be tranquil and alone,' Corbett said. 'We went out along the River Wye, Tintern way. Simply drove. An occasional stop. Brilliant under the moon.'

'Ah, sylvan Wye,' he replied.

'That's it,' Corbett said.

'Wye, my eye. This is make-believe, yes?' Floyd went on. He was in a brilliant red roll-top shirt, not his colour. 'You've been negotiating her out of one of those random passions she gets. A true deal this time?'

'We might go away somewhere,' Corbett replied.

'Because he – whoever – might come back into the picture?'

Henrietta said: 'We found we both love the Wye, Daddy. Possibly other rivers, too. We'd never spoken of this. It must have been always a subconscious bond.'

'Well, you'll be all right financially for your trip,' Floyd remarked, nodding towards the closed cases under the bed.

'I'd like to sleep a little more, if you don't mind,' Henrietta told her father.

'This all needs some sort of consummation, does it?' Floyd asked. 'Make as much noise as you like, what with the traffic outside at this hour and so on.'

'We've got a few things we want to forget,' Henrietta replied.

'Those increase as you get older,' he said.

They slept for a couple of hours and then Henrietta packed and Corbett loaded the car with her luggage and the money cases.

'Where will you go?' Floyd said.

'It could be anywhere,' Corbett answered.

'We're free,' Henrietta said.

'All this jugged hare here,' Floyd replied.

'I'd like to go back to the cottage at Tongwynlais, Jule,' Henrietta said in the car. 'In case Otis came.'

'And if he did? If he's there?'

'I'll say goodbye.'

'If he's not?'

'Well, no problem.'

'It could be dangerous for me, Henrietta.'

'I know. I'd like to go, though.'

He drove right up there this time. They saw a Sierra parked half out of sight behind the cottage and when they went in found Drinkwater sitting in the chair where Corbett had slept during the wait. The drapes on the bed were open and he had pulled back the covers to expose Hamer's face. Drinkwater did not move.

'I stayed until the end, Otis,' Henrietta said. 'Well, *we* stayed.'

'I knew you would. Thanks. No doctor would come. Lance had given me up – thought I would never show?'

'He was certain you would,' Henrietta replied.

'Totally,' Corbett said.

'We were uncertain. But Lance never wavered,' Henrietta told him. 'His belief in you kept him going longer than anyone could have expected – with those injuries.'

'Right,' Corbett said. 'It gave him spirit. You ought to get away, Otis. All this activity up here – someone's going to alert the police.'

'Yes.' He remained motionless in the chair.

'Did you get rid of your gun?' Corbett asked.

'My bullets are in Lance. That what you mean, Jule?'

'Best get rid of the gun,' Corbett replied.

'I might have hit someone else, as well.'

'Probably. They'll be able to tie the two.'

'Possibly Billy. Poor Don.'

'Where will you go, Otis?' Henrietta asked.

'I'll be all right.'

'Get abroad,' Corbett said. He went out to the car and, putting his hands into a money case, brought out two good helpings. When he returned to the room, Henrietta was pulling the clothes back over Hamer's face. It did not look as if she had been close to Drinkwater during this short absence by Corbett, but who could tell? He put the notes in Drinkwater's lap.

'It's not certain I hit Lance,' Drinkwater said. There was a plea in his voice.

'Of course it isn't,' Corbett replied.

'There was other firing,' Drinkwater said.

'Why you must get clear,' Corbett replied. 'Even a place as remote as this – the shooting could have been heard.'

'We're going, anyway,' Henrietta told him. 'Possibly towards the Wye.' She went out and Corbett heard the car door slam.

Drinkwater said: 'Jule, be honest, be honest with me twice. Do you think I hit him? And did he give me up – die thinking I'd ditched him?'

'Yes, of course. Both, you dumb shit.'

31

In Bullfinch's office at Division, Brade just about managed to say: 'Both Glyndwr and I, sir, think it was remarkable insight of yours to spot that Tommy Samson did indeed do them.'

'Quite remarkable, sir,' Jenkins trilled.

'He really did?' Bullfinch replied. 'You're not just saying it because one mentioned promotion as a possible accompaniment to a quick and quiet wrap-up? Nor to distract from that uproar about whores living at your place, Dave? Actually living there! Church officials with formal protests.'

'Not at all, sir,' Brade said. 'It all seems to hold water. The girls have left now. A bizarre interlude. They considered it had become reasonably safe again on the patch.'

'I feel they may well continue calling on you there, though,' Bullfinch replied. 'I mean, knowing the way you are, Dave. This sort of thing could have some bearing on the promotion prospects, I fear. Yours, I mean, not Glyndwr's.'

'Of course, sir,' Brade replied.

'He was only sheltering them,' Jenkins said.

'Exploiting is the word I'd use,' Bullfinch replied.

'I expect it is,' Jenkins said.

'Watch it,' Bullfinch replied.

'It's all right, Glyn,' Brade said.

Bullfinch grew genial, as far as you could with eyes like that. He was in rolled shirt-sleeves, the skin of his arms radiant. 'Dave, I take no credit for the way this has turned out. I've got a talent for the obvious, that's all. What policing's about, fortunately. You probably thought I was on the take?'

Nobody spoke.

'No, afraid not, lads,' Bullfinch went on. 'But, look, Dave, feel no pain. It was you who cracked it, proved it. Mine was mere flair. You're the one they talk to and bargain with and trust. Dockland – it's still your place.'

'Oh, yes, sir, I know my place.'

Bullfinch stood and pulled a jacket on. He was away to something crucial. 'This Samson family, jinxed? I gather they've brought Tommy's brother's body out of the sea.'

'Billy, yes, sir,' Brade replied. 'We had an anon call about that – suggesting we compare the bullets from Billy and that character found shot in bed in Tongwynlais, Lance Hamer. They matched. The caller told us Hamer's boyfriend, an ageing villain called Otis Drinkwater, did both and would be trying to get out of Britain. He was stopped at Heathrow, on his way to Ecuador. He wasn't daft enough to have the weapon with him, but did have approaching twenty grand in traceable notes from a Bristol bank raid. The caller also told us to look out for the money. We're assuming Drinkwater and Hamer were part of a team and warred over the cut.'

'The rest of the team?'

'Not really our concern, sir. The bank raid was off our ground.'

'I like it,' Bullfinch remarked, leaving.

32

Yeo found he was spending more and more time on the *Splott*. As owner, he had a cabin at the stern where he could look after visitors and which he used as an office – or as a sitting-room sometimes these days, and nights. Highcross seemed big and empty now Carol had gone. When the *Splott* was moored at Cardiff or Newport he would often go aboard, on the face of it to check all was well, but really because the ship could still always make him feel solid, a real part of the scene. This was a vessel that could load a thousand tons of graded sand or gravel near Flat Holm, dock, discharge and be out again on the same tide. She meant something. She was part of the big future. He felt as if he meant something, too, when he was aboard, no matter how he helped finance her, and even though he was alone. There might be another ship soon. Bristol had paid less than forecast, but there would be new openings.

He was below deck messing about with one of the diesel pumps when he thought he heard footsteps above. Occasionally, before they were living together, Carol used to come down and drag him away for a drink from work on the *Splott*, and he listened for a moment now, then hurried up the steel stairway. Rushing to meet her and reclaim her was like coming up from some dark pit into the light, into happiness again. He was wiping his hands on a rag, longing to embrace her. For a moment, he saw nobody. 'Carol,' he called.

'Paul, I'm here.' But it was a man's voice. For a second, Yeo felt a ripe mixture of despair and rage. Instead of his life being put back together again, this was an intruder on his boat.

'It's Graham, Gray Flanders – I'm always appearing out of nowhere.' Flanders gave a chuckle, but it did not sound too genuine. He was crouched down alongside the sand hold, keeping his head below the bulwarks. 'I've got to see you. They've identified me.'

Yeo turned and walked towards his cabin, then sat on the bunk and waited. In a moment, Flanders appeared and closed the door.

'I went up to your house and found it empty. They told me at the pub you'd probably be here.'

'You've been asking around in the Starboard Light?'

'Not making a big deal, or anything.'

Someone new in the pub and everyone knew. Someone new in the pub making inquiries and you might as well advertise on telly. 'Who's identified you, Gray?'

'Well, we were spending a bit over there, Mark and I.'

'Police noticed?'

'Some of the Bristol notes were noisy.'

'I've got them in deposit boxes for a while.'

'Clever. I thought it best to get out. I wasn't actually at Bristol, no, but if they start circulating stuff about a possible bank raid

214

lad with big glasses up will come Blackpool on the screens. Even under a balaclava they'd be visible.'

'Yes.'

Flanders looked around the cabin. Yeo had pictures of the *Splott* on the walls and some designers' drawings of hull sections. 'This is your realm, Paul.'

'It's a job.' Yeo opened the cabinet and brought out a bottle of Barolo. He had an idea that wine gave a sweeter touch of class than whisky or rum, especially on a boat, and especially a rich red. He poured a couple of drinks.

'I'm a disappointment? You were expecting Carol?' Flanders said.

'You're welcome here, Gray.'

'But you'd prefer Carol?'

'Oh, she's the past.'

'This early tip: I had to get out very, very fast, Paul.'

So, surprises, it was about money. 'Without funds?'

'Most of the funds are gone, anyway. It's feverish over there. You've got to keep pace.'

'Lucky you.'

'And I took only forty per cent of a quarter, didn't I? I need just a bit – to get out of the country for a while. It's best for everyone. I could lead to all sorts, couldn't I?'

'Lead? Only if you talked.'

'Would I talk?' He made his face turn hard. 'Do I drop friends in it? But they could be up to so many tricks – put me on parade for a spotting, even trace associates. They're not dim. And now I hear they've named Tommy for some killings down here. This is very complex, Paul, very close.'

Yeo did a calculation or two. 'What are you saying, Gray?'

'Enough to get abroad for a spell.'

'I'm building a down payment for another vessel. I'm already behind on my financial plan. I must get somewhere near the big league. That's important to me. Even more now Carol's gone.'

Flanders lowered his head. He had on a three-quarter length tan leather coat which must have taken some lump of his Bristol cut. 'Yes, I'm a disappointment – a pain,' Flanders said, with another thin chuckle. 'But you know how it always is with Gray Flanders. It comes and goes, the loot.' Flanders waved an arm. Such carefree charm.

215

'Within limits I can do something, Gray.' This time it was more than a duty. It was wisdom. This lad talked bold, but this lad went into panics.

Now, Flanders gave a real, deep smile. 'That's great, Paul. You know, you were the only one I could come to.'

Yes, he did know. If you picked up a leadership role, you played it, and went on playing it. 'Couldn't you have gone straight to France from Jersey?'

'What's France without cash?'

'I've got a bit in the house.' They drove to Highcross. On the way, Yeo said: 'There's a car in the garage for you. An Escort.'

'Safe?'

'Enough. It was Carol's. She rang a while ago to say pick it up from a street in Hounslow.'

'Why there?'

'It will get you to the hovercraft.'

'Well, if she rang why can't you – ?'

'No number to ring back, no address except London.'

'That's cruel. You still want her?'

'I want her. But she's not coming back.'

'Thanks for the vehicle, then.'

'You'll be doing me a favour. I'd like it gone but couldn't bear to sell it, in case.'

'Don't they cut loose these days, though?'

These must have been really great houses once. Yeo liked the size of the rooms and the solid doors and dark wooden fireplaces.

Don Samson said: 'The fact is, Paul, there's a real problem getting a team together these days. Look, that's not why I asked you – not just because I'm up against it. I know you're top class. But you can see my difficulties. Tommy, Billy gone. And then the culture – they really wrote me off after Billy was found like that. What they say, I fell down on settling up after Tommy, so next is Billy. They think I deserved it, for ignoring the rule book. Billy's funeral? Four people and a dog and three of the people were me, his mother and Amiable.'

'Depressing,' Yeo replied.

'It's good of you to come to London and my place for a

meeting. Shows willingness, shows a positive side, shows courage.'

'Don, I owe you one – I owe you more than I can ever pay. Tommy.'

'Yes, well – I think I can tell you something now. Tommy had lost a lot of interest in life since his girl was killed. That's the one down there – Olive something? He's got – he had – another girl, too, yes, New Cross way, and a kid. But this Olive – well, a tart, no question, but he was really struck. Maybe he was sick of himself, desperate, through ditching one girl and a baby for another, and then seeing her killed. Oh, he kept going like normal – the Elvis turns, and working, Tommy could always switch it on – but he wasn't the same. Sometimes I wonder, did he loiter about deliberately on that job, blasting off at nothing for no reason, not caring if he was hit himself? I don't say suicide, but very careless risk. Not like him. You got caught up in that, maybe. Not all your fault.'

Yeo felt glad he was sitting down. He had begun to shake with shock. 'But they've got Tommy named for doing that girl. There's a top officer – this is above street level, real clout – this one's closed the case, with Tommy supposed to have killed her and Sweet Bachelor Percy.'

'Well, I know, I know. It's how police work. But this minder guy killed Olive because she'd heard somehow that he'd been bought to see off his boss, Bachelor – bought by us, as a matter of fact, so no mystery how she heard. Tommy could be slack. Bachelor had turned out unsuitable for the job, but he wouldn't let go. Well, we recruited the minder. Plus we think little Olive had heard who employed Bachelor, and us, down there. These girls pick up a lot from big-talk clients, besides the clap.'

'This is Ivor Lestocque?'

'Him. And there was some sex in it for Ivor – he was having Bachelor's lady from way back. Also, there was her money.'

Yeo said: 'You've known all this from the start, then?'

'Of course. I level with you now because we're going to work together. Naturally I put out different hints about what might have happened when I was speaking to other folk – say to Corbett – people who talk. Clouding the water, that's all. We've still got an operation to run in the Bay, and I can't afford to be dragged into the shit for procuring Lestocque, can I?' He had a sad chuckle. 'So, do we seek a Queen's pardon for Tommy?' Samson had a long laugh.

'But you might seek Lestocque – for wiping out Tommy's girl?'

Samson waved a hand towards – towards who knew what? You could read it how you liked.

Yeo said: 'And Tommy didn't go after Ivor himself?'

'As I hear it, Lestocque disappeared, went to ground. Perhaps that helped make Tommy desperate. If he'd gone on looking he might have found him eventually – but he didn't have an eventually, did he, Paul? In a way, of course, what Lestocque did on Olive was right – from our business operation's point of view. It meant nothing would stop him getting rid of Bachelor for us. Tommy would have been split – his own grief and interests, and the family's. More despair.' He switched tone suddenly, left the reminiscences and moved back into the present and future, his voice brisk. 'Listen, I'm not going to find any local helpers for a new money-snatch job, that's the long and short of it. And I can't ask Amiable. His girl turned inquisitive after we used her car in a difficult expedition. Nice but inquisitive. He's had to tell her he'll behave.'

'Which expedition's that, Don?' Yeo asked.

'Very tough,' Samson replied.

Amiable said: 'It's a promise I made her – for a while.'

'I'm glad to be asked,' Yeo told Samson.

'My thinking is, the culture says I should have seen off you and yours following Tommy, and they freeze me because I didn't. So fuck them, I go the whole hog and ask you in on an operation. I don't even try to recruit local. They can whistle for it.'

'I'm needing some capital,' Yeo replied.

'Plus I like mixed geography in a team. It gives the police headaches. This is well off your home ground, so nobody's going to connect you,' Samson said. 'I heard you insist on that. This cements things once and for all, Paul.'

'I know cement. I like the whole concept,' Yeo told him.

'I'll get the drawings.' Samson crossed the big, panelled living-room. A hired morning suit hung in a plastic cover from the picture rail and he flicked it with his fingers as he passed. 'My first wife's getting married again the day after tomorrow. Some piss artist called Clifford Simms-Makins DSO and Bar from near her in Chislehurst. Name like that, am I going to be buying his booze for ever afterwards? No wonder we all need work.'

He brought a street plan from concealment inside a cookery book and spread it on the table. 'Lincoln, central. Here's the bank. Some traffic congestion possible I must admit, but Amiable's contact says a very heavy cash load there on the 22nd and 23rd, so we swallow the risk.'

Yeo suddenly had the feeling of doom that had stopped him going with Magnificent Martin to the bank in Manchester. He had half experienced it before Blackpool, and not at all before Bristol. This was the full dark portion.

'Exceptionally heavy cash delivery,' Amiable said.

'I reckon this is a four job, Paul,' Samson said.

'Including Wheels,' Amiable said.

'I'll handle the driving myself,' Samson said.

'You've done that before?' Yeo asked.

'I'll be all right. Excuse me, Paul. You've driven, I know. Well, of course I know. This is sort of delicate.'

'That's all right.'

'I'm not alleging anything at all. It's a closed book. But I'll feel happiest if I'm the car man. You can lead inside, naturally. This could be a very tough exit.'

'And it's not ground I know,' Yeo said.

'You're taking it like a real trouper, Paul. It's no problem.'

So, this was probably going to be one of those jobs where chaos was a principal partner. Chaos almost always was. You put up with that to reach peace and solidity and stature when it was over, and occasionally you did reach them, for a while, at any rate. Should he exit now, as he did from Magnificent's party? Could he? This was different. Hadn't he hurt this family enough, whatever Samson said about Tommy's weariness with life? They were standing by him, regardless, offering needed work. He blocked off the drab notion of doom.

Samson stood: 'I'll make some tea. Mugs all right? I don't get the real crockery out since Eloise left.'

'I heard about that,' Yeo said.

'With someone who'd been sniffing a while, I found afterwards. They get upset by the stress, don't they, Paul? Well, you know. Of course, it'll never last with Eloise. I won't have her back, though. Not after a thing like that.'

'I mean, could he?' Amiable asked.

'And then I thought about Julian Corbett for our party,' Samson said, 'leaving me one more to find. Jule's got flair, yes? Plus he's useful with armament? I've tried to reach him. No luck.'

'Jule? Oh, he went away with Henrietta. Nobody knew where. Italy? Tunisia? But he was in touch with me the other day, looking for work. He's bored senseless. Henrietta's really settled down – like a wife. Gives it only to Jule. That terrifies him.'

'Did he ever speak to you about a deal, Paul?'

'Deal?'

'Never mind. I expect he would have, when he thought the time was right. It's the past now.'

'What deal?' Yeo asked.

'That bloody Jule. Who trusts him?'

'Few.'

'He's all right on a job, though?'

'As good as most,' Yeo said.

'I'd like to be coming myself,' Amiable said, 'but my girl would go spare.'

'Now and then you've got to see things from the woman's point of view,' Samson replied.

33

Almost fully dressed, Erica and Petronella were dancing slowly together in Brade's flat to an oldie disc, 'Somewhere along the way'. It was Sunday morning. Louise had taken to attending the cathedral services regularly, and the other two would come and wait for her in Brade's place, talking and so on, occasionally dancing or playing Monopoly. Louise apparently had a history of church-going, and recently let out to Brade that when she disappeared in London she was at a convent retreat. 'It's not something I usually talk about,' she said. Cliffy Hale-Garning must be at the cathedral, too, or he would have heard the music through the floor and come down to join the party, probably bringing Enid, his blow-up doll.

For some of the morning in bed Erica and Petronella had argued about Brade's tattoos. Erica thought they cheapened him, cheapened him even more, and should be removed. Petronella liked them. The two girls had become quiet now as they danced. Petronella was younger but taller and took the man's part. Obviously a bandanna person, she had put today's back on as soon as the three of them left the bedroom. This bandanna was gold, not crimson, and just as striking with her red hair.

Brade, reading the Agony Column in *Wales on Sunday*, said from the settee: 'And do you think you'll be able to put up long-term with Max, Petronella?'

'He's ace,' she replied, 'and almost fit again.'

'A tyrant?' Brade asked.

'Not a bit. Only one rule – apart from handing over the money intact, obviously.'

'Oh?' Brade said.

'I mustn't go with this certain guy. Max worries about me.'

'Maniac?'

'It's *him* that's in bad peril, but Max thinks I might get hit, too, by accident.'

'Yes?' Brade replied.

'Like a foreign name but Welsh to start. A black.'

'Ivor Lestocque?' Erica asked.

'Like that,' Petronella replied.

'What's Max got against Ivor?' Brade said.

The girls sat down, Petronella next to Brade on the settee. She pulled his shirt off to look at the tattoos again. 'Max says some London people will come after him. Some family.'

Erica said: 'Max has lost one girl. Two would be carelessness.'

'What family?' Brade asked.

'Max said this family blame Lestocque for something very bad.'

'For what?' Brade asked.

'Oh, Max didn't tell me that. Just stressing the hazard. Or didn't tell me very much. This Ivor killed some boy's girl – a boy from this family.'

Erica, seated on the hearth rug, said: 'Do you hear what I hear, Dave? Have we all been wrong thinking Tommy Samson did them? Instead, Tommy driven to despair by Olive's murder? Is this the family Samson, Pet?'

'Oh, Max would never mention names. He's so careful,' Petronella replied, sliding her hand slowly back and forth over Brade's pre-Raphaelites. 'But Olive? You mean the girl before me with Max – that terrible stabbing? My God, Dave.'

'Don't be troubled,' Brade replied.

Erica said: 'The way I see this, Dave, is Olive had picked up something Ivor didn't want broadcast. Sort of thing that can happen in our trade. Like he'd been paid to leave Bachelor exposed.'

'Or worse,' Brade said. All at once cripplingly sad, he would have liked to pace the room as distraction from his pain. But Petronella had her head on his chest. He cried: 'Jesus, this is what I foresaw and dreaded – the old minor, decent villainies displaced by something bigger and fouler. Fat London money pays Lestocque to kill his own boss, his friend. To shoot his eye out! Plus a kid like Olive gets it for hearing too much. Are we already into the pit? I must work on dear Ivor again.'

Petronella howled: 'No, no, please don't have these ladies scrubbed off or whatever, Dave. It won't be the same.'

'So, what did Max tell you in that private meeting at the hospital, Erica?' Brade asked.

'Nothing, except things were sliding, sliding, and to keep quiet or none of us had any hope. The enemy was too big.'

'He's been sitting on this the whole time?' Brade said.

'Max is not a talker,' Erica replied.

'But love talk, yes, oh, yes,' Petronella said. 'Fluency. Depth.'

Louise came in in her hat and full of a sermon from *Jude* about strange flesh.

Erica said: 'I thought Bullfinch had drawn a line under the inquiries. Will he let you restart them, Dave?'

'Why he banned any more digging into Fiona's death. He wants Miriam to carry it, so Lestocque is given no hard time. Ivor has to be looked after. Ivor must be kept clear of pressure questioning in case something else comes out.'

'What?' Louise asked. 'Are you saying Bullfinch had, has, an interest in Sweet Bachelor's death, Dave?'

'I can't discuss a senior officer with you, I'm afraid,' Brade replied.

222

'Bollocks,' Louise said.

'Anyway, weren't you convinced it was her jealous daddy?' Erica asked.

Brade said: 'Maybe I was off balance, from jealousy myself.'

'Jealousy? Oh?' Petronella replied. 'Oh? Did you like her so very much, Dave? Nobody, not even Louise and Erica can come as close? Or, perhaps . . .?' She stood up and paraded in front of him, smoothing her hips, movingly. As Maximilian said, Life renewed itself.

'Well, possibly in due course,' Brade replied. 'First, though, I think I'll squeeze Lestocque. To cleanse we must know the truth.'

'I've already had the sermon for today,' Louise replied.

Brade said: 'I'll tell Bullfinch I've received new information from an immaculate source. He'll hate it, see it as Brade stirring again. Yes, maybe fuck up his special pay packet. Great. Probably, Ivor really was doing things with Bachelor's wife a long time before he was found in the water.'

'Of course,' Louise replied. 'Wake up, Dave, or we'll all lose interest in you, even Petronella.'

'You're supposed to be a mind, Dave, as well as all the rest of it,' Erica said.

Knuckles tapped the door gently and Brade went to open up. Hale-Garning wearing full canonicals and carrying a prayer book peered in around Brade's bare chest at the girls: 'I heard voices. A session? Room for one or two more?'